THE LION
⊰ AND THE ⊱
THRONE

Stories from the Shahnameh of Ferdowsi

Volume I

PROSE RENDITION
by Ehsan Yarshater

TRANSLATED FROM THE PERSIAN
by Dick Davis

ILLUSTRATING A *SHAHNAMEH*
by Stuart Cary Welch

Mage Publishers
Washington, DC
1998

THIS IS A MOHAMMAD AND NAJMIEH BATMANGLIJ BOOK
PUBLISHED BY MAGE PUBLISHERS, INC.

A COMPLETE LIST OF ILLUSTRATIONS, CREDITS AND
ACKNOWLEDGMENTS CAN BE FOUND STARTING ON PAGE 259.

LIBRARY OF CONGRESS CATALOGING-IN-PUBLICATION DATA
Yar-shater, Ehsan
The lion and the throne: stories from the Shahnameh of Ferdowsi /
prose rendition by Ehsan Yarshater ;
translated from the Persian by Dick Davis ;
Illustrating a shahnameh by Stuart Cary Welch.
p. cm.
ISBN 0-934211-50-7 (cloth)
I. Davis, Dick, 1945– .
II. Firdawsi. Shahnamah.
III. Title.
PK6457.Y37 1997
891'.5533--DC21
96-44432
CIP

Printed in Korea

ISBN 0-934211-50-7

MAGE BOOKS ARE AVAILABLE AT BOOKSTORES OR DIRECTLY FROM THE PUBLISHER.
TO ORDER OR TO RECEIVE OUR CURRENT CATALOG
CALL 1-800-962-0922 OR 202-342-1642
OR VISIT MAGE ON THE WORLD WIDE WEB AT WWW.MAGE.COM

❧ CONTENTS ❧

⇥ INTRODUCTION ⇤

The tales included in this volume are taken from the first quarter of the Persian national epic, Ferdowsi's *Shahnameh*, which is the largest repository of pre-Islamic myth and legend still extant in Persian culture. In the form in which they appear in the *Shahnameh*, these legends and myths were written down in verse by the poet Ferdowsi at the end of the tenth and the beginning of the eleventh century, some 350 years after the Arab conquest which had destroyed the Sasanian Empire and Persian political independence, and brought to the country the new religion of Islam. Ferdowsi's poem is at one and the same time a gathering of folk memory, a nostalgic record of a lost imperial civilization, and a definition by precept and example of a perceived cultural identity that had seemed in danger of being eroded by the new civilization, social values, and religious concerns that emerged in Islamic Iran.

The *Shahnameh* begins with the creation of the world and continues until the successful Arab conquest of Persia in the seventh century A.D. The narrative as a whole is more or less framed by stories that evince a deep suspicion of Arab civilization. Near the opening, Ferdowsi gives us the story of the Arab demon-king Zahhak (page 29), and just before the end of his immense poem, a character prophesies at length and in detail the terrible results of the coming Arab conquest. But despite this framework, the Arabs and their civilization are mostly noticeable by their absence. Unlike virtually all other Persian writers of his time who concerned themselves with the country's pre-Islamic past, Ferdowsi makes no attempt to integrate the chronology of ancient and legendary Persia with the chronology sanctioned by the Qur'an; the creation myths he recounts are wholly Persian, and for the purposes of his poem Ferdowsi simply ignores the Islamic version of the early history of the world.

In the poem's later parts (to be covered in volumes II and III) the tales often correspond, sometimes closely, sometimes less so, with the historical record. The chief external focus of the Persian monarchs' concern is the West—the Greeks and later the Romans, whose lands are collectively known as "Rum," a word which in the *Shahnameh* can refer to the area now covered by modern Turkey, or the Byzantine Empire and the countries of the eastern Mediterranean, or the West in general. But in the earlier parts of the poem, from which the tales collected here are taken, Persia takes little heed of the West. Its gaze is largely directed eastward, to India and Afghanistan (where the chief heroic family of the poem's opening section has its fiefdom), and north, into central Asia beyond the Oxus, from which threats to Persian independence continually come. The stories of this section belong to such a nebulous time period that the historical record has virtually nothing to say as to their accuracy. Whatever core of historical truth some of them may once have had has been overlaid and obliterated by the accretions of legend and myth, so that kings routinely live for over a hundred years, great heroes can live for many generations and serve as many as nine such monarchs, and the supernatural is never far away, either as a malign threat or as a source of help and comfort.

The myths recorded at the opening of the poem show links to both Indian and European (especially Greek) mythology and must derive from the Indo-European myths which were common to all three civilizations before the migrations that established these peoples in the geographical locations where their cultures diverged and which are now associated with their names. For example, the Persian king Jamshid, whose story figures prominently in the *Shahnameh*'s opening pages, has been identified with Yama, the Indian god of the underworld. The same king's introduction of the arts of civilization, and his rebellion against God have clear parallels with the Greek story of Prometheus, and Prometheus's punishment (being chained in torment to a rock) recalls the ultimate fate of Zahhak, the king who defeats Jamshid.

The poem's beginning is therefore more like a cosmogony than an epic, dealing as it does with the creation of the world and the introduction of the customs and arts of civilization. It is significant that the first of these customs to which Ferdowsi draws attention is that of a divinely sanctioned kingship. The institution of kingship was seen by the ancient world as one that the Persians had made peculiarly their own (this is largely how Herodotus, for example, differentiated the Persians from his own Greek peoples), and this emphasis had been made into an instrument of state propaganda by the Sasanians. The Sasanians were defeated by the Arabs more than three centuries before Ferdowsi wrote the *Shahnameh*, but much of the ideological and social matrices of many of the stories, even the earliest ones, can be seen as anachronistically Sasanian in emphasis. As well as the general concern with the notion of a sacred kingship, there is also the specific identification of Iran's enemies to the north, beyond the Oxus, as "Turks," a designation which only became generally accurate in Sasanian times, long after the earliest stories of the poem supposedly occurred.

The importance of kingship in the *Shahnameh* is evident in the very name of the poem, which means "King-Book" or "The Book of Kings," and the poem is structured according to these kings' reigns, exactly fifty of which are recorded, a satisfyingly round number which seems to emphasize the quasi-mystical centrality of kingship to the work. But the stories themselves often seem strongly resistant to Sasanian attempts to sanitize them in the service of notions of a sacred and infallible monarchy. Many of the kings prove ethically unsatisfactory. It is true that the most unsatisfactory of all—Zahhak—is not an Iranian, and this makes it possible for him to be a dreadful king without reflecting directly on the Persian monarchy itself, but others who are unequivocally identified as Persian are almost as bad, most notably, in the early part of the poem, Kay Kavus. Generally well-intentioned kings can make grave errors of judgment that have disastrous results (Feraydun); they can be overcome by the destructive effects of hubris (Jamshid) or destroyed by vacillating incompetence (Nozar). Very frequently in the *Shahnameh*, Iran and its kings are in need of a savior.

The saviors are in general drawn from one family, the clan of Nariman, which rules in an area called variously Sistan, Nimruz, Zavolestan, or Zabolestan, the central town or inhabited district of which is referred to as Zabol. Sistan's whereabouts are vague, but one border of the area is identified as the River Hirmand (now Helmand, in modern Afghanistan, flowing west from the region of Kandahar to a marshy area near the present Iran-Afghan border). The greatest hero of this clan, and the savior of Iran and its monarchy on innumerable occasions, is Rostam.

Rostam is a complicated and equivocal figure. Superficially he is the Iranian hero par excellence, and his ancestry is partly Iranian (i.e., from the ruling house of Sistan), but it is also partly from the Arab demon-king Zahhak and partly from the Indian-Afghan princess Rudabeh, who is his mother. His relations with the Iranian kings are marked by increasing exasperation on both sides and there are even suggestions that he may be a direct threat to the kingship—his son Sohrab attempts to usurp Iran in his father's name, and Rostam's last great victory is over a crown prince of Iran, Esfandyar, and results in the prince's death.

Rostam is clearly an ancient figure from an early stage of the evolution of Persian mythology: He is protected by magic, he is possessed of supernatural strength, the weapons especially associated with him are of the simplest, most ancient and primitive kind—the club, or mace, and the lariat. Further, scholars have speculated that the dark-skinned demons with whom the Iranians often fight in the early stories of the poem are a characterization of the indigenous peoples of the area with whom the Iranian branch of the Indo-European peoples had to contend when they entered the Iranian plateau at some time in the second millennium B.C. Given this, it is remarkable how often Rostam's enemies, especially in the early stories of his legend, are characterized as "white." He does battle with a white demon, a white elephant, and a white mountain, and his son fights against a white castle. There is too the strange importance given to his father Zal's white hair, as if whiteness always signaled disaster or evil for this family. It may be that elements of the Rostam story were originally indigenous to the Sistan area and preceded the coming of the Iranians to the land of Iran; Rostam was then co-opted, as it were, to the Iranian cause and mythology. This would go some way toward accounting for Rostam's generally un-Iranian (and somewhat demonic) genealogy, for his often uneasy relations with the Iranian monarchy, and for his sometimes being on the "wrong" side in the white-black supernatural confrontations, which have been interpreted as struggles for the control of Iran between an indigenous dark-skinned people who were overrun by the lighter skinned Iranians from central Asia.

Be this as it may, Rostam and his legend have become a kind of symbol of the Persian chivalric and heroic virtues. He is presented as a hero of immense strength, appetites, and martial ability but also as selfless and honorable; he is relentless in war but merciful in victory and compassionate toward suffering. Much of the tension of the heroic parts of the narrative comes from the way in which Rostam and other selfless heroes like him are called on to serve kings who are often their moral inferiors; this is most noticeable during the reign of Kay Kavus, to whose reign Ferdowsi devotes more space than that of any other king in the poem.

Heroism and the martial virtues are not by any means the only human qualities celebrated in the poem. Against the freebooting and always potentially anarchic valor of independent heroes like Rostam, the more sober virtues of justice and social order are frequently invoked. The poem is also remarkable for its many scenes of tenderness; these occur most obviously in the narratives concerned with young love (in this volume, in the wonderful tale of Zal and Rudabeh), but we are also given glimpses of the mutual concern of husbands and wives, of monarchs and their champions, of fathers and their children (the reluctance fathers feel when faced with separation from their daughters is a frequently mentioned topos). And the poem includes a gallery of varied portraits of heroines, which is remarkable in a work supposedly devoted to the severely masculine world of martial valor and public warfare. In the stories given here we see the youthful, guileless love of Rudabeh, the coolheaded strength of purpose of Sindokht (her rather henpecked, would-be macho husband, Mehrab, is a beautifully judged companion piece), the extravagant devotion of Sudabeh, the valor and shrewdness of the amazon Gordafarid, Tahmineh's passion for Rostam and then her maternal anxiety.

It is Tahmineh who leads the reader into the last story of the present volume, that of Rostam and his son Sohrab, the best known of all the tales in which Rostam figures and probably the only one that is reasonably well known in the West, in Matthew Arnold's idiosyncratic and very Victorian version. This story is one of a number in the *Shahnameh* which involve tragic misunderstandings and/or violence between father and son. The story of Rostam's father, Zal, and his suffering at his father Sam's hands prefigures the Sohrab tale in some ways. Later in the *Shahnameh*, Rostam is involved, partly as a bystander, partly as a surrogate father, in other equally tragic father-son conflicts. In such tales and elsewhere in his poem, Ferdowsi weaves public, dynastic, familial, and private concerns into narratives of extraordinary emotional resonance. He does this with such unobtrusive but effective skill that an English-speaking reader is almost inevitably reminded of Shakespeare's preoccupations in his Roman and chronicle plays. These, rather than the more frequently invoked and generically related works of Homer, are perhaps the closest Western works, in terms of thematic depth and complexity, that we can put beside Ferdowsi's *Shahnameh*.

Most of the present book is a translation of Professor Ehsan Yarshater's well-known retelling in modern Persian prose of the opening narratives of the *Shahnameh, Bar Gozideh-ye Dastanha-ye Shahnameh az aghaz ta piruzi-ye kay kavus bar shah-e mazanderan (Selections from the stories of The* Shahnameh: *From the beginning until the conquest of Kay Kavus over the king of Mazanderan).* The last two narratives, those of Kavus's expedition to Hamaveran and his marriage to Sudabeh, and of Rostam and Sohrab, have been rendered into English directly from Ferdowsi's *Shahnameh.* Professor Yarshater included short passages of direct quotation from Ferdowsi in his retelling, and these I have translated as verse in English; I have followed this same system (of giving brief passages in verse) in the stories rendered directly from Ferdowsi.

At the end of the book the reader will find four appendices: A glossary of names in the text and their pronunciation, a summary of the complete *Shahnameh*, an essay on illustrating a *Shahnameh*, and a guide to the illustrations used in this volume and their sources.

DICK DAVIS

⊰ THE FIRST KINGS ⊱

Kayumars and Siamak

In the beginning, men lived in a scattered, haphazard way, without true culture or civilization. Kayumars was the first leader who emerged among such people, and it was he who established the institution of kingship. He took his place on his throne on the first day of spring, when the youthful world was renewed. In those days life was simple and uncomplicated; men knew nothing of clothes and their diet was plain and straightforward. Kayumars dwelt in the mountains, and he and his kinsfolk dressed themselves in leopard skins. But Kayumars was endowed with the divine *farr*, a glory reserved for great kings; he had immense power and all the men and animals of the earth obeyed him, and he was men's guide and teacher.

The king's chief source of joy and pride was his son, Siamak, a handsome, dexterous, ambitious youth. Kayumars was extremely attached to the boy, and he found the thought of being separated from him intolerable. Time passed, and Siamak grew confident and powerful, and Kayumars's rule was strengthened by his presence.

The Hatred of Ahriman

Everyone loved Siamak, except for one individual; this was the malevolent Ahriman, who hated the earth and its people, and who was an enemy of everything in the world that was fine and noble. But out of fear he kept his malevolence hidden. He became envious of Siamak's youth and splendor and glory, and evil thoughts tormented him. Ahriman had a son, who was as vicious and fearless as a wolf. Ahriman collected an army together for this lad and sent him to Kayumars, as if honoring the king and out of love for him. Envy seethed in the heart of this devil's spawn, and Siamak's good fortune made all the world dark and dreary to his eyes. The demon began to spread slander and to plant his evil thoughts here and there, wherever he could. But Kayumars knew nothing of all this and did not realize that he had such a malicious individual present in his court.

The angel Sorush, the messenger of the great god Hormozd, appeared before Kayumars and revealed to him the enmity of Ahriman's son and his desire to destroy Siamak.

As soon as Siamak learned of this foul demon's malevolence, he roused himself in fury and gathered an army together and, wearing the skin of a leopard as battledress, set out to make war on the devil's brood. When the two armies were drawn up face to face, Siamak, who was both brave and noble, demanded to fight his adversary in single combat. Then he stripped and grappled with the demon. But the demon tricked him and rent him with his claws, and stretched the noble Siamak in the dust.

> *Now in the dirt he laid the king's son low,*
> *Clawed at his gut, and struck the fatal blow:*
> *So perished Siamak—a demon's hand*
> *Left leaderless his people and his land.*

When Kayumars heard the news that Siamak had been killed by this demon, sorrow darkened all the world before his eyes. He descended from his throne and began to weep; the sound of mourning arose from the army, and all the tame animals and wild animals and birds gathered there and made their way weeping and crying into the mountains. For a year men mourned in the mountains, until the glorious Sorush brought a message from God, saying, "Kayumars, weep no more, but be of sound mind again. Now it is time for you to gather an army together and fight against this malevolent demon and purify the face of the land of this evil." Kayumars raised his face toward the heavens and gave thanks to God and cleansed his eyelashes of their tears. Then he roused himself to thoughts of vengeance for the death of Siamak.

Hushang's Pursuit of Vengeance

Siamak had a noble son called Hushang; he was a living reminder of his father and Kayumars loved him dearly. When the time for vengeance had come, Kayumars called Hushang before him and told him of all that had happened and of the evil that had befallen Siamak, and said, "Now I shall raise a great army and gird up my loins to take revenge for the death of my son Siamak. But you must lead this expedition, since you are young and I am full of years; you are to be the commander of this army." Then he raised a great army. All the tame animals and wild animals, such as lions and tigers and leopards and wolves, as well as the birds of the air, joined him in their desire for vengeance. Ahriman too came forward, a fearful and appalling monster swooping and swirling through the air, together with his army, and the two hosts fell on one another. The host of animals triumphed and overcame Ahriman's demons. Then the brave Hushang was like a lion that stretches out its claws, and he made the world dark before the son of Ahriman's eyes. Hushang bound his body in chains and cut off his head and threw his lifeless trunk on the ground.

When vengeance for the death of Siamak had been taken, the life of Kayumars came to an end, and he passed away after a reign of thirty years.

The Reign of Hushang

Hushang was a wise and provident king and he set to work to make the world fit for civilized habitation. Hushang was the first person to know of iron and to extract it from its rocky home. When he discovered this wonderful metal, he established the blacksmith's craft and fashioned axes and saws and hatchets from iron. Once he had accomplished this task, he established the principles of agriculture. First he turned his attention to irrigation, to the digging out of canals and waterways in plains and deserts. Then he taught men the crafts of sowing, and the rearing of crops, and how to harvest them, and he appointed skilled artisans to be farmers. In this way men's food supply was put on an ordered basis, and each man was able to have bread in his house. In matters of faith and religion Hushang followed the example of his grandfather Kayumars. The notion that fire is sacred and to be approached with awe and praise also began in Hushang's time, since it was he who first brought fire forth from flint.

The Discovery of Fire

This happened in the following manner: One day Hushang and a group of his companions were on their way to the mountains when suddenly in the distance a terrifying, black serpent appeared, coming swiftly toward them. Two red eyes glowed on its head and smoke billowed from its mouth. Bravely, nimbly, Hushang seized a rock, dashed forward, and flung it at the serpent with all his strength.

Before the rock reached him, the serpent writhed to one side, and the rock struck against another rock. As the two smashed against one another, sparks spurted forth in every direction, so that the landscape was lit up in brilliant splendor.

Although the serpent escaped, the secret of fire had been revealed. Hushang gave thanks to the world's Creator, saying, "This splendor is a divine splendor; we must revere it and rejoice in its presence."

When night fell he gave orders that his men produce sparks from rock in the same manner. They lit a huge fire, and in honor of the divine splendor which had been revealed to Hushang, they instituted a festival of rejoicing. This is called the Sadeh festival, and it was celebrated with great reverence by the ancient Iranians, and the custom is still observed as a memorial of that night.

This was not the last of Hushang's efforts on behalf of humanity. The divine *farr* was with him, and this enabled him to carry out mighty projects. It

was Hushang who separated domesticated animals, such as cows and donkeys and sheep, from animals that are hunted, such as deer and the wild ass, both so that they would be a source of food for men and also so that they could be used to plow the land and for other agricultural purposes. Among creeping animals, he singled out those that have warm, fine fur—such as squirrels, ermines, foxes, and sables—so that men might use their skins to clothe themselves. Hushang spent his life in this fashion, always striving to bring civilization to the world

and comfort to its inhabitants, so that he left the world to his son Tahmures in a far more flourishing state than he had received it.

Tahmures

Despite the defeat which his forces had suffered at the hands of Hushang, the evil Ahriman did not give up his malevolent and wicked ways. Constantly he attempted to transform the world, which had been created by God, into a place of ugliness and filth, to torment mankind and destroy their happiness and well-being, to make the earth's animals and plants sicken and die, and to spread lies and oppression wherever he could. Tahmures pondered the matter and set before his wise, benevolent, and God-fearing chief minister, Shidasb, the nature of Ahriman's labors. Shidasb said, "We must counter this unclean devil's work with sorcery." Tahmures did as he suggested, and by powerful spells he humbled this lord of the demons and made him his obedient slave. Then he rode on him, just as one would ride on a horse or a donkey, and journeyed about the world in this fashion.

When Ahriman's demonic companions saw how weak and helpless their leader had become, they rose up in anger; they rejected the yoke of Tahmures and gathered together, fomenting rebellion. Tahmures was well aware of their activities; he lifted his heavy mace to his shoulders and prepared for war against them. On their side, the demons and their magicians also prepared for war, crying out to the heavens and raising great clouds of smoke and vapor. Once again the prescient Tahmures resorted to sorcery; by sorcery he bound in chains two-thirds of Ahriman's army (and for this he was afterward known as "Tahmures, the Binder of Demons"), and the other third he shattered with his heavy mace, laying them prone in the dust. When the demons saw how soundly they had been defeated, they begged for quarter, crying out, "Don't kill us, spare us and we shall teach you skills as yet unknown." Tahmures spared the demons, and they too became his slaves; then they revealed the mystery of writing to him, and they taught him almost thirty different kinds of script, among them the scripts of Pars, of the West, of the Arabs, of Pahlavi, of Soghdia, and of China.

Tahmures followed in his father's footsteps, adding to the knowledge and skills of mankind. It was he who first taught men how to spin sheep's wool and then how to weave this wool into clothes and carpets. It was he who took grass and straw and barley as fodder for domesticated animals. It was he too who first selected hunting animals; he tamed the dog and the lynx among the wild animals and the hawk and the falcon among the birds of the air, and he taught men how to train them for hunting. It was also Tahmures who domesticated roosters and hens. But life was primitive as yet, and there was still much to learn. Tahmures was succeeded by Jamshid, and Jamshid, by his intelligence and with the help of the divine *farr*, gave the habits and customs of life their true dignity and glory, and taught mankind the new knowledge that was needed then.

Jamshid

Jamshid was crowned with great splendor and became the monarch of the whole world. All demons and birds and angels were his to command and they lived together in amity. Jamshid was both a king and a religious leader, since the great god Hormozd had placed both worldly and spiritual matters in his hands. The first thing Jamshid undertook was the manufacture of weapons, so that he would be secure through them and able to block the spread of evil. He rendered iron pliable and from it made helmets, breastplates, chain mail, body armor, and barding. He spent fifty years laboring at this and laid up stores of weapons.

Then Jamshid turned his mind to what men should wear, and he spent a further fifty years fashioning clothes suitable for feasting and fighting, banquets and battles. He made clothes from linen, silk, and wool, and he taught mankind all the crafts associated with cloth, such as spinning, weaving, sewing, and how to dye clothes.

When this task too was completed, he regulated men's professions and trades, gathering the men of each occupation about him. He divided mankind into four large groups. One consisted of those whose lives were devoted to religion, whose work was the praise of God and the conduct of spiritual affairs. He assigned these men places in the mountains, since in ancient times Iranians had no temples or mosques and worshiped God in open spaces on the tops of hills and mountains. Another group consisted of warriors; these were noblemen and soldiers, and their might maintained peace and concord in the land. A third group consisted of farmers, men who tilled the soil and sowed and reaped crops, who lived in freedom by their own efforts, who were indebted to none for wages or favors, and through whose labors the world was made fruitful and flourishing. The fourth group consisted of men who labored with their hands at the various

crafts of mankind. Jamshid spent a further fifty years arranging these matters, until everyone's work and rank and status were established.

Then Jamshid gave his mind to the problem of where men should live, to houses and buildings, and he ordered the demons who were at his command to mix earth and water together and to pour the mixture into molds and so make bricks. They also called stone and plaster to their aid and in this way constructed houses, public baths, castles, and palaces.

When these labors had been accomplished and the basic necessities of life had been satisfied, Jamshid turned to thinking of how men's lives could be adorned and given dignity and glory. He split the cores of rocks and brought forth from them various jewels, such as sapphires and rubies, and precious metals like silver and gold, adorning men's lives with splendor and delighting their hearts. Then he gave his mind to fine scents and perfumes, and so discovered rose water, sandalwood, musk, and camphor.

Then Jamshid turned his attention to travel; he built boats and set sail upon the world's waters and traveled by boat from country to country. So passed a further fifty years.

The Festival of No-Ruz

And so in this manner Jamshid became skilled in all arts and crafts and considered himself to be unique throughout the world. Then even loftier and grander ambitions swelled in his heart, and he began to think of how he could journey through the skies. He ordered that a costly throne studded with jewels be built for him. He sat upon the throne and then commanded the demons who were his slaves to lift the throne from the ground and raise it up toward the heavens. Jamshid sat there splendid as the shining sun, and thus he traveled through the skies. He did all this through the strength of the divine *farr*. The world's inhabitants were astonished by his glory and power. They gathered together and praised his *farr* and good fortune, and rained jewels upon him; they called this day, which was the first day of the month of Farvardin, No-Ruz, or the New Day, and they called for goblets and wine and sat together feasting and rejoicing. From then on, this day was celebrated with rejoicing and pleasure every year. This was the origin of the festival of No-Ruz.

Jamshid reigned in this fashion for three hundred years, and during this time mankind knew neither suffering nor death. Jamshid had discovered cures for illness and sickness; he knew the secrets of good health and taught them to mankind. During his reign the world was at peace and men were content; the demons were men's slaves and served them. All the world danced to pleasure's tune, and God was Jamshid's guide and teacher.

THE DEMON-KING ZAHHAK

Jamshid's Ingratitude

Jamshid reigned for many long years. All animals, both wild and domestic, together with the demons and mankind itself, were under his command, and from one day to the next his glory and splendor grew greater, so that pride found its way into Jamshid's heart and he set out down the path of ingratitude.

> Jamshid surveyed the world, and saw none there
> Whose greatness or whose splendor could compare
> With his: and he who had known God became
> Ungrateful, proud, forgetful of God's name.

He called his elders and army commanders and priests before him and spoke at length, saying, "It was I who introduced the skills and arts of living into the world, I who adorned the world with such splendor, and I who drove out death and disease. There is no leader or king in all the world but myself. Man's food and sleep and clothes and joy and security all derive from me, and the life and death of all men lies in my hands. Since this is so, I should be called the world's creator, and whoever does not agree to this is a follower of Ahriman."

The nobles and priests all bowed their heads in assent. No one could question or oppose Jamshid, since he was a mighty and powerful king and the divine *farr* was with him. But

> By saying this he lost God's farr, *and through*
> The world men's murmurings of dissension grew.

Since Jamshid had forfeited the divine *farr*, his schemes began to fail, and his nobles and courtiers turned away from him and scattered throughout the earth. Twenty-three years passed, and each day Jamshid's power and splendor diminished. However much he asked for pardon before the throne of God, he could not revive his power, and as his fortune declined, so his terror increased, until Zahhak the Arab appeared on the scene.

بنفشیٔ زلبیان و سبوکند من
چیان اینشدکه دنترمال او هرکزید

باندکرود و ستی سیوکند و سند
برسیدکین جاریه نامن نکوی

The Story of Zahhak and His Father

Zahhak was the son of a fine, good-natured nobleman called Merdas. But Ahriman, whose sole business in the world was to stir up trouble and discord, decided to lead the young Zahhak astray. To further his ends he appeared before Zahhak in the guise of a pleasant, personable man and set about cajoling him with fine deceitful words. And Zahhak was indeed deceived by him.

Then Ahriman said, "My dear Zahhak, I want to share a secret with you. But first you must swear that you will not reveal this secret to anyone." Zahhak swore as Ahriman required him to.

When Ahriman was assured of his prey, he said, "Why should your old father rule all the while that you're a young man? Why are you so unambitious? Get rid of your father and become the ruler yourself. Then his palace and wealth and army, everything, will be yours."

Zahhak was a foolish youth, his heart was easily led astray, and he joined with Ahriman in plotting to kill his father. But he didn't know how to go about it. Ahriman said, "Don't worry, I'll take care of how it's to be done."

Merdas owned a charming garden. At dawn each morning, before sunrise, he would rise and pray in this garden. Ahriman dug a pit there, where Merdas normally walked, and covered it with leaves and branches. On the next day, when the unfortunate Merdas went to pray, he fell into this pit and was killed, and the ungrateful Zahhak ascended his father's throne.

Ahriman's Ruse

When Zahhak had become king, Ahriman disguised himself as an intelligent, talkative young man, presented himself before Zahhak, and said, "I'm a skillful person, and my particular skill is the ability to cook wonderful, truly royal food."

Zahhak entrusted him with the preparation of his food and the management of his meals. Ahriman produced a marvelous colorful spread of various kinds of delicious foods made from birds and animals. Zahhak was well pleased with all this. On the next day an even more colorful spread was laid before him, and so it went on, with Ahriman providing finer food with each day that passed.

On the fourth day the gluttonous Zahhak was so overjoyed that he turned to the young man and said, "Ask me for whatever you desire." Ahriman had been waiting for precisely this opportunity and said, "O king, my heart overflows with love for you and I desire nothing but your happiness. I have only one wish, and that is that you will allow me, as your slave, to kiss your two shoulders." Zahhak gave his permission for this. Ahriman placed his lips against the king's two shoulders and then, suddenly, he disappeared from the face of the earth.

Snakes Grow from Zahhak's Shoulders

From Zahhak's shoulders, where Ahriman had placed his lips, two black snakes emerged. They cut the snakes off at the base, but immediately in their place two more snakes appeared. Zahhak was distraught and searched high and low for a remedy. But however much his doctors tried, they could do nothing.

When all the doctors had shown themselves to be powerless, Ahriman disguised himself as a skillful physician, presented himself to Zahhak, and said, "There is no point in cutting the snakes from your shoulders. The cure for this illness is human brains. The one way to quiet the snakes and keep them from doing any harm is to kill, every day, two people and to prepare food for the snakes from their brains. Perhaps if you do this the snakes will ultimately die."

Now, Ahriman hated mankind and he hated men to be happy, and he hoped in this way to deliver the whole of mankind over to be murdered, and to wipe out their seed forever.

The Capture of Jamshid

It was while all this was going on that Jamshid became arrogant and lost the divine *farr*. Zahhak saw his chance and attacked Iran. Many Iranians who were searching for a new king welcomed Zahhak and, ignorant of his cruelty and tyranny, made him their king.

Zahhak drew up a huge army and sent it to capture Jamshid. For a hundred years Jamshid hid himself from men's eyes, but finally he was trapped on the shores of the China Sea. Zahhak gave orders that Jamshid's body be sawn in half, and he himself became the owner of Jamshid's throne and crown and wealth and palaces. In all, Jamshid had ruled for seven hundred years and, although no king ever reigned with such *farr* or such glory, he finally departed this world ignominiously, with his splendor eclipsed.

Jamshid had two beautiful daughters, Shahrnavaz and Arnavaz. These two became prisoners of the evil Zahhak, and fear forced them to obey him. Zahhak took both of them to his palace, and he set them, along with two others, as the guardians and nurses of the snakes growing from his shoulders.

Every day Zahhak's agents would seize two men and bring them to the royal kitchens, where their brains were to be made into food for the snakes. But Shahrnavaz and Arnavaz and their two companions, who were kindhearted people who could not tolerate such cruelty, each day let one of the captives go, sending him into the plains and mountains, and in place of his brains they would use a sheep's brains to prepare the food.

Zahhak's Dream

Zahhak reigned as an evil and unjust king for many years, and during this time many innocent men were put to death in order to serve as food for the snakes. Many men's hearts harbored a longing for revenge, and anger against him gradually spread and increased. One night as Zahhak was sleeping in his royal palace, three warriors suddenly appeared before him in a dream, turning their faces toward him. The youngest of the three, who was a valiant fighter, lunged at him and brought his heavy mace crashing down on Zahhak's head. Then he bound his arms and feet with leathern straps and dragged him toward Mount Damavand while a great crowd of people ran after them.

Zahhak writhed in his sleep and woke in an anguish of terror. He screamed so violently that the very pillars of his palace trembled. Jamshid's daughter Arnavaz, who was sleeping beside him, started up and asked him what had caused his terror. When she learned that Zahhak had had such a dream, she said that he should call the wise and learned from every corner of the world and have them offer their interpretations of it.

Zahhak did as she had suggested and called wise men and learned dream-interpreters to his court and described his dream to them. All of them remained silent, except for one man who was less fearful than the others. He said, "Your Majesty, the interpretation of your dream is as follows: Your days have come to an end and another shall sit on the royal throne in your place. One Feraydun will come forth, he will be eager to possess the royal crown and throne, and with his heavy mace he will topple you from your position and imprison you."

When he heard this speech, Zahhak fell back unconscious. After he came to himself, he began searching his mind for some way out. His first thought was that his enemy was this Feraydun, and so he gave orders that the country be scoured for Feraydun and that he be delivered to the court. From that time forth he could neither sleep nor feel at ease.

The Birth of Feraydun

There was a noble Iranian, by the name of Atebin, who was descended from the ancient Iranian kings and traced his lineage back to Tahmures, the Binder of Demons. His wife was called Faranak. A fine, handsome boy was born to them and they named him Feraydun. Feraydun was like a shining sun and he possessed the splendor and royal *farr* of Jamshid.

Atebin was deeply afraid of what Zahhak was planning and he fled. But finally agents of Zahhak, searching for men to be used as food for Zahhak's snakes, met up with Atebin. They bound him and delivered him to the executioner.

Feraydun's mother, Faranak, now had no husband, and when she learned that Zahhak had dreamt that he would be overthrown by Feraydun, she became very fearful. Feraydun was still a young child, and she took him to the grassy uplands where a famous ox that bore the name of Barmayeh grazed. She begged the oxherd who grazed his animals there to accept Feraydun as his own son and to rear him with Barmayeh's milk, so that he could be kept safe from Zahhak's tyranny.

Zahhak Learns of Feraydun's Whereabouts

The oxherd took Feraydun and watched over him and reared him with Barmayeh's milk. But Zahhak did not give up his search and finally learned that Barmayeh was nourishing the young Feraydun in the grassy uplands. He sent his men to capture Feraydun. Faranak realized what was afoot and hurried to the uplands; fearful of Zahhak, she took Feraydun and set out for the desert, fleeing toward Mount Alborz.

In the Alborz Mountains, Faranak entrusted Feraydun to the care of a wise and noble man who had forsaken the world. She said to him, "My lord, I appeal to your goodness; the father of this child was a victim of Zahhak's snakes. But Feraydun will one day be a leader of men who will exact vengeance from the evil Zahhak. I ask you to be as a father to Feraydun and raise him as your own son."

This wise and noble man accepted the boy and set about his education.

Feraydun Learns of His Lineage

A few years passed and Feraydun grew apace. He became a tall, strong, fearless youth. But he did not know whose son he was. When he was sixteen he descended from the mountains to the plain and went to his mother, and asked her to tell him the name of his father and what his lineage was.

Then Faranak revealed her secret to him and said, "O my brave son, your father was a noble Iranian. He was of Kayanid descent and his lineage reached back to the renowned king Tahmures, the Binder of Demons. He was a wise, kindhearted, and good man who hurt no one. The tyrant Zahhak delivered him over to the executioners so that they could make food for Zahhak's snakes from your father's brains. And in this way I was left without a husband, and you without a father. Then Zahhak had a dream, and his astrologers and dream-interpreters

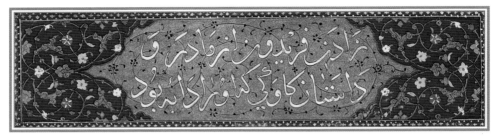

said that it meant that one Feraydun would rise up from among the Iranians to do battle with him, and that this Feraydun would smite Zahhak with his mighty mace and topple him from the throne. Zahhak set about searching for you. Out of fear I entrusted you to a shepherd in the uplands, so that he could nourish you with milk from the wonderful ox which he possessed. But news of this reached Zahhak. Zahhak killed the innocent, dumb ox and destroyed our house. I had no choice but to flee, and, out of fear of that tyrant and his evil snakes, I hid you for safekeeping in the Alborz Mountains."

Feraydun's Rage

When Feraydun had heard this tale, his blood seethed with fury; he writhed in inward torment and a flame of vengeance was kindled in his heart. He turned toward his mother and said, "Mother, just as this tyrant Zahhak has darkened all our days and destroyed so many Iranians, so shall I darken his days. I shall lift up my sword and in one stroke I shall reduce his castles and palaces to rubble."

Faranak said, "O brave son of mine, this is not a wise way to talk. You cannot fight against the whole world; Zahhak is a powerful man, possessed of a huge army, and whenever he wishes he can summon from every country a hundred thousand warriors all prepared to do his bidding. Don't be so naive and impetuous, don't disregard a mother's advice, and until you have found a means and a method to proceed in this venture, don't think of drawing your sword."

Zahhak's Terror

And for his part, thoughts of Feraydun ran in Zahhak's head and terrified him, so that from time to time his lips would fearfully form Feraydun's name. He knew that Feraydun was alive and that Feraydun thirsted for his blood.

One day Zahhak gave orders that a royal audience be arranged at the court. He sat upon the ivory throne, the turquoise crown on his head, and commanded that the country's priests be summoned before him. Then he turned to them and said, "You are aware that I have a mighty enemy who, although he is still young, is a brave and ambitious youth who seeks to overthrow my crown and throne. Thinking about this enemy has left my soul in a constant state of terror. A solution must be found. A document must be drawn up stating that I am a just and generous king who has done only righteous and noble acts, so that this malevolent enemy will have no excuse to seek revenge. All the nobility, all those who are in any way distinguished, must sign this document."

Zahhak was tyrannical and quick-tempered. From fear of him no one dared object, and all signed the document attesting to the justice and righteousness and generosity of the evil tyrant Zahhak.

Kaveh the Blacksmith

As this was going on, a great outcry was heard resounding throughout the court; a man came forward, distractedly beating his hands against his head and fearlessly demanding justice. He cried out, "O tyrant king, I am Kaveh, Kaveh the blacksmith. Where are this justice and righteousness of yours? Where is your generosity, your care for your subjects' welfare? If you are no tyrant, why have you slaughtered my sons? I had eighteen sons. All but one of them have been seized by your agents and handed over to the executioner. Enough of such tyranny and malevolence! What evil have I ever done to you that you did not spare my sons' lives? I am a simple, harmless blacksmith; why should I suffer such violence and cruelty at your tyrannous hands? What excuse can you have for such behavior? Why should seventeen of my sons be sacrificed to your snakes? And why will you not release that one son who is remaining to me? This last remaining child, the light of my eyes, the prop of my old age, and the reminder of his dead brothers— why should he too be sacrificed to an evil monster like yourself?"

Zahhak was astonished by this fearless talk and his terror increased. He pondered what to do, and assuming a smiling face, he spoke kindly to Kaveh. He gave orders that the man's last remaining son be released to him. Then Zahhak said to Kaveh, "Now that you have seen my generosity and tasted my justice, you too must sign this document which the nobles and elders of this land have written concerning my just dealings and benevolence."

The Revolt of Kaveh

When Kaveh read the document he felt his blood boil within him. He turned toward the nobles and elders who had signed it and shouted, "O wretched, spiritless men, this demonic tyrant has scared the wits out of every one of you; in accepting his terms like this you have sold your souls to hell. I shall never sign such a lie and I shall never call a tyrant a righteous man." Then he leapt forward and ripped the document from top to bottom and flung it from him; wild with rage, he took his one remaining son by the hand and stormed from the court. He fixed his leather apron to the head of a lance and went down to the marketplace and cried, "The tyrant Zahhak and the snakes that grow from his shoulders are an evil that must be cleansed from the earth. Join me, so that together we shall save ourselves from this filthy demon; let us take the nobly born Feraydun as our leader and seek revenge for our dead sons and loved ones. How long is Zahhak to oppress us while we make no murmur in reply?" His vehement words found willing listeners.

Feraydun's Leadership

People who could tolerate no more of Zahhak's injustice flocked to Kaveh's call, and a great crowd gathered. Kaveh strode ahead, bearing aloft his leather apron high on the lance, with a multitude of men crying out for justice and revenge following in his wake, until they reached the court of Feraydun.

As they drew near, Feraydun saw the huge crowd of men crying out for justice and revenge, with Kaveh at their head bearing aloft his leather apron on a lance. Feraydun took this leather banner as a favorable omen. He went among the crowd and listened to the words of those who had been oppressed. His first order was to have Kaveh's leather apron adorned with silks and gold and jewels; it was then named "the Kaviani banner." Then he placed the Kayanid crown on his head, dressed in his armor, and, thus accoutred for war, appeared before his mother Faranak. He said to her, "Mother, the day of vengeance is at hand. I leave for war, and with God's help I shall destroy the tyrant Zahhak's palace. I place you in God's hands and entreat you not to let fear invade your heart."

Faranak's eyes filled with tears. She entrusted her son to God, sending him out to battle.

The Ox-Headed Mace

Feraydun had two older brothers. When he was ready for battle, he went to them first and said, "My brothers, the day of our triumph and the defeat of Zahhak and his snakes has dawned. Righteousness will be victorious throughout the world. The Kayanid crown and throne are ours by right and will be ours once again. Now I shall set forth to do battle against Zahhak. Get me skillful blacksmiths and metalworkers who can fashion me a mace."

The brothers went to the blacksmiths' quarter and brought Feraydun the finest masters of the craft. Feraydun took a staff and drew in the dust a mace with a head like that of an ox, and the blacksmiths set about making such a weapon. When the ox-headed mace was ready, Feraydun grasped it in his hand, mounted his great horse, and, at the head of the ever increasing army of Iranians, set out for Zahhak's palace.

The Envoy of God

Feraydun rode forward until nightfall, his warlike heart filled with the longing for vengeance. Then the army pitched camp and Feraydun dismounted. In the darkness a beautiful young man with an angelic face appeared before him; he spoke to Feraydun and taught him how he could undo Zahhak's magical powers and break the chains Zahhak had wrought. Feraydun knew that this youth was an envoy from God and that Good Fortune was now his friend. He rejoiced, and when dawn broke he once again set out toward Zahhak.

When he drew near the River Arvand, he sent a message to the ferrymen who worked there, saying they should provide him with boats and rafts to take his army across the water. The head of the ferrymen said that he was sorry, but he could not accept any orders without Zahhak's permission. Feraydun was enraged by this reply; mounted on his horse, he fearlessly plunged into the river. His commanders and their soldiers followed his example. The ferrymen fled, and in a short while Feraydun and his army reached dry land and made for the city.

The Taking of Zahhak's Castle

When they were within a mile of their destination, Feraydun saw a palace fair as a new bride; it was magnificently adorned and its pinnacles seemed to reach to the heavens. He knew that this was the palace belonging to the tyrant Zahhak. He grasped his ox-headed mace firmly and strode into the palace grounds. Zahhak himself was not present in the city. The palace guards rushed forward like raging devils, but Feraydun brought his great mace down on their heads and destroyed them. And so he went forward, sending Zahhak's companions sprawling in the dust, until he reached the audience hall where Zahhak's throne was. He seized the throne and sat himself upon it, and his soldiers occupied the palace.

Then Feraydun went to Zahhak's private quarters, where many beautiful girls were kept imprisoned. He freed the prisoners, and among them were Shahrnavaz and Arnavaz, Jamshid's daughters, who, fearful for their lives, had submitted to Zahhak. Jamshid's daughters rejoiced at their freedom and with tearful faces said, "For years we were prisoners in the clutches of this vile Zahhak and suffered because of his snakes. Now we thank God that we have been freed by your power."

Feraydun took his place on the throne and sat Shahrnavaz and Arnavaz beside him, one on his right and one on his left, and promised that the land of Iran would soon be cleansed of all trace of Zahhak.

Kondrow's Report to Zahhak

The keys to Zahhak's treasures were in the hands of a man named Kondrow who, although he had no great love for injustice, was extremely loyal to Zahhak. Zahhak's palace had been entrusted to his care. Now when he entered the palace, he saw a young man seated upon Zahhak's throne; the youth was strong and elegant as a cypress tree, he carried an ox-headed mace in his hand, Shahrnavaz and Arnavaz were seated on either side of him, and he gave every sign of enjoying his good fortune.

Kondrow went gently forward, made his obeisance, and greeted Feraydun. Feraydun summoned him and gave orders for a celebration at which there were to be singers and musicians and a sumptuous banquet was to be served.

Kondrow accepted the command and provided all that Feraydun had requested. But at daybreak he stole away, mounted a horse, and galloped swiftly to Zahhak, to whom he said, "O king, it is clear that Good Fortune has turned her face from you. Three courageous young men of Iran, together with a great army, have attacked your castle. Of these three, the youngest carries a huge mace that is like a fragment of a mountain; he shines with sunlike splendor, and everywhere they go he leads the others. He has taken over your castle and sat upon your throne, and all your people and followers are now his to command."

Zahhak could not believe that his fortune had deserted him. He said, "There's no cause for concern; perhaps these three have come as guests. We should rejoice at their arrival."

Kondrow said, "Your majesty, what kind of guest is it who arrives at a banquet with an ox-headed mace with which he then proceeds to beat the palace guards about the head, and who sits on your throne and turns all your protocol and ceremonial functions upside down?"

Zahhak said, "Don't trouble yourself about this. A little presumption in a guest can be taken as a good omen."

Kondrow cried out, "Your majesty, if this is a noble guest, what business has he being in your private quarters? What kind of guest is it who drags your women Shahrnavaz and Arnavaz out of their apartments and proceeds to whisper secrets to them and make love to them?"

When Zahhak heard this he leapt up like a wolf and in his rage violently cursed Kondrow. Then he precipitously mounted his horse and with a great army set out by trackless, unknown ways to confront Feraydun.

The Battle of Zahhak and Feraydun

When Zahhak arrived at the city with his army, he saw that everyone there, young and old alike, had deserted him and accepted Feraydun as their leader. As soon as the populace learned of the arrival of Zahhak's army, they attacked it, and Feraydun's army came to their aid. From the city's roofs and walls they threw rocks and bricks, as thick as hail, down on Zahhak's army. The battle was so fiercely fought that the sky was darkened by the dust.

Zahhak writhed in anguish, tormented by envy and rage. When he realized that his army would avail him nothing, he stole away from the soldiers and secretly made his way into his castle, which had fallen into Feraydun's hands. Where he himself had once reigned, he saw Feraydun giving orders and distributing gold and jewels, and Shahrnavaz and Arnavaz were there serving him. The fire of his jealousy flared up; he drew a glittering dagger from his belt and leapt toward Jamshid's daughters, intending to kill them. But Feraydun was not taken unawares; like the wind he ran to their side and brought his huge ox-headed mace down upon Zahhak's head. Zahhak's helmet shattered beneath this terrible blow and the tyrant fell helpless to the ground. Feraydun was about to destroy him with another blow when once again a messenger from God appeared before him and said, "Do not kill him; bind him and imprison him beneath Mount Damavand. It is not yet time for him to be killed."

Zahhak Is Imprisoned

And so Feraydun took straps made from lion skin and tightly bound Zahhak's arms and legs with them and then had him ignominiously dragged behind a horse toward Mount Damavand. There was a deep cave beneath the mountain. Feraydun gave orders that huge nails be prepared. Then the wicked king Zahhak was imprisoned in the cave; the nails were driven into the rock face, securing the chains that held him, so that the world was delivered from the burden of his evil existence.

Then Feraydun summoned nobles and freemen to him and said, "For many years the tyrannous Zahhak has practiced oppression, forgetful of God

and the ways of justice and benevolence, dragging the people of this region through blood and filth. God sent me to cleanse the face of the earth of this vile tyranny. May God be praised that I have found success and overcome the tyrant. You will see nothing from me but benevolence, justice, and godliness. Now I ask all of you to give thanks to God, to lay aside your weapons, and to return peacefully and at rest to your homes and families."

Those present rejoiced and did as he commanded. Feraydun seated himself on the royal throne and began to rule with benevolence and justice. The ways of injustice were laid aside, and the world was at peace again.

THE STORY OF FERAYDUN AND HIS THREE SONS

The Festival of Mehregan

Feraydun was enthroned and placed the Kayanid crown upon his head, on the first day of the month of Mehr, which falls at the autumnal, equinox. The Iranian people rejoiced to see his reign; they lit fires and drank wine and inaugurated a great celebration, and they designated the day as a festival. This festival has been passed down through the years to the present and is called the Festival of Mehregan.

As yet Feraydun's mother, Faranak, knew nothing of her son's coronation. But when she learned of it, she praised God and bathed her face and body and made her way to Feraydun's court. There she bowed her head in homage and gave thanks to God and rejoiced. Then she turned her attention to the poor and deprived; in secret, for seven days, she distributed wealth to beggars and to the needy, so that no one was left in poverty. Then, to offer thanks for the fall of Zahhak, she gave a great banquet for the nobility and the learned. Next she revealed the treasures that she had kept hidden until then and presented cloth, jewels, saddlery, weapons, crowns, and belts, together with untold wealth, to her sovereign son.

The champions and leaders of the army praised Feraydun and Faranak and gave thanks. They gathered together gold and jewels which they heaped before Feraydun and his mother, calling down God's blessing on Feraydun's crown and splendid throne, and wishing him long life and good fortune.

When Feraydun felt his sovereignty to be secure, he traversed the world, toiling to spread the arts of civilization and to uproot evil and ugliness. He lived for fifty years and during his reign the world was a place of happiness and splendor, and the depredations of Zahhak were healed.

Feraydun's Sons

In the first fifty years of his life Feraydun had three sons,

Stately as cypresses, fair as the spring,
The image of their father and their king.

In no time Feraydun's sons were young men, and when he looked at them he saw that each was noble and brave and deserving of a crown and throne. He began to consider to whom they should be married.

Feraydun had a wise, experienced councillor called Jandal. He summoned Jandal and placed the matter before him, saying, "My sons have grown and it is time they were married. We must find girls who are worthy of them. You are wise and learned and I entrust this mission to you; you are to search until you find three sisters who share one father and mother; they should be beautiful and of noble lineage."

Jandal selected a number of trusty companions and set off on his long journey, asking whomever he met for help, until he arrived in the Yemen and there heard a description of the Yemeni king's daughters. He made diligent inquiries and realized that these girls were worthy to be the brides of Feraydun's sons.

Jandal and the King of the Yemen

He made his way to the king's court and asked to be received in audience. The king asked him why he had come to their country. Jandal kissed the ground and made his obeisances before the king, and said, "I bear a message from Feraydun, the king of Iran. Feraydun sends you his greetings and says: 'In all the world nothing is dearer than a son; I have three sons and each of them is more precious to me than my eyes. It is now time for them to be married, and, to the wise, nothing is more important than that their sons be married to worthy brides. My country is a flourishing and noble one, and my three sons are wise and learned and worthy of the crown and sovereignty. I have heard, O king, that you have three chaste and beautiful daughters. I rejoice at this news, since I see that our children are of a lineage worthy of one another and that it would be fitting if we arranged their marriages with all due pomp and ceremony.'"

When the king of the Yemen heard Jandal's words, his face clouded over and in his heart he thought, "My daughters are the light of my eyes, my prop and support in every undertaking. If they are not here beside me, my days will be as dark as night. I must answer circumspectly and give myself time to think of a way out of this."

He granted Feraydun's messenger a suitable lodging at the court and asked him to wait until a fitting answer could be prepared. Then he summoned his experienced advisors and put the matter before them, saying, "Feraydun has asked for the hands of my daughters in marriage, on behalf of his sons, but you are aware of how dear my daughters are to me. I don't know how to free myself from this predicament. If I say I am pleased at this development, I will not be telling the truth, and it is not acceptable for a king to lie. Besides, if I hand my daughters over to him, how will I be able to endure the fire in my heart, the tears in my eyes, and all the sorrows of separation? But if I refuse, how shall I be safe from his rage? Feraydun is lord of the world and you have heard how he dealt with Zahhak. Provoking his enmity would be no light undertaking. Now, what do you propose that I do?"

The nobles of the Yemen replied, "We do not see why you should twist and turn with every breeze that blows. Feraydun may be a great king, but we are not wretches and slaves to do his bidding:

> To give good counsel's our appointed task
> But spears and steeds are all the faith we ask;
> With daggers we will make the earth blood red
> And crowd the sky with lances overhead.

If you approve of Feraydun's sons and consider them worthy of your daughters, accept and stay silent. But if you want to find a way out of this and at the same time remain secure from the wrath of Feraydun, demand conditions from him that it will be difficult to fulfill."

Then the king of the Yemen summoned Jandal and spoke with him at length, saying, "Bear my greetings to Feraydun and say to him that I am the great king's obedient servant and that I accept in my heart whatever he may command me to do. If it is the king's desire that my daughters be honored by such a marriage, then I rejoice at his command. But just as the great king's sons are dear to him, so too my daughters are the apple of my eye, the light of my life, and if the great king were to ask me to hand over my kingdom and crown and throne, or my very eyes, this would be easier for me than that I should exile my daughters from my side. But despite all this, since this is indeed the great king's wish, what he desires will be done. I ask only that his sons come to me here in the Yemen, so that my eyes may see them and rejoice, and so that I may become acquainted with their justice and righteousness; then I shall grasp their hands as a sign of our union and hand over to them the light of my eyes."

Jandal kissed the throne and made his farewells and took the king of the Yemen's message back to Feraydun's court; there he repeated what he had heard.

Feraydun's Advice to His Sons

Feraydun summoned his sons, told them what had happened, and said, "Now you must prepare to leave for the Yemen, from whence you will return with the king of the Yemen's daughters, whose loveliness and charm have no equal. But see that you are wise and circumspect, that you act with due decorum and speak well, and that you show your nobility, purity, and wisdom, for the king of the Yemen is a knowledgeable, perspicacious, and enlightened king, possessed of great armies and wealth. He must not see you as weak and stupid, since he might be tempted to play some trick on you. On your first full day there he will hold a banquet and he will have his three daughters ranged in all their glory and finery on thrones in front of you. These three beauties are of the same height and appearance, and there are very few who can tell which is the youngest and which the oldest. But the youngest daughter will sit at the front and the oldest daughter at the back, and the one in the middle will sit between them. The youngest of you should sit beside the youngest daughter, and the oldest beside the oldest daughter, and the one in the middle should sit with the daughter who sits between the other two. The king of the Yemen will ask you, 'Which of these girls is the oldest, which the youngest, and which the middle girl?' And you should answer as you have found it to be, so that he sees how wise you are."

His sons left their father's presence, and, full of confidence and joy, they prepared themselves for the journey; they equipped a great army and set off for the king of the Yemen's court.

The king of the Yemen came out with a large force of soldiers to welcome them, and the people of the Yemen, both men and women, ran out to see the princes, scattering gold and jewels and musk and saffron before them, and passing goblets of wine from hand to hand in their happiness. The horses' manes were saturated with musk and wine, and the procession went forward, stepping on the gold and coins that had been scattered in its path.

The king of the Yemen put a splendid palace at the princes' disposal and on the next day, just as Feraydun had said, he held a banquet and brought his daughters out in their finery, hoping that the princes would not be able to distinguish between them and that he could use their ignorance as an excuse to annul the agreement.

But the sons were aware of his ruse and they answered wisely, distinguishing the girls exactly as their father had told them to. The king of the Yemen and his courtiers were astonished and realized that trickery would not work against these young men. When he saw that no pretext remained, the king gave his consent to the marriage of Feraydun's sons with the princesses of the Yemen, and his beautiful daughters then returned to their quarters.

The Spell Wrought by the King of the Yemen

But the king of the Yemen, who was familiar with spells and magic, could not bear the thought of being separated from his daughters. He thought of another plan, a way of testing Feraydun's sons by magic, hoping that if he could entrap them by some spell, his daughters would be free of them and would remain with him.

Deep into the night they drank wine in celebration of the marriage. When wine had overcome the guests and made everyone sleepy, the king gave orders that the brothers' beds were to be made in an orchard, beneath a tree that scattered blossoms and beside a channel that flowed with rosewater.

When the brothers had fallen asleep, the king of the Yemen left the orchard and cast a spell by which suddenly a violent wind sprang up and severe cold seized the orchard, so that everything froze motionless in an icy grip. But the Iranian princes had learned how to break spells from their father, Feraydun, and as suddenly as the wind had sprung up, they awoke from their sleep and by means of the divine *farr*, which protected the royal family, they were able to neutralize the spell and so remain unharmed by the severe cold.

On the next day, when the sun rose above the mountain peaks, the magician-king came to the garden, expecting to find the three princes frozen and lifeless, their faces blue with cold. But he was astonished to see the three princes seated on thrones, their faces bright and shining as the new moon.

رسیده ست با ما بدیشان ملوک

همه گرزداران پرخاشخن

He realized that his magic would have no effect and that his daughters now belonged to Feraydun's three sons. Since there was no other way for him to proceed, he accepted what had happened and set about preparing fitting trousseaux for the brides. He opened the doors of his ancient treasury and brought out quantities of gold and jewels; these, together with untold wealth of other kinds, he loaded on the backs of pack animals and then, together with the princes and their brides, he set out in state toward Feraydun's court.

> News came of their return: without delay
> King Feraydun set out to block their way—
> He longed to know their hearts, and by a test
> Lay all his mind's anxieties to rest.
> He took a dragon's form, one so immense
> You'd say a lion would have no defense
> Against its strength; and from its jaws there came
> A roaring river of incessant flame.
> He saw his sons, dust rose into the sky,
> The world re-echoed with his grisly cry:
> First he attacked the eldest prince, who said,
> "No wise man fights with dragon-foes," and fled.
> Seeing his second son, he wheeled around—
> The youth bent back his bow and stood his ground,
> Shouting, "If combat's needed I can fight
> A roaring lion or an armored knight."
> Lastly the youngest son approached and cried,
> "Out of our path, fell monster, step aside,
> If you have heard of Feraydun then know
> That we're his valiant, lionlike sons—now go,
> Or I'll give you a crown that you'll regret!"
> He saw how each son took the test he'd set
> And disappeared. He left them there, but then
> Came out to greet his princes once again—
> Their king now, and the father whom they knew,
> Surrounded by his royal retinue.

Then he gave each of the Yemeni princesses Persian names: He called the wife of Salm, the oldest son, Arezu (Desire), and he called the wife of Tur, the middle son, Mah (Moon), and he called the wife of Iraj, the youngest son, Sahi (Tall and Slender).

⊰ THE STORY OF IRAJ ⊱

Feraydun Divides His Kingdom

After the marriages of Salm, Tur, and Iraj had been celebrated with great pomp and splendor, Feraydun summoned astrologers to his court and had them read his sons' horoscopes. When it came to Iraj's horoscope, they saw war and dissension there; Feraydun was saddened by this and fell to brooding on the unkind, inauspicious fate foretold by the skies.

In order to obviate any discord between his sons, Feraydun divided his vast domains into three areas. Rum and the lands of the West he gave to the oldest of the brothers, Salm. China and Turkestan he bestowed upon Tur, and Iran and Arabia he handed over to Iraj.

Salm and Tur both set off for their respective lands and Iraj took his place upon the throne of Iran, which was the most favored of the countries ruled by Feraydun.

Salm Is Envious of Iraj

Many years went by. Feraydun grew old and his strength and glory faded. The demon of greed found its way into Salm's heart. Salm became dissatisfied with his own portion; he grew envious of Iraj and evil plans preoccupied him. He sent an envoy to China, to Tur, with the following message: "O king of Turkestan and China, may you live always in joy and contentment. But look how unjustly our father has erred in the way he divided up the lands between us. We were three brothers, and I was the oldest. But our father favored the youngest of us and gave the throne of Iran to him and sent you and me off to the East and the West. Why should we stand for such injustice? How are you and I less than Iraj?"

When he heard these words, greed and desire crept into Tur's heart and his head whirled as in a wind. He chose an eloquent messenger and sent him to his older brother, saying, "Yes, you are right, we have been unjustly dealt with, and when Feraydun made his division of the land, we were

deceived. Brave men do not patiently accept deceit and injustice. You and I must sit down face to face and look for a solution to this."

In this fashion the curtain that had been hiding the brothers' secret desires was drawn aside. Shortly after this, Salm set off from the west and Tur from the east, their hearts filled with hatred for Iraj. When they met they withdrew together and discussed what should be done.

The Message Sent by Salm and Tur

Then they chose a persuasive, intelligent messenger and told him to make all speed to Feraydun's court and there to announce their message to Feraydun

openly. First the messenger was to present the two brothers' greetings and then to say, "O king, now that you have reached old age, it is time that you were mindful of the fear of God. The great God bestowed all the world on you, and from the shining sun to the dark earth all beings obeyed you. But you did not carry out the orders of God; instead you followed only your own desires and acted with impiety and oppression. You had three sons, all wise, all noble. One of these you elevated and the other two you treated with contempt. You gave the land of Iran, with all its wealth and treasure, to Iraj, and you sent the two of us wandering off to the East and the West. Iraj has no more ability than we do, and as regards lineage, we are not less than him. Well, whatever injustice you have done against us is done, but now you must recompense us and follow the ways of justice. You must either remove the crown from Iraj's head and send him wandering off to some corner of the earth, as you did to us, or you must prepare for battle. If Iraj remains on the throne, we shall attack Iran with a mighty army of Turks and Chinese and Western warriors, and we shall wreak vengeance on Iraj."

As soon as the envoy had heard the message he mounted his horse and sped to Feraydun's court. When his eyes beheld Feraydun's palace, the might of his army, and the splendor of his courtiers, he gazed at them, lost in astonishment.

Feraydun was told that a messenger had come from his sons. He ordered that the curtain that screened kings from the eyes of the vulgar be drawn aside and the man be granted audience. The messenger saw a great and glorious king, radiant as the sun, seated upon his throne. He made a deep obeisance and kissed the ground. Feraydun welcomed him with kindness and motioned him to a place of honor. Then in a gentle voice he asked after his sons' health and happiness, as well as of the hardships the messenger had suffered along the way to his court.

The envoy greeted Feraydun with all due respect and then said, "May the king live forever; your sons are alive and well and I have brought a message from them to you. Should the message be harsh, I am no more than the messenger, a mere slave of the court. May the king forgive this impertinence, for if the message is intemperate, this is no fault of the messenger. If the king orders me, I shall tell him the message these hotheaded youths have sent."

The king gave his permission and the envoy repeated the message of Salm and Tur.

Feraydun's Answer

When Feraydun heard the envoy's words and became aware of Salm's and Tur's ingratitude and malevolence, his blood boiled within him. He turned to the envoy and said, "You have no need to apologize, I should have foreseen this. Tell my two ungrateful sons from me: 'With this message you have revealed your true nature. Ungratefully and foolishly you think to take advantage of my old age. You have no shame before me, and you have erased the fear of God from your hearts. But remember the turning of the heavens and the ways of fate. I too was young once, my stature upright and my hair black as pitch. The heavens that have turned my hair white and bowed my back are still in their place and they will not leave you young forever either. Consider the days of your weakness and frailty. I swear by the great God, by the shining sun, and by the royal throne, that I have done no evil to you, my sons. Before I divided up my kingdom I consulted with learned priests and councillors. All my endeavors were made in a spirit of justice and righteousness. I have never given either ill will or injustice a place in my heart. I wanted the world to remain a place of joy and civilized order, and I divided it between my three sons, whom I considered the light of my eyes. My hope was that my sons would avoid all discord and dissension. But Ahriman has misled you; greed and ambition have found their way into your hearts so that you have forgotten all shame, rising up in anger against your ancient father and selling your younger brother's love for a fistful of earth. I fear that the heavens will not look kindly on this venture of yours. I am an old man now and this is not the time for me to think of anger and strife. But you have many long years before you. Try not to soil your minds with greed and malice. When the heart is emptied of all greed, treasures and dust are but one. Strive to do such things that they will be the means of your salvation on Judgment Day."

Iraj's Humility

After Salm and Tur's messenger had returned to his masters, Feraydun brooded on what should be done. He summoned Iraj and said to him, "My child, your brothers have cast all love for you from their hearts; they have chosen to follow the ways of malice and hatred. The desire for wealth and power has turned their heads; each of them has prepared an army and they intend to attack from both sides simultaneously and destroy you. From the beginning, their malevolence and ingratitude were written in the stars. You must take all precautions; open the doors of your treasury and equip an army so that you will be ready for their attack, since if you answer malevolence with kindness, you will only make them even more overbearing."

Iraj was a kind, humble youth, content with whatever fortune gave him. He said, "O king, why should we plant seeds of dissension, why should we pollute our friendship and happiness with spite and injustice? In this brief moment of life that Fate has allowed us, is it not better that we act kindly toward one another? Time whirls by like wind, scattering the dust of old age upon our heads; our stature is bent double, our cheeks fill with wrinkles, and the pillow all of us finally rest upon is the dust. Why should we plant the tree of hatred? We did not bring the usages of monarchy and sovereignty into the world; before we came here, there were kings and mighty leaders. Their way was not the way of vindictiveness and anger. If my lord will agree, I shall renounce the throne; I shall win my brothers over by such kindness that all vindictiveness and anger will be expelled from their hearts."

Feraydun replied, "O my wise son, such an answer is worthy of a man like you: It is no surprise if the moon radiates moonlight. But though you follow the way of love, your brothers are seeking the path of war. To act kindly toward a malevolent enemy is liking placing one's head in a snake's mouth in order to show it friendship. What other outcome can there be besides a venomous bite? But if in spite of all this you intend to act in a conciliatory way toward Salm and Tur, I shall write a letter to them and send it with you. I hope you return safe and sound."

Iraj Visits His Brothers

Then Feraydun wrote a letter to Salm and Tur, saying, "My sons, I no longer have any need for the royal throne or for treasure or an army. All my desire is for my three sons' happiness and welfare. Iraj, with whom you were so angry, has come hoping to see you. Although he has done no one any harm, in order to satisfy you he has stepped down from the royal throne and stands ready to serve you. Iraj is your younger brother; you should act kindly toward him. See that you treat him well and show him no anger; then, after a few days have elapsed, send him back to me with all due honor, and safe and sound."

Accompanied by a few traveling companions, Iraj set off toward his brothers. When he drew near them, Salm and Tur, together with a great army, came out toward him. Iraj greeted his brothers with kindness, warmly embracing them. But their hearts were full of hatred for him.

When their soldiers saw Iraj's splendid face and stature, they were astonished and said to themselves, "Iraj is worthy of the crown and throne; he is every inch a king, deserving of sovereignty." Iraj's kindness struck a chord in the soldiers' hearts, and his name passed among them from one to another.

Salm watched his soldiers; he realized that Iraj had won their hearts and that they were talking about him. He frowned and, his heart filled with hatred, entered his royal tent. He gave orders that he and Tur be left alone. Then he sat down to take counsel with Tur and said, "Our soldiers have given their hearts to Iraj. When we were coming back with Iraj, they couldn't take their eyes off him. We had worries enough, and now we have to worry about our armies, too. As long as they're so enamored of Iraj, our soldiers will not accept us as their kings. If we allow Iraj to remain alive, our sovereignty will not last long."

The Murder of Iraj

All night, until dawn, the two brothers brooded on the crime they contemplated. When the sun rose they banished justice from their hearts, washed their eyes of all shame, and set off quickly for Iraj's tent. Iraj was at the tent's entrance, watching for his brothers. When he saw them, he ran forward, greeting them warmly.

They answered him coldly and entered the tent with him, and laid their grievances before him. Harshly, Tur opened the conversation, "Iraj, you are younger than both of us. How is it that you should possess the crown and throne of Iran and have our father's treasure at your disposal, while we, who are both senior to you, should spend our days in China and the western provinces? When he divided up the countries between us, our father acted honorably only toward you; to us he acted unjustly."

Kindly, Iraj said, "O my brother, why do you torment yourself in this way? If you desire to be sovereign of Iran, I will resign the Kayanid crown and throne to you. What use are treasures and glory if they annoy one's brother? All of us in the end come to nothingness. Even if we were to subdue the whole world to our desires, our head's final resting place is the dust of the grave. What point is there in oppression and injustice? Come, let us look kindly on one another and tread the paths of goodness and chivalry. If hitherto my signet ring has given me lordship over the realm of Iran, I hereby renounce my power and hand over to you throne, crown, army, and authority. And I do not desire China or the West either. I have no quarrel with you, and I ask you not to harbor hatred for me, not to torment my heart in this way. You are both senior to me and deserving of greatness. I would not exchange your happiness and contentment for all the world. And so I ask that you also act kindly toward your younger brother and put aside such angry talk."

But Tur was determined to fight with his brother, and Iraj's kindness and attempts at reconciliation only further infuriated him. Again he spoke harshly and violently to Iraj, every now and then jumping up from his place and striding back and forth and then sitting down again. Finally anger and violence so ripped away all sense of shame that he sprang up, grasped the golden throne on which he had been seated, and brought it crashing down on Iraj's head.

Iraj realized that his brother intended to kill him. He asked for mercy and cried out: "Have you no fear of God, nor no shame before our aged father? Let me live, don't stain your hands with my blood. How can your heart let you murder me? My blood will be on your head forever:

You have a soul yourself—how can you say
That you will take another's soul away?
Pity the ants that toil beneath your feet;
They have their souls—to them their souls are sweet.

If you cannot forgive me at least remember our aged father and do not torment his old age and weakness with the death of a son. And if you care nothing for our father, remember the world's Creator and do not include yourself among the murderers. If you desire treasures and the crown and my seal of office, I have given them to you; have mercy on me and do not spill my blood."

Black-hearted Tur returned no answer. He drew a poisoned dagger and plunged it into Iraj's body; blood stained the young prince's cheeks, and his angelic stature buckled and he lay stretched on the ground. Then Tur cut off his brother's head and gave orders that it be wrapped in camphor and musk and sent to Feraydun.

Having carried out their crime, Salm and Tur set off triumphantly for their own countries, one toward China and the other toward Rum and the West.

Feraydun Learns of Iraj's Death

Feraydun was waiting anxiously for Iraj. When the time for his son's return had come, he gave orders that the city be splendidly decked out for his welcome, that a turquoise throne be prepared for him, and that everyone watch for his approach. The whole town gave itself up to pleasure, with musicians and singers playing and singing to the crowds, when suddenly a plume of dust became visible in the distance. A messenger, energetically urging his horse forward, emerged from the dust. As he drew near the Persian army, he cried out in a loud voice full of pain and sorrow and laid the casket he was carrying with him on the ground. They opened the casket and, pulling aside the silk they found there, saw the young prince's severed head.

Feraydun fell from his horse and cried out, tearing the clothes from his body. The warriors and nobles who were present heaped dust on their heads in anguish, and the soldiers wept bitter tears, grieving for the death of their renowned lord.

The sound of wailing spread throughout the city, and everywhere cries and lamentations could be heard. Feraydun clasped the head of his beloved son in his arms and carried it, stumbling and reeling, to Iraj's castle. There he saw the throne that had no lord, the army that had no leader, and the paradisal garden given up to grief and sorrow. He closeted himself in the castle and sat weeping and moaning, "Alas, alas for you, my luckless prince, slaughtered by the dagger of vengeance. Alas, alas for you, my beloved son, unjustly murdered. Alas for your bravery and splendor and royal *farr*, alas for your greatness and magnanimity. O God, Creator of this world, just judge of all, look on this innocent victim whose blood has been vilely spilt on the earth. O great God, grant my desire and allow me life enough to see one of Iraj's descendants rise up to avenge his father, and may he sever the heads of those two vile creatures just as they have unjustly severed the head of this sweet youth from his body. This is my one petition before your throne, I have no other need or hope."

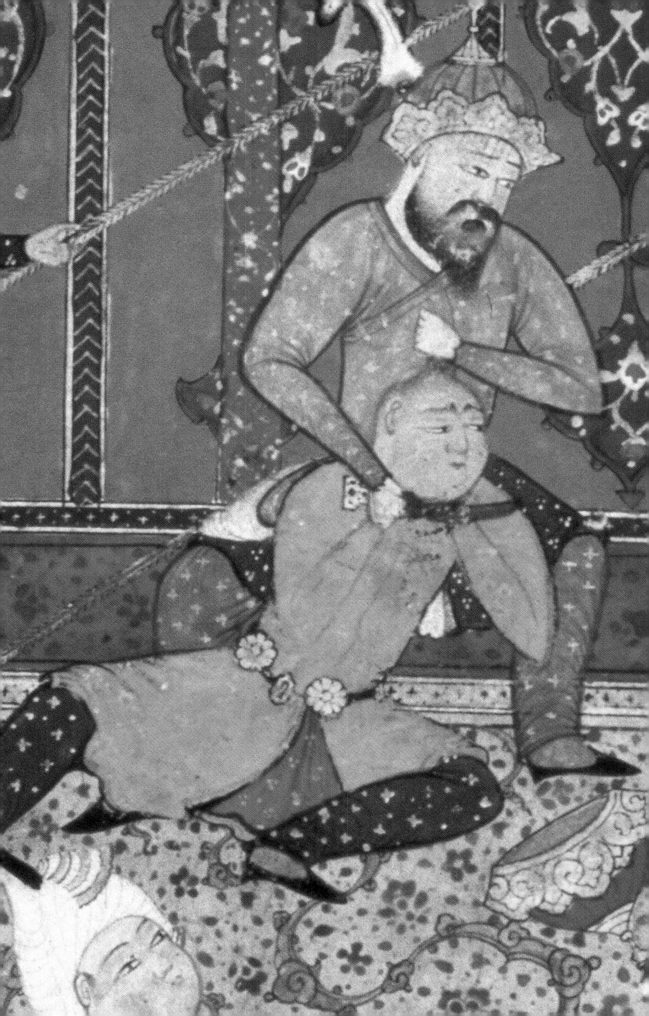

☙ THE VENGEANCE OF MANUCHEHR ❧

Manuchehr's Birth

At the time that Iraj was killed by his brothers Salm and Tur, one of his wives, who was called Mah-Afarid, was pregnant by him. When Feraydun, the emperor of Iran, learned of this, he rejoiced and made much of Mah-Afarid. Mah-Afarid gave birth to a beautiful daughter who was brought up gently and graciously until she grew into a fine young woman, with the stature of a cypress tree and a face as lovely as a wild tulip. Feraydun married this young woman to his nephew, a courageous Persian prince named Pashang.

From the union of Pashang and Iraj's daughter, Manuchehr was born. Feraydun rejoiced so much at the sight of Manuchehr that it was as if his own son Iraj had been restored to him. He had a great celebration organized, with much feasting and revelry; in his joy at Manuchehr's birth he distributed large quantities of gold and jewels and every year from then on a festival was held on that day. He gave orders that special pains were to be taken with his education and that he was to be taught everything becoming to a lord and a noble warrior.

In this way some years passed. Manuchehr became a brave, noble, and cultivated young man. Then Feraydun convoked a council of the nobles and warriors and elders of Iran and, in their presence, seated Manuchehr on the throne and made him king of Iran in Iraj's place, bestowing the crown and royal seal on him. The army accepted his authority and the nobles and champions of the country proclaimed him as their king. Qaren, the commander of the Persian armies, Garshasb, the great cavalry leader, and the fearless champion Sam all declared their heartfelt loyalty to him; they swore fealty to the young king and pledged themselves to join with him in seeking revenge against Salm and Tur for the slaying of their brother Iraj.

Salm and Tur's Message

News reached Salm and Tur that Manuchehr had ascended the royal throne, that he had drawn up an army, and that the whole country supported him.

The brothers' hearts were filled with fear. They consulted together and decided to send someone to Feraydun, hoping that by asking for pardon and by flattering him they would be able to escape Manuchehr's desire for revenge. So they chose a clever, eloquent messenger and picked out a great many gifts from their treasuries—ivory thrones, golden crowns, pearls, jewels, silver and gold coins, musk, ambergris, brocade, silk, and fur—piled all these on the backs of elephants and set off for Feraydun's court, sending their envoy ahead with the following message: "May the brave Feraydun live forever; we have no desire in life other than our father's happiness. If we have acted unjustly and oppressively toward our younger brother, we now regret this injustice and have come to ask for pardon. In these past long years our hearts have been tormented by the injustice we did to our brother, and this has been a terrible punishment for our evil acts. If we have sinned, it was Fate that ordained this, and there is no escape from the will of Divine Fate; even lions and dragons, for all their strength, cannot escape the claws of Destiny. And then we were overcome by the demon of greed, so that the malevolent Ahriman led us astray, and our councils were darkened and we turned to evil and injustice. Now all this is in the past, and we offer ourselves as slaves, ready for service. If the emperor sees fit, may he send Manuchehr to us, together with his army, so that we may stand before him as his inferiors, ready to do his bidding; we shall shower wealth and precious stuffs upon him and wash away the sorrows of his heart with our tears."

News reached Feraydun that the envoy of Salm and Tur had arrived. He gave commands that he be granted an audience. When the envoy entered the court, he was astonished by the splendor and royal *farr* of Feraydun and by the nobility gathered there. Feraydun was seated on the imperial throne, wearing the Kayanid crown, and Manuchehr was seated next to him, wearing the royal crown. On either side of them were ranged nobles and elders, arrayed in gold and jewels and iron and steel. The envoy went forward, made his obeisance, asked permission to speak, and then repeated the brothers' message.

Feraydun's Answer

When Feraydun heard the malevolent brothers' message, he cried out, "I have heard the message of this vile pair. This is my answer. Tell those unjust and evil criminals that there is no point in their pursuing their lies. Say, 'Your malevolence is not hidden from me. What's happened now to make you so kind to Manuchehr? Do you wish now to destroy Manuchehr too by such tricks, to act toward him as you acted toward my son Iraj? Oh yes, Manuchehr will come to you, but not like Iraj, careless of his safety, unarmed and alone. This time he will come with the Kaviani banner, with a

mighty army, with armor and lances and swords, with champions and war-
riors who destroy their enemies; warriors like Qaren who is ever eager for
battle, Garshasb who shatters armies, warlike Shidush, brave Sam, and
courageous Qobad. Manuchehr will come seeking revenge for his grandfa-
ther's death; he will come to punish your fratricide. If through all these
years you have remained unpunished, it is because I did not consider it right
to make war on my own sons. But now a noble shoot has sprung from the
tree which you so unjustly felled, and Manuchehr will come with an army
mighty as the thundering ocean; he will destroy you, root and branch, and
wash away the sorrows of his heart in your blood. As for your declaring that
it was Divine Fate and Destiny that persuaded you to act unjustly, know that
whoever plants the seeds of injustice will reap a harvest of sorrow and dark-
ness. It is your punishment that is fated by God. Have you no shame, to

speak so deceitfully and smoothly when your hearts are black with evil desires? And as for your sending treasure and wealth and gold and jewels so that I will forget about vengeance, I shall not sell the blood of Iraj for gold and jewels. Anyone who would sell his son's life for gold is of a monstrous lineage, but my lineage is human. Who told you that gold and wealth will make your old father forget about revenge for his son's death? I have no need of your treasures and jewels. For as long as I live I will devote my energy to seeking revenge for Iraj, and I shall not rest until I see you punished.'"

Trembling, the envoy rose from his place, kissed the ground, and left the court. He hurried back to the two brothers, who were in their tent discussing the situation when he entered. They questioned him, asking for information on Feraydun, his army, and his realm. The envoy repeated what he had seen of Feraydun's splendor and royal *farr*, of his great castle and serried army, of his bursting treasury and the bellicose warriors of his court; he told them of Qaren-e Kavian, leader of the Persian army, of Garshasb and brave Sam, and then he related Feraydun's message to them.

The brothers' hearts were gripped by fear and their cheeks grew pale. Finally Salm said, "It's clear that our asking for pardon has had no effect and that Manuchehr is determined to revenge his grandfather's death. We should not have expected anything else from someone who is descended from Iraj and has been brought up by Feraydun. We must muster our armies, forestall their plans, and attack Iran."

Manuchehr Makes War on Salm and Tur

News reached Feraydun that the armies of Salm and Tur had united, that they had crossed the Oxus and were bearing down on Iran. Feraydun summoned Manuchehr and said, "My boy, the time has come for war and vengeance. Equip your army and prepare for battle." Manuchehr said, "Great king, whoever opposes you in battle is ill-fated and will be destroyed. Now I shall put on my armor, and I shall not remove it from my body until I have taken revenge for my grandfather's death. I shall do such things to Salm and Tur that they shall never be forgotten."

Then he gave orders that the army was to be drawn up and the royal pavilion pitched on the plains. Little by little the army assembled. The plains were filled with tumult. The battle cries of the warriors, the neighing of horses, the clatter of drums and squeal of trumpets—all rose echoing to the heavens. Great warriors were drawn up in ranks on the army's two flanks. The center was held by Qaren-e Kavian and three hundred thousand warriors. The left flank was commanded by Garshasb, and Sam, the son of Nariman, together with Qobad, held the right flank. Wearing their massive body armor and with drawn swords, the champions moved forward; the army, like a mountain on the move, set off toward Turan.

News reached Salm and Tur that the Persian army, with all its heroes and champions and warriors, was nearby. The brothers drew up their own armies, ready for battle. From the Persian side Qobad rode out to observe the situation and strength of the enemy. From the other side Tur also rode forward and shouted out: "Heh, Qobad, go back to Manuchehr and tell him that Iraj's child was a girl, so how did he manage to seat himself on the throne, and where did he get the crown and royal seal from?" Qobad shouted back, "I'll report your message just as you said it, but see that you wait until you get an answer worthy of such childish prattle. When the Kaviani banner moves forward, and the Persian lions with their swords in their fists fall among you foxes, your hearts will burst with terror of our heroes, and the very beasts of the field will weep for you poor devils."

Then Qobad rode back and gave Tur's message to Manuchehr. Manuchehr laughed and said: "The wretch doesn't know that Iraj is my grandfather and that I'm the son of that girl. But the moment I urge my horse into battle it'll be clear who is descended from which lineage. I swear by the divine *farr* and by the sun and moon that I shall not give him respite enough to blink his eyes. I shall shatter his army and cut his worthless head from his body with my sword. Thus will I take revenge for the slaughter of Iraj."

As night was departing, Qaren-e Kavian, the leader of the Persian army, stood before his troops and cried out, "O far-famed warriors, the battle which lies before us is a battle between God and Ahriman. We have come seeking vengeance and must remain alert and vigilant. The world's Creator is with us. Whoever is killed in this battle will be rewarded with Paradise, and whoever lays his enemies low will live renowned for his exploits and be given land and wealth by the king of Iran. When dawn unsheathes its sword you must all be ready for battle, but do not stir from your positions until you hear the command."

With one voice the army answered, "We are yours to command; our lives and bodies are at the king's service. When the order comes we are ready to plunge our swords into our enemies and to leave the plain awash with their blood."

The Combat between Shirui and Garshasb

As dawn broke, Manuchehr came forth from the center of the army. He wore his body armor and his crown, and with his drawn sword in his hand he was as splendid as the sun rising from behind a mountain. As they caught sight of him, all the army burst forth with shouts and cries of "May the king live forever"; they thrust their lances into the air and the whole army became as tumultuous as a roaring ocean. The two hordes advanced toward each other, and the din of their war cries rose into the air.

When the sun had passed its high point in the heavens, Manuchehr became impatient with the length of time their combat was taking. He gripped his horse with his thighs, stretched out his hand, and grabbed at Kakui's belt; he lifted his opponent's mammoth bulk from the saddle and dashed it to the ground, then plunged his sharp sword into his chest.

Salm Is Killed

With the death of Kakui, the back of Salm's army was broken. Scenting victory, the Iranians violently attacked their enemies. Salm realized that he could not overcome Manuchehr, and he fled toward the Fortress of Alanan to take refuge there and be safe from his enemy's attacks. Manuchehr understood what Salm was about to do and followed him with a mighty army. When Salm arrived at the seashore he saw no sign of the fortress; everything was burned and laid waste, leveled in the dust. His hopes faded and he and his army prepared to flee, but the Iranians drew their swords and fell on the retreating warriors.

Manuchehr was always on the lookout to take revenge for the death of Iraj, and when he caught sight of Salm, he urged his horse forward in order to get close to him. Then he cried out, "Vile, unjust wretch, you killed your

brother out of desire for his throne and crown. Hold your ground now, for I have brought you your throne and crown. The tree of malice and greed that you planted has borne fruit, and now you must taste that fruit. I shall do to you as you did to my grandfather Iraj. Stand now, and see a people's revenge." Having said this he charged forward, drawing his sword, which he brought down on Salm's head, cleaving him in two. Manuchehr gave orders that Salm's head be severed from its body and spitted on a lance.

When Salm's soldiers saw their leader's head on the lance, they lost all heart and scattered like a flock in a storm, fleeing in separate bands to byways and mountain strongholds. Finally they asked for quarter, sending to Manuchehr a humble, eloquent man who said, "O king, we are all your slaves and yours to command. If we fought against you, this was not our choice. We are mostly shepherds and farmers and war is not our business. But we were ordered to the battlefield. Now we trust in your justice, throwing ourselves on your mercy. Accept our repentance and grant us our worthless lives."

When Manuchehr heard their envoy's words, he said, "Far be it from me that I should harass the helpless. I fought in order to take revenge for Iraj's death. Thanks be to God I have accomplished my goal and visited condign punishment on the evil. Now my commands are that my former enemies live in peace and security, and that every man return to the land of his birth and there follow the ways of righteousness and religion."

The armies of China and Rum praised the king and blessed his name. They took off their armor and came in scattered bands to Manuchehr, kissing the ground before him and handing over their weapons—their swords and lances and spears, cuirasses and breastplates, helmets and shields, maces and daggers and barding. Then, praising him, they departed, each for his own country.

Manuchehr's Return

Manuchehr dispatched a swift messenger, bearing Salm's head, to Feraydun; he sent too a message describing the recent battle and announcing his own imminent return.

Feraydun, together with the nobles and lords of Iran, came out with their armies to welcome him, and Feraydun and Manuchehr met with great splendor and pomp; festivities were held and the two distributed gold and silver to their troops.

Then Feraydun entrusted Manuchehr to Sam, the renowned champion of Iran, and said, "I am not long for this world. I hand my great-grandson over to your keeping; see that you are the prop and support of his reign." Then he turned his face to the heavens and said, "O great God, I offer here my gratitude to you. You bestowed the crown and royal seal upon me and you have been my support in all that I have done. With your help I have followed righteousness and striven for justice and I have achieved all my desires. And finally, two malicious criminals have received their just deserts. But now I am sated with life. Fate has decreed that I see the heads of my three dear sons severed from their bodies. What was fated took place. Free me now from this world, and send me to another place."

Then Feraydun placed Manuchehr on the imperial throne, where he himself had sat, and with his own hands he set the Kayanid crown on Manuchehr's head.

> Having done this, he bowed to Fate's decree—
> The leaf was withered on the royal tree.
> He lived his life in mourning; ceaseless tears
> And constant grief consumed his final years.
> Weeping, the great king said, "My heart's delight,
> My sons, have turned my days to endless night—
> My sons slain wretchedly before my eyes,
> Since all my plans were evil and unwise . . ."
> And so, heartbroken, weeping for the past,
> He lived tormented till Death came at last.
> O world, from end to end, unreal, untrue—
> No wise man can live happily in you.
> But bless'd is he whose good deeds bring him fame,
> Monarch or slave, he leaves a lasting name.

❧ THE TALE OF SAM AND THE SIMORGH ❧

The Birth of Zal

Sam, the son of Nariman, was the lord of Zabol and the preeminent champion of Iran, but he had no sons, and this was a source of great grief to him. At last a beautiful woman of his entourage became pregnant by him and she gave birth to a handsome son. But although the baby had rosy cheeks and black eyes and a fine face, his hair was as white as snow. His mother was very distressed by this. No one dared go to Sam and say that he had a son whose hair was as white as that of an old man.

Finally the boy's wet nurse, who was a courageous woman, conquered her fear and went to Sam and said, "My lord, I bring good news. You have a handsome, healthy son as splendid as the sun. And if he has white hair, well, this was your Destiny fated by God. You must rejoice and not grieve about this."

When he heard the wet nurse's words, Sam descended from the throne and went to the women's apartments. He saw the rosy-cheeked, splendid baby whose hair was like an old man's. He was deeply perturbed and, turning his face to the heavens, said, "O just Lord, what sin have I committed that you have given me a white-haired son? If now the nobles here should ask, 'What is this baby with black eyes and white hair?' how am I to answer? How can I lift my head up with such shame in my family? The champions and nobles will laugh at Sam, the son of Nariman, saying that after so long he finally had a son who has white hair. How can I stay in my own country with such a son?" Saying this, he passionately turned his head aside and left the apartments.

The Simorgh

A short while later he gave orders that the baby be taken from its mother and carried to the foothills of the Alborz Mountains, where it was to be exposed. The little baby was left on the ground, bereft of its mother's love, with no comfort or companion, without food or clothes. It gave a cry and began to weep. The Simorgh had a nest on a summit of the Alborz. As she was flying on her search for food, she heard the sound of the crying baby. She flew low and saw the baby lying on the ground, crying and sucking its thumb. She had intended to treat the child as prey, but maternal love stirred in her heart. She reached down with her claws and lifted him up to take him to her own fledglings.

When the Simorgh's fledglings set eyes on the crying baby, they were astonished; they acted kindly toward him and made much of him.

A voice came from God to the Simorgh, saying, "O king of the birds, nourish and look after this splendid child." The Simorgh gave the child food and brought him up with her own young.

Many years passed. The child grew up and became a brave, noble youth. Caravans passing that way would occasionally glimpse the mammoth-bodied young man with white hair, as he moved nimbly among the crags and foothills of the mountains. Rumors of the youth passed from mouth to mouth, until the world was full of talk of him and the news reached Sam, the son of Nariman.

Sam's Dream

One night Sam was asleep in the inner apartments of his castle. In a dream he saw an Indian warrior, mounted on a galloping horse, who came to him and gave him the good news that his son was alive. Sam started up from sleep and summoned the wise men and priests of his court and told them of his previous night's dream and said, "What is your opinion of this? Can we believe that a defenseless child could survive the cold of winter and the heat of summer and stay alive until now?"

The priests considered the matter carefully and then reproached the king, saying, "My lord, you have acted ungratefully, despising the gift given to you by God. Consider the beasts of the field, the untamed beasts of the thicket, the birds of the air, and the fish in the sea, and see how loving they are to their offspring. Why did you take his white hair to heart in this way and not consider his innocent body and divine soul? Now it is plain that God has preserved your son, and one whom God preserves cannot be destroyed. You must follow the path of remorse and seek out your son."

The next night Sam saw in a dream that a young man carrying a banner had appeared at the head of an army in the mountains of India, and that he was accompanied by two learned priests. One of these two came forward and began to speak harshly to him, "O presumptuous, heartless man, had you no shame before God that you exposed on a mountainside the son for whom you had begged God? You despised him for his white hair, but look, your own hair has turned as white as milk. What kind of a father do you call yourself, that a bird has had to bring up your child?"

Sam started up from sleep and immediately made all preparations necessary for a journey, and set off for the Alborz Mountains. He saw a high peak whose summit touched the heavens. On the top of the peak rose the Simorgh's nest, as tall and strong as a castle, and around it walked a nimble-bodied, noble youth. Sam realized that this was his son. He wanted to climb up to him, but for all his efforts he could not find a way up the mountain. The Simorgh's nest seemed to be placed as high as the stars themselves. He scattered dust on his head and bowed before God, repenting his former actions, and said, "O just Lord, place a way before my feet so that I can reach my child again."

The Return of Dastan

Sam's repentance was accepted in the world Creator's court. The Simorgh looked down and, glimpsing Sam on the mountainside, she realized that this was the father come in search of his son. She went to the youth and said, "O brave young man, until today I have brought you up as if I were your nurse, and I have taught you speech and the ways of virtue. Now it is time for you to return to your own birthplace. Your father has come searching for you. I have named you Dastan (The Trickster) and from now on you will be known by this name."

Dastan's eyes filled with tears, and he said, "Have you grown tired of me, that now you are sending me to my father? I have become used to the nests of birds and the high mountain peaks, and I have found comfort in the shade beneath your wings; after God himself, there is no one to whom I am more grateful than you. Why do you want me to return?"

The Simorgh said, "I have not lost my love for you, and I shall always be your kindhearted nurse. But you must return to Zabolestan and there fight and be a brave warrior. Birds' nests are no longer of any use to you. But take a memento of me: I give you this feather from my own wing. Whenever you are in trouble and need aid, fling the feather into fire, and without delay I shall make haste to help you."

Then the Simorgh lifted Dastan up from the mountain peak and placed him on the ground next to his father. The youth seemed so noble and illustrious that Sam wept to see him; he embraced his son and thanked the Simorgh and begged for forgiveness.

The army flocked about Dastan, rejoicing and praising his mammoth body, his strong arms, and his cypress stature. Then Sam and Dastan and the other warriors who were with them set off in high spirits for Zabolestan. From that day forth, because of his white hair, Dastan was called Zal-e Zar (The Golden Graybeard).

❧ THE TALE OF ZAL AND RUDABEH ❧

Zal Travels to Kabol

The demons of Mazanderan and the refractory warriors of Gorgan rose in rebellion against Manuchehr, supreme lord of Iran. Sam, the son of Nariman, entrusted the lordship of Zabolestan to his brave son, Zal-e Zar, and set off for the court of Iran, to offer his services in battle against Manuchehr's enemies.

One day Zal decided to spend time in the pleasures of the chase, and with a few companions and a group of soldiers, he went out to the plains looking for game. Every now and then they stopped beside a stream or in the foothills of the mountains, and Zal would call for singers and musicians and pass the time drinking wine with his friends; and so they went forward until they reached the land of Kabol.

The ruler of Kabol was a sensible, courageous man called Mehrab who paid tribute to Sam, the king of Zabolestan. Mehrab was descended from Zahhak, the Arab who had ruled over Iran and committed so much injustice there, and who had finally been deposed by Feraydun. When Mehrab heard that the son of Sam had arrived near Kabol, he was very pleased. At dawn he went out to greet Zal, accompanied by his army and well-paced horses and nimble slaves, and he bore precious gifts with him.

Zal welcomed him warmly and gave orders that a celebration begin; he called for musicians and entertainers, and he and Mehrab sat happily down to feast together.

Mehrab looked at Zal. He saw a tall, noble, brave youth, with ruddy cheeks, black eyes, and white hair, and with the body of a mammoth and the courage of a lion. He gazed at him in wonder, openly expressing his admiration, and to himself he thought, "To have such a son would be like being lord of all the world."

When Mehrab rose from the feast, Zal saw that he had the trunk and stature of a male lion, and he said to his friends, "I don't think a more elegant and handsome and noble individual than Mehrab can be found in any country anywhere."

During the celebrations one of the courtiers remarked that Mehrab had a daughter, and said of her:

> "In purdah, and unseen by anyone,
> He has a daughter lovelier than the sun.
> Lashes like ravens' wings protect a pair
> Of eyes like wild narcissi hidden there;
> If you would seek the moon, it is her face;
> If you seek musk, her hair's its hiding place;
> She is a paradise arrayed in splendor,
> Glorious, graceful, elegantly slender."

When Zal heard the description of Mehrab's daughter, love found its way into his heart and deprived him of all rest. All night he thought of her, and sleep did not visit his eyes.

One day when Mehrab came to Zal's tent, Zal welcomed him warmly and made much of him and told him that if he had any wish hidden in his heart, he had only to ask. Mehrab said, "My lord, I have only one desire and that is that you show your magnanimity to one as unworthy as myself, and that you do me the honor of coming to my house as my guest."

Although Zal's heart was preoccupied with Mehrab's daughter, he thought for a moment, then said, "My lord, ask me anything but this and it shall be done. But my father, Sam, the son of Nariman, and Manuchehr, the lord of Iran, will not look kindly on my entering the abode of one who is of the seed of Zahhak, or of my sitting down to eat as his guest." Mehrab was saddened by this answer; he made his obeisance before Zal and went on his way. But Zal could not rid himself of thoughts of Mehrab's daughter.

Sindokht and Rudabeh

After returning from Zal's camp, Mehrab visited his wife, Sindokht, and his daughter, Rudabeh, and rejoiced to see them. In the midst of their conversation, Sindokht asked about Sam's son and said, "How did he seem to you, and what was it like to eat as his guest? Is he worthy of the royal throne? Has he taken on human habits? Does he know how to act with noble warriors, or is he still the Simorgh's wild child?" Mehrab began to praise Zal, saying, "He is a fine, magnanimous nobleman, and as a mighty warrior he has no equal. He is,

> As ruddy as the pomegranate flower—
> Youthful, and with a young man's luck and power;
> Fierce in revenge, and in the saddle he's
> A sharp-clawed dragon to his enemies;
> Possessed of mammoth strength, a lion's guile,

> *His arms are mighty as the flooding Nile;*
> *He scatters gold when he's in court, and when*
> *He's on the battlefield, the heads of men.*

The one strange thing about him is that the hair on his head and face is completely white. But then, this whiteness suits him and gives his face a kind appearance." When Rudabeh heard these words, her cheeks blushed bright red and she longed to see Zal.

Rudabeh Tells Her Secret to Her Companions

Rudabeh had five close friends who were her confidantes. She told them her secret and said, "I think of Zal night and day, I long to see him, and his absence has reft me of rest and sleep. You must think of some way to make me happy by catching a glimpse of Zal."

Her companions reproached her, saying that in all the seven climes of the world, there was no one as beautiful as she was, and that everyone who heard of her longed for her. And how was it that she should long for someone with white hair and refuse the great lords and nobles who came seeking her hand?

Rudabeh shouted at them, saying that they should not talk so foolishly and that their opinions were all worthless. She went on "If I should fall in love with a star, what use is the moon to me? I long for Zal because of his virtues and bravery, and his face and hair are of no importance to me. When I think of his kindness and goodness, the lord of Rum and the Khaqan of China are as nothing to me.

> *Oh may my heart admit no one but him*
> *And see you mention to me none but him;*
> *I do not love him for his hair and face*
> *But for his virtue and his godly grace."*

When her companions saw that Rudabeh was so firm in her love for Zal, they said with one voice, "O princess, lovely as the moon, we are all yours to command. May a hundred thousand like us be sacrificed for one hair of your head. Tell us what must be done. If we must practice magic in order to bring Zal to you, we shall do this, and if we must give up our lives for one such as you, then so be it."

The Companions' Plan

Then the companions thought of a plan. Each of the five dressed herself in her most attractive clothes and together they made their way over to Zal's camp. It was the month of Farvardin, when spring is at its most beguiling, and the plain was green with new grass and bright with wild flowers. The companions went to a stream, where Zal's tent was pitched on the other side. They began to wander up and down, picking flowers. When they reached a point opposite Zal's tent, the hero caught sight of them and asked, "Who are these girls who are so fond of flowers?" And the answer was, "They are the companions of Mehrab's daughter, who come each day to pick flowers beside the stream."

Zal's head began to whirl and he felt his self-control slip from him. He called for his bow and arrows and, taking a servant with him, strolled alongside the stream. Rudabeh's companions were busy on the opposite bank. Zal looked for some excuse to talk to them, so that he could ask about Rudabeh.

A duck was swimming in the stream and Zal grasped his bow and took aim at it. The duck flew into the air, toward Rudabeh's companions. Zal released his arrow and the duck fell lifeless at the companions' feet. Zal told his servant to cross the stream and retrieve the duck. When Zal's servant reached them, Rudabeh's companions asked him, "Who is he that shot the arrow, for we have never seen such a tall and handsome man?" The

youth answered, "Have no fear, for this is the famous Zal-e Zar, son of the brave warrior Sam. There is no one in the world with his strength and splendor, and no one has ever seen a finer-looking person than him."

The oldest of the companions laughed and said, "This is not so. Mehrab has a daughter who is lovelier than the sun and the moon." Then gently she added, "These two would seem to suit one another, for one is the champion of the world, and the other the most beautiful woman alive.

> *How fitting it would be in every way*
> *If Zal became betrothed to Rudabeh."*

The young man rejoiced at this and said, "What could be finer than that the sun and moon be linked in partnership?" He picked up the duck and returned to Zal and told him what he had heard from Rudabeh's companions.

Zal was very pleased and gave orders that the companions be given jewels and fine robes. They said in reply, "If the hero has anything to say, he should tell us." Zal approached them and enquired after Rudabeh and asked questions about her face and form and habits and character, and as he heard her

described, his love for her grew ever stronger. When the companions saw the hero so eager in his interest they said, "We shall talk to our mistress, and we shall see that she looks kindly on you. In the evening you should come to Rudabeh's castle and delight your eyes with her moon-like beauty."

Zal Visits Rudabeh

The companions returned and brought Rudabeh the good news. When night fell, she secretly sent a servant to Zal to guide him to the castle, while she herself went up on the castle walls to watch for his arrival.

When the brave hero appeared in the distance, Rudabeh called out, greeting him warmly and welcoming him. To Zal it seemed as though he saw the sun itself shining from the castle walls and his heart beat faster with joy. He greeted Rudabeh and declared his love for her.

Rudabeh unloosed her lovely hair and let it down from the castle walls, as if it were a rope for Zal to climb. Zal kissed her tresses and said, "God forbid that I should use your musky hair in this way." Then he took a lariat from his servant and threw it up so that it looped over the battlements; nimbly he sped up the rope and gathered Rudabeh into his arms and embraced her and said, "I love you, and I desire no one but you as my wife; but what can I do—my father Sam, the son of Nariman, and Manuchehr, the king of Iran, will never agree that I marry someone descended from Zahhak."

Rudabeh grieved to hear this and tears stained her cheeks. She said, "If Zahhak was unjust, how is this my sin? Ever since I heard the stories of your bravery and greatness and magnanimity, my heart has been yours. Many nobles and famous warriors have sought my hand in marriage. But I have given my heart to you, and I desire no husband other than you." Zal gazed at Rudabeh with loving eyes and stayed silent for a moment, thinking. Finally he said, "O my beloved, do not grieve. I shall pray to God, asking that he wash away all thoughts of hatred and revenge from the hearts of Sam and Manuchehr, and that they look on you with affection. The lord of Iran is a great and magnanimous man and he will not act unjustly toward me."

Then Rudabeh swore that she would accept no husband in all the world but Zal and that she would give her heart to no one else. These two noble souls swore eternal, binding love to one another; then they said their farewells and Zal returned to his camp.

Zal Consults with the Priests

Zal thought constantly of Rudabeh, and there was no moment when her image was not before him in his mind. He knew that neither Sam, his father, nor Manuchehr, the king of Iran, would agree to his marrying the daughter of Mehrab.

At dawn the next day, hoping to find a solution to his problem, Zal had priests and elders and wise men summoned before him. He told them his heart's secret, saying, "The Lord of the world has established marriage as an institution among mankind, so that children be born and the world be populated and civilization endure. It would be wrong if the lineage of Sam, the son of Nariman, and Zal-e Zar did not continue and if their customs of chivalry and bravery should be lost. I have decided to ask for the hand of Rudabeh, the daughter of Mehrab, in marriage, since my heart is filled with love for her and I know of no one more beautiful or more noble than she. What is your opinion of this matter?"

The priests remained silent and looked at the ground, since they knew that Mehrab was descended from Zahhak and that Sam and Manuchehr would not agree to this marriage.

Once again Zal spoke, "I know that you disapprove of what I am saying, but Rudabeh is so dear to me that I cannot live without her; without her I will find no joy in life. I have pledged my love to her. You must find some way forward for me and help me to achieve my desires. If you do this, I shall act more generously to you than any lord has ever done before to his subjects."

Seeing him so determined in his love for Rudabeh, the priests and wise men said, "My lord, we are all yours to command and we want nothing but your happiness and well-being. There is no shame in wishing for a wife, and although Mehrab is not your equal in greatness, he is a brave and renowned man who has the dignity of kingship; and although Zahhak was tyrannical and was responsible for countless injustices against the people of Iran, he was a powerful and formidable king. Your best course is to write a letter to Sam, telling him what you have in your heart, and to persuade him to support you. If Sam agrees, Manuchehr will not oppose his views."

Zal's Letter to Sam

Zal wrote a letter to Sam: "My lord, may God keep and preserve you. You know of my past, and you know the injustices I have suffered. When I was born, I was left alone and friendless on a mountainside; the companions of my youth were the birds of the air. I suffered from exposure to wind and dust and sun and had no knowledge of a father's love or a mother's embraces. While you lived lapped in silk and brocade, I was seeking a bare subsistence among mountain crags. But this was my destiny ordained by God, and it could not be gainsaid.

Finally you sought me out and welcomed me back to your love. Now I have a wish whose fulfillment is in your hands. My heart is filled with love for Rudabeh, the daughter of Mehrab, and night and day I find no rest from thoughts of her. She is a noble, good, and beautiful woman. No houri of Paradise could be so lovely or so charming. I wish to take her as my wife, according to the customs of our people. What is my noble father's opinion concerning this matter? Do you recall that when you brought me down from the mountains you swore before an assembly of nobles and champions and priests that you would oppose no desire of mine? This now is my desire, and as you well know, it is not worthy of a chivalrous man that he break his word."

Sam's Answer

When Sam saw Zal's letter and had understood what it was that his son wished for, he froze in terror and astonishment. How could he agree to a union between his own family, descended from Feraydun, and the family of Zahhak? He was deeply perturbed by Zal's wish, and he said to himself, "Zal has finally shown his true colors. Such irresponsible selfishness is only to be expected from someone brought up by a bird in the mountains."

He had received the letter while hunting, and he sadly returned home from the chase. Anxiously he thought, "If I refuse my son my permission I will be breaking my oath, and if I agree . . . well, how can poison and sweetness be mixed in one draught? What kind of a child would be born from parents, one of whom was brought up by a wild bird and the other is descended from demons? Into whose hands will the sovereignty of Zabolestan fall then?"

Saddened and tormented by these thoughts, he retired to bed. When day broke he summoned wise men and astrologers, told them what had passed between Zal and Rudabeh, and said, "How can two lineages as disparate as fire and water be mingled? How can a union be effected between the families of Feraydun and Zahhak? Consult the stars and cast my son Zal's horoscope and see what Fate has in store for our family."

The astrologers spent a day casting the horoscope. Finally they reappeared with joyful smiles on their faces, saying that they brought good news, since the union of Mehrab's daughter and Sam's son was an auspicious one. From these two, they said, a splendid son will be born. His sword will dominate the world and he will be the protector and obedient servant of the kings of Iran; he will drive evil and malice from Iran and he will overcome the forces of Turan. He will punish the enemies of the land of Iran, and through him its champions will become renowned throughout the world.

> Iran will trust in him and in his fame,
> Her champions will rejoice to hear his name;
> Throughout his life the monarchy will thrive,
> In times to come his glory will survive;
> Before his name, inscribed on every seal,
> Iran and Rum and India will kneel.

Sam rejoiced to hear the astrologers' words; he gave them presents of silver and gold coins, summoned Zal's envoy, and said to him, "Give my lion-conquering son this message: 'I had not expected such a request from you; however, since I have promised you that I would oppose none of your desires, I find happiness in your happiness. But permission must come from the king. This very night I shall hurry to his court and find out his opinion of the matter.'"

Sindokht Learns of What Rudabeh Has Done

There was a cunning woman who used to act as a go-between for Zal and Rudabeh, taking messages from one to the other. When his envoy came back from Sam, Zal sent this woman to Rudabeh with the good news that his father had agreed to their marriage. Rudabeh was overjoyed and gave the woman jewels and fine clothes; she also gave her a valuable ring which she was to take to Zal together with Rudabeh's greetings.

When this sly woman left Rudabeh's apartments, Sindokht, Rudabeh's mother, caught sight of her. Sindokht became suspicious and asked the woman who she was and what she was doing there.

The woman was afraid and said, "I'm a harmless woman who takes clothes and jewels to rich people's houses in order to sell them. The daughter of the king of Kabol wanted some expensive trinkets. I took them to her and now I'm leaving." Sindokht said, "And where's the money that Rudabeh gave you for them?" The woman was taken aback and said, "She will pay me tomorrow." Sindokht grew even more suspicious and began to cross-examine the woman and to search her. She found the clothes and the ring that Rudabeh had given her; she recognized them and exploded in fury, hitting the woman and dragging her before Rudabeh. She said, "My child, what kind of behavior is this? For your whole life I have been a loving mother to you and I have given you everything you have ever asked for, and now you're keeping secrets from me? Who is this woman and why did she come to see you? You are of royal stock, and there is no one who is lovelier or more beautiful than you; why don't you give some thought to your good name instead of upsetting your mother like this?"

Rudabeh hung her head; tears trickled down her cheeks as she said, "Dearest mother, I am caught in the toils of love for Zal-e Zar. When this noble warrior came from Zabol to Kabol, I became enchanted by his bravery and greatness, and without him I can find no rest. We have sat together and sworn our love for one another, but we have said nothing that was not right and proper. Zal wishes to marry me, and he dispatched a messenger to Sam. At first Sam was angry, but finally he agreed to his son's request. This woman brought me the good news, and I gave her this ring to give to Zal as a token of my gratitude and happiness."

When she had heard her daughter's secret, Sindokht remained silent and amazed. Finally she said, "My child, this is not a wise course of action. Zal is a renowned warrior, the son of Sam, the foremost champion of Iran, and a member of the house of Nariman. He is magnanimous and generous and wise. If you have given your heart to him, well, there is no wonder or sin in that. But if the king of Iran should hear of this secret he will turn on our whole family in fury and raze Kabol, for between the houses of Feraydun and Zahhak there is an ancient enmity. It would be better if you bore this in mind and did not set your heart on things that can never be."

Next, Sindokht turned to the go-between and treated her kindly and, admonishing her to keep the secret hidden, sent her on her way; then she retired to bed, weeping and grieving for Rudabeh's grief.

Mehrab's Fury

When Mehrab returned to his castle that night, he saw Sindokht crying distractedly. He asked her, "What has happened to upset you so much?"

Sindokht replied, "My heart is wrung with thinking on the ways of Fate. Of this great castle, and our fine army, and dear friends, of our joy and our pleasure—what will remain? We planted a sapling with such care and nourished it with such love and took such pains on its behalf, until it bore fruit and spread its shade above us. But hardly can we rest a moment in its shade before it will be laid low in the dust, and from all this pain and desire and hope not a jot will remain in our hands. It is thoughts such as these that have made me so sad. I see that nothing is stable in this world, and I do not know what will become of us."

Mehrab wondered at this speech and said, "You are right, such are the ways of Fate. Before us, those who rejoiced in their castles and power have trodden just such a road. This world is not a place of stability. One comes and another leaves and we cannot fight against Fate. But this is not a new theme; the world was ever thus. What has happened to make you think of such things tonight?"

Sindokht hung her head, tears flowing from her eyes, and she said, "I hinted at my meaning, but I cannot tell you my secret. But how can I keep a secret from you? Zal, Sam's son, has spread all sorts of snares in Rudabeh's path; he has captured her heart and Rudabeh can find no rest away from Zal. All my advice was useless. She can talk only of Zal's love."

Mehrab sprang up and grasped his sword and, shuddering in his fury, cried, "Has Rudabeh no shame or sense, that she would swear to things in secret, flinging our family's honor to the winds in this way? I shall spill her blood on the ground this very minute!" Clinging to his skirts, Sindokht cried out, "Wait for a moment and hear me speak and then do whatever you wish, but do not shed innocent blood."

Mehrab flung her to one side and roared, "Would that on the day she was born I had laid Rudabeh in the ground; better her death than that she make promises to strangers and bring disaster down upon our heads. If Sam and Manuchehr realize that Zal has fallen in love with a girl descended from Zahhak, they will not leave one soul alive in all this land; they will see to it that we are utterly destroyed."

Sindokht snapped back, "Forget your fear, Sam knows of this secret and is travelling to Manuchehr's court to expedite the matter."

Mehrab paused in astonishment and then said, "Woman, tell me the truth and do not hide things from me. How can I believe that Sam, the first of Iran's champions, would agree to this desire of theirs? If Sam and Manuchehr had no objection, then there would be no better son-in-law in all the world than Zal. But how can we be sure we are safe from Manuchehr's fury?"

Sindokht said, "Dear husband, I have never said anything to you but the truth. Believe me, Sam knows of this secret, and the king himself is quite likely to agree to it. Didn't Feraydun seek the daughters of the king of the Yemen as brides for his sons?"

But Mehrab was still angry and would not calm down. He said: "Tell Rudabeh to come to me."

Sindokht was afraid he would harm their daughter and said, "Before I call her, you must first swear to me that you will not injure her in any way, and that you will send her back to me healthy and unhurt." Mehrab had to agree.

Sindokht took the good news to Rudabeh, saying, "Your father has learned of the matter, but he's not going to hurt you." Rudabeh lifted her head high and said, "I have no fear of the truth, and I remain strong in my love for Zal." Then she bravely went in to her father. Mehrab was still in a rage and shouted harshly at her and reviled her. Faced with her father's anger Rudabeh held her breath; tears flowed from between her tightly closed eyelashes as she listened to his rage. Then, weeping and distraught, she fled back to her own rooms.

Manuchehr Learns of What Has Happened

News reached Manuchehr that Sam's son had fallen in love with the daughter of Mehrab. The king frowned, knitting his brows together, and thought to himself, "For many long years Feraydun and his people sought to curtail the power of Zahhak's family. And now if there is to be a union between these two clans, who is to know what the result might be? Zal's son is quite likely to take after his mother's family; he might well take it into his head to make

a bid for the crown and throne of Iran, throwing the country into chaos. It's better that I try to head off this possibility by forbidding Zal to go ahead with the union."

At this time Sam was returning from his war with the demons of Mazanderan and the rebels in Gorgan, in order to see Manuchehr. Manuchehr sent out his son Nozar, together with a group of courtiers and a splendid detachment from the army, to welcome him and conduct him to the court. When Sam arrived, Manuchehr made much of him and motioned him to a throne beside his own; next he made enquiries about the difficulties of his journey as well as about his victories in Dilman and Mazanderan. Sam recounted the story of his battles, going over his victories, the rout of their enemies, and the killing of Zahhak's descendant Kakui. Manuchehr treated him very kindly, praising his bravery and skill.

Sam wanted to take advantage of the king's pleasure at what he had done and bring up the matter of Zal and Rudabeh, hoping for a favorable response. But the king forestalled him by saying, "Now that you have destroyed Iran's enemies in Mazanderan and Gorgan and delivered a crushing blow against Zahhak's clan, it's time that you led your armies into Kabol and India and got rid of Mehrab, who is also a descendant of Zahhak. You should subjugate Kabolestan in the name of the king of Iran, and in this way put my mind finally at ease."

Sam's words stuck in his throat and he made no answer. He could not disobey the king's command. He had no choice but to make his obeisance, kiss the ground, and say, "Since the king of all the world so wishes, it shall be done." Then with a mighty army he set out for Sistan.

Zal Complains

The king's intentions became known in Kabol. The town was thrown into a frenzy of anxiety; Mehrab's family gave themselves up for lost and Rudabeh wept day and night. They went to Zal, saying, "What kind of injustice is this?" Zal was enraged and deeply distressed; grim-faced, his heart filled with foreboding, he set out to intercept his father's army.

His father sent the leaders of the army out to welcome him. His heart filled with resentment and grief, Zal entered his father's tent, kissed the ground, and said, "My lord, may you live forever. Your chivalry and courage are renowned throughout all the land of Iran. Knowing of you, all men rejoice, but I cannot rejoice. All men experience justice from you, and I experience injustice. I was brought up by the Simorgh, and I have seen much suffering. I have done no one any evil and I wish no one any evil. My only sin is that I am Sam's son. When I was born, you separated me from my mother and had me exposed on a mountainside; you caviled about black and white hair and rose up against God's will, isolating me from a mother's love and a father's care. But the great God watched over me and the Simorgh nurtured me until I grew to be a young man, and I became strong and skilled in the ways of the world. Now among all the champions of Iran there is none who is my equal in stature and pride and martial spirit. Constantly I have carried out your orders and striven to serve you. From all the world I have chosen to love Mehrab's daughter, who is both beautiful and possessed of royal *farr* and splendor.

"Once again I did nothing except what you had commanded me; I did not act stubbornly or impetuously but asked for your will in this matter. And had you not sworn before our assembled people that you would not harm me and that you would oppose none of my desires? And now that I have declared my desire, you come from Mazanderan and Gorgan with an army ready for war? Is this the justice you offer me, is this how you keep your word to me? I stand here as your slave to command, and if you are

angry with me, then my body and soul are yours to dispose of as you wish. Give orders that my body be hacked in two, but do not say a single word about Kabol. Do with me whatever you wish, but I will not be a party to any action taken against the people of Kabol. While I live, no harm shall come to Mehrab. If you wish to march on Kabol, you must first give orders that my head be severed from my body."

Sam remained silent, deep in thought. Finally he raised his head and answered, "O my brave son, you have said nothing but the truth. I have not acted toward you according to the ways of love; I have been unjust to you. I swore that I would carry out whatever you desired. But the king ordered me here, and I had no choice but to obey. Now, put all grief aside; relax the frown that knits your brows together. Let us think of some way to resolve this matter, some way in which I can soften the king's heart and persuade him to look kindly on you."

Sam's Letter to Manuchehr

Sam had a scribe summoned and gave orders that he write a letter to the lord of all Iran, saying, "O king, I have served you for one hundred and twenty years. During this time I have taken cities and routed armies in your name. Everywhere that I have found enemies of the land of Iran I have smashed them to pieces with my mace, and I have leveled with the dust all who wish the kingdom ill. As a horseman, as a warrior, and for lionhearted service, there has never been such a hero as myself. I destroyed the demons of Mazanderan who had revolted against the king's rule, and I made the rebels of Gorgan plead in the dust for mercy.

"If I had not been ready to serve you, who would have dealt with the dragon that emerged from the River Kashf? The whole world lived in terror of it; neither bird nor beast was safe from its depredations. It plucked fierce monsters from the depths and swift-winged eagles from the air, and it devoured countless animals and men. But in the king's name I grasped my mace and went to battle with the dragon. All who knew of this foresaw my death and bade me a last farewell. When I drew near the dragon, I seemed to be walking through a sea of fire, and when it saw me, it gave such a roar that the whole world shook. Its great tongue lolled from its mouth like a black tree trunk, blocking my path. With God's help I fought off fear and set an arrow of white poplar wood, tipped with a diamond point, against my bowstring. I released the string and pierced one side of the dragon's tongue, pinning it to his palate. Then I released another arrow, and pinned the other side of the tongue in the same fashion. The dragon writhed and screamed, and I shot the third arrow deep into its throat. Blood welled forth from its vitals and it writhed again and came toward me. I drew my ox-headed mace and urged my huge horse forward, and with the help of God and the king's good fortune, I struck so violently against its head that it was as if a mountain had fallen on the beast. The brains burst forth, and poison spewed out like a mighty river, and smoke and vapor filled the air. When I returned from that encounter my armor was in tatters and my body was seared in various places by the dragon's poison. All the world sang my praises, and from that time forth the world returned to its untroubled life and men were once again at peace.

"I will say nothing of my brave deeds in other places. You yourself know what I did to your enemies in Mazanderan and Dilman, and how I have

dealt with ungrateful rebels against your rule. Wherever my horse has trod, the very lions have cowered in fear, their hearts quaking within them, and wherever I have drawn my sword, the severed heads of your enemies have toppled to the ground.

"Through all these long years my pillow has been my saddle, and my place of rest the battlefield. I have never pined for my homeland, and I have always rejoiced in the king's victories and sought nothing but his happiness.

"But now, my lord, the dust of old age has settled on my head, and my once upright stature has bent double. I am content to have spent my life obedient to my king's commands and to have grown old in his service. Now it is the turn of my son, Zal. I pass on to him the burden of service and chivalry, so that from now on he may do the things that I have done, making his king's heart happy by his skill and bravery against our enemies, for he is a brave, able, and martial youth, and his heart is filled with love for his king.

"Zal has a request to make of you. He will come to offer his services, to kiss the ground and rejoice in the sight of his king, and to tell you what it is he wishes. The king is aware of the oath I have sworn to Zal; before our people I swore to him that I would fulfill whatever wish he might have. When, as the king had commanded, I set out for Kabol, Zal came to me distressed and seeking justice, saying that it was better I split his body in two than that I march on Kabol. His heart is filled with love for Rudabeh, Mehrab's daughter, and without her he knows neither rest nor sleep. I send him to your court so that he himself may tell you of his suffering. Great king, I entreat you to deal with him magnanimously. There is no need for me to say more. The king would not wish his courtiers to break their oaths or to harm those to whom they have sworn them; for I have only this one son in all the world, and I have no other helpmate or companion than him. May the king live forever."

Mehrab's Rage

For his part, when Mehrab learned of Sam's march on Kabol, he turned in fury on Sindokht and Rudabeh, saying, "You have acted like fools, offering our country up to the lion's maw; Manuchehr has sent an army to lay waste Kabol, and who can stand and fight against Sam? We shall all be utterly destroyed. The only way to calm Manuchehr's rage is for me to sever your heads with my sword in the public marketplace, and then he may pause in his desire to sack Kabol. By this means men's lives and property may be delivered from the threat of destruction."

Sindokht was an intelligent woman who was rarely at a loss for ideas. She threw herself on Mehrab's mercy, saying, "Hear me out my lord, and then, if you wish, kill me. Catastrophe now stares us in the face; our lives and country are in danger. Open the doors to your treasury; be liberal with your jewels and give me permission to take rich gifts to Sam, so that I may talk to him, seeking some way out of this situation; I may be able to soften his heart and so deliver Kabol from the king's wrath."

Mehrab answered, "What are wealth and treasure when our lives are at stake? Take the keys to the treasury and do whatever you wish."

Sindokht extracted a promise from Mehrab that while she was away he would do Rudabeh no harm. Then she set out for Sam's court, taking with her treasure and precious stuffs, gold, a quantity of jewels, thirty Arab horses, thirty Persian horses, sixty goblets of gold filled with musk, camphor, rubies, and turquoise, a hundred red-haired dromedaries, a hundred swiftly pacing camels, a crown worked with royal gems, and a throne of pure gold, as well as many other rich gifts.

The Meeting of Sam and Sindokht

Sam was told that a messenger bearing many rich gifts had arrived from Kabol. Sam granted the messenger audience and Sindokht entered the royal enclosure, kissed the ground, and said, "I have brought a message and gifts from Mehrab, the king of Kabol." Sam looked and saw that the slaves, horses, camels, elephants, and treasure and wealth that Mehrab had sent stretched for two miles. He was unsure what he should do. If he accepted Mehrab's gifts Manuchehr would be angry, since he had sent Sam to take Kabol and he had instead accepted presents from the enemy. And if he did not accept them, his son would be distressed; once again he thought of the oath he had sworn to him.

Finally Sam lifted his head and said, "Place all these horses and slaves and gifts in Zal-e Zar's treasury." Sindokht was overjoyed and ordered her attendants to strew jewels before Sam's feet. Then she delivered her message: "O my lord, in all the earth there is none who is your equal. The great bow their heads before you and your authority runs throughout the world. But if Mehrab has sinned against you, what sin have the people of Kabol committed that you come threatening them with war? The people of Kabol all love and support you, they live rejoicing in your happiness, and the dust beneath your feet is as kohl for their eyes. Be mindful of God, who made the moon and the sun and life and death, and do not shed innocent blood."

Sam was amazed by her eloquence and thought, "How is it that Mehrab, with all the men and brave warriors he can call on, has sent a woman to me as his envoy?" He said: "Woman, answer my questions truthfully. Who are you, and what is your relationship to Mehrab? And tell me what kind of person Rudabeh is, as regards her intelligence, behavior, wisdom, and beauty. And how is it that Zal fell in love with her?"

Sindokht said, "O renowned warrior, before I tell you what you wish to know, first promise I shall not be harmed." Sam gave her his promise. Then Sindokht opened the secrets of her heart to him: "Then know, O champion of the world, that I am Sindokht, the wife of Mehrab and the mother of Rudabeh, of the clan of Zahhak. In Mehrab's castle we all support you and sing your praises and our hearts are filled with love for you. I have come to you now to know what it is you would do. If we have sinned, and are of an evil race, and are unworthy to be allied with kings, then I stand before you here, helpless and alone. If I am worthy to be killed, kill me, and if I am worthy of chains, bind me. But do not harm the innocent inhabitants of Kabol; do not blacken their days with sorrow, bringing sin upon your own soul."

Sam looked keenly at her and saw a woman like a lioness, noble, of comely stature, wise and perspicacious. He said, "Honored lady, set your mind at rest and know that you and your family are safe with me and that I agree to the union of your daughter and my son. I have sent a letter to the lord of all Iran asking him to grant us what we wish for. And now I shall strive even more to bring this about. Do not allow anxiety to find its way into your heart. But tell me, what kind of wonder is this Rudabeh that she has captured the heart of brave Zal so thoroughly? Show her to me, too, so that I can see what kind of person she is."

Sindokht rejoiced to hear Sam's words and said, "If in your magnanimity you would do us the honor of visiting our house, with your companions and your army, then you can make Rudabeh's heart happy by seeing her. If you come to Kabol, you will find the whole city at your service."

Sam laughed and said, "Have no fear, I shall grant you this wish too. As soon as the king's command arrives, I and the lords of Zabol, and the leaders of its army, will come as guests to your house."

Happy and with her heart at rest, Sindokht brought the good news to Mehrab.

Zal at Manuchehr's Court

Meanwhile, as soon as Sam had written his letter to Manuchehr, Zal took it and, riding as swiftly as he could, traveled to Manuchehr's court. When news of his approach came, a band of courtiers and warriors hurried out to greet him, and then, with much splendor and pomp, they escorted him to the king's presence. Zal kissed the ground, made his obeisance to the lord of all Iran, and handed over Sam's letter to him.

Manuchehr made much of him and questioned him closely and gave orders that his face be cleansed of the dirt of the journey and that he be sprinkled with musk and ambergris. When he had read Sam's letter and learned what it was that Zal desired, he laughed and said, "Well, young man, you have added to my troubles by asking for something that is difficult for me to grant. But although I don't rejoice at your request, there's no denying whatever the aged Sam wishes for. Stay here with me for a while and let me consult the priests and elders about this business, and then I will grant your desire." Then a banquet was set out and a royal celebration began and the lord of all Iran sat down to wine and feasting with his courtiers.

On the next day Manuchehr gave orders that astrologers were to look closely at the course of the stars and to inform him whether or not a marriage between Zal and Rudabeh would be auspicious. The astrologers took three days casting the horoscope. Finally they returned to the court in high spirits, saying that it was clear from the stars that the outcome of this union would be to the king's satisfaction. From these two a son would be born who would have the heart of a lion and the strength of an elephant, and who would uproot the enemies of Iran,

> Strong, tall, and fierce, no lion would withstand
> The arrows shot from his unerring hand;
> No eagle would outsoar him and no lord
> Would be his equal: with his glittering sword
> He'd make the air weep and his food would be
> A wild ass roasted, spitted on a tree;
> Prompt in his monarch's service, prompt to fight,
> Persia's protector and stout-hearted knight.

Manuchehr's face radiated pleasure and he gave orders that the priests and wise men of his court should gather together and put Zal's wisdom, knowledge, and shrewdness to the test.

Zal Is Tested

When the priests had arrived, the lord of all Iran granted an audience for the testing of Zal; he sat Zal down before the priests so that he could answer their questions and display his wisdom.

The first priest asked, "I saw twelve flourishing trees, each of which had thirty branches. What is the meaning of this?"

The next priest said, "I saw two swiftly galloping horses, one as white as snow and the other as black as pitch. Each hurried after the other, but neither could reach the other. What is the meaning of this?"

The next priest said, "I saw a beautiful green meadow through which a man moved with a sickle, harvesting that which was fresh and that which was withered, and neither tears nor entreaties moved him in any way. What is the meaning of this?"

The next priest said, "I saw two tall cypress trees that rose from the ocean and on each of them a bird had built a nest. In the day it would sit on one and in the night on the other. When it sat on one of the cypresses, that tree would flourish, and when it flew up again, the tree would wither and become dry and leafless. What is the meaning of this?"

The next priest said, "I saw a beautiful land next to which was a thorn-covered waste. People took no account of the beautiful land and built their houses in the thorny waste. Then suddenly they began to weep and wail, longing for the beautiful land. Now tell us, what is the meaning of this?"

For a while Zal remained deep in thought, and then he lifted his head and said, "The twelve trees, each of which has thirty branches, are the twelve months, each of which has thirty days, and the passage of time is measured by them. The two swift horses, one of them black and the other white, are night and day, which follow one another swiftly but never reach one another. The two cypresses on which the bird has its nests are the two halves of the year, and the bird is the sun. For half of the year, in the spring and the summer, the world rejoices and is green and verdant. During this half of the year the bird of the sun lives in six of its twelve mansions. In the other half of the year, during the autumn and winter, the world is cold and dry and the bird of the sun lives in the other six of its mansions. The man who passes through the meadow and who cuts down the fresh and the withered, making no distinction between them, is Death, who is unmoved by our tears and entreaties, who is merciful to none when their time has come, taking from this world the young and the old, the mighty and the helpless. And that beautiful land is the eternal world while the thorny waste is the fleeting world in which we live. While we are in this world, we take no thought of the eternal world and are content to be among these thorns and weeds, but when Death comes, wielding his sickle, we remember the eternal world and regret that we had given no thought to it before."

When Zal finished speaking, the priests were astonished by his wisdom and eloquence; they gave him high praise, and the king's heart was filled with pleasure by his words.

Zal Shows His Skill

On the next day, at sunrise, Zal appeared before the king to receive permission to set out on his return journey; he was impatient to see Rudabeh again and was ready to leave. Manuchehr laughed and said, "Stay here with us for today, and then tomorrow I shall send you off to your father in a manner that befits a young hero like you."

Then he gave orders that drums and cymbals be sounded to summon warriors and champions to the public meeting ground where they could

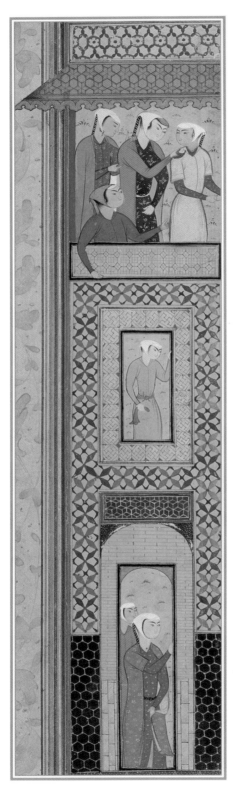

display their skill with the bow, shield, sword, lance, and javelin.

Zal, too, took up his bow and arrows and laid out his weapons in readiness, and, mounted on his horse, set off for the meeting ground. There was a very ancient tree in the middle of the open space. Zal notched an arrow on his bowstring, urged his horse forward, and let the arrow fly. The arrow pierced the tree and came out of the other side of the trunk. A great cry of congratulation rose on all sides.

Then Zal laid his bow aside and picked up his javelin and rode against a group of shield-bearers and with one blow shattered the shields into pieces. Manuchehr was astonished at the strength of Zal's arm. To test him further, he ordered that a group of horsemen with spears wheel around and attack him. With one charge, Zal scattered the whole band. And then Zal turned toward the one among them who seemed to be the strongest and the most courageous and, urging his horse forward, caught up with him and reached out and grasped him by the belt; then he nimbly swung him up into the air and flung him down on the ground. A roar of approval went up from the spectators. The lord of all Iran congratulated him and gave him a robe of honor as well as gold and jewels.

Zal Returns to His Father

Manuchehr gave orders that a letter be written to the hero Sam, saying, "Your envoy has come and I am aware of what it is that the world's great hero desires. I have also put your courageous young son to the test. He is a wise, brave, and skillful youth. I grant his desire and I send him back to his father rejoicing. May evil never harm the brave and may you always live in happiness and contentment."

Zal was so happy that he did not know his head from his feet. Immediately he chose a swift courier and sent the following message to his father: "Greetings, and rejoice that the lord of all Iran has granted our desire." Sam was overjoyed and came out with his courtiers and chief warriors to greet his son. The two heroes warmly embraced, and then Zal kissed the ground in homage and praised his father's wisdom.

Sam gave orders for a celebration; a banquet was laid out and the group fell happily to their wine. Sam sent a message to Mehrab and Sindokht, saying, "Zal has returned with the king's approval for the marriage. And now, as I promised, I and my entourage will come to your house as your guests."

The Marriage of Zal and Rudabeh

Mehrab's face glowed with joy. He called Sindokht to him and gently caressed her and said, "Your plan was a good one, and all has turned out well. We shall be united with a great and splendid family; we have found honor and good fortune. Now open the doors to our treasury and scatter jewels and decorate the court; have a throne worthy of a great king made, and summon singers and musicians so that we shall be ready to receive the king of Zabolestan."

In a short time the brave Sam and his noble son and their army arrived. When Sam saw Rudabeh, she seemed like a celestial being to him; he wondered at her beauty and loveliness and warmly congratulated his son.

Thirty days passed in celebration and rejoicing, and no one slept for joy and happiness. Then Sam set out for Sistan, returning home in triumph. Zal stayed for one more week in Mehrab's palace. Then he too returned to Zabol, taking with him Rudabeh and Sindokht and a band of courtiers and nobles.

The city had been decorated in their honor, and Sam organized further celebrations and scattered gold and jewels in gratitude to God for the young people's marriage. Then he sat Zal on the throne of Zabolestan and, as the lord of all Iran had ordered, unfurled his martial banner and once more marched on Mazanderan.

◈ ROSTAM, THE SON OF ZAL-DASTAN ◈

The Birth of Rostam

A short while after the marriage of Rudabeh and Zal, Rudabeh became pregnant and her body grew heavy. Every day her face became paler and her belly more plump, until the time for her baby's birth drew near. She writhed in the pain of labor, but to no effect. It was as if she had iron within her or her belly were filled with stone. The doctors' efforts were of no avail and finally Rudabeh fainted away from the intensity of the pain. No one knew what to do, and they told Zal of what had happened. His eyes filled with tears, Zal hurried to Rudabeh's bedside and saw everyone there weeping and groaning. Suddenly he remembered the Simorgh's feather and took comfort from this; he told Sindokht that he knew a way out of their difficulty. He ordered that a fire be lit and then burned a little of the feather in the flames. At that very moment the air grew dark and the Simorgh descended from the heavens. Zal told the Simorgh of his distress, and the Simorgh replied, "This is no place for sorrow or grief, why should a lion of a man like you have eyes wet with tears? You should rejoice, for a lion-hearted son, eager for fame, will be born to you.

> He'll master all the beasts of earth and air,
> He'll terrify the lion in its lair;
> When such a voice rings out, the leopard gnaws
> In anguished terror its unyielding claws;
> Wild on the battlefield that voice will make
> The hardened hearts of iron warriors quake;
> Of cypress stature and of mammoth might,
> Two miles will barely show his javelin's flight.

But, for this noble child to be born you must prepare a sharp knife and summon a wise and experienced doctor. Then have her attendants make Rudabeh drunk with wine, so that she forgets her fear and becomes insensitive to pain. Next the doctor must cut open the mother's womb and bring this lion

cub forth; then he must sew up the womb. Meanwhile, you must grind certain herbs that I shall name, together with musk and milk, and dry the mixture in a shady place; then reduce it to powder and apply it to the scar, which you must also stroke with one of my feathers. The mixture is a healing one, and my feather will ensure its effect; Rudabeh will soon be out of pain and danger. Be happy now, and drive all fear and sorrow from your heart."

The Simorgh plucked a feather from its wing and gave it to Zal and flew up into the air. Zal followed the Simorgh's instructions, and while Sindokht stood by weeping for her daughter, the skillful doctor brought forth from Rudabeh's womb a tall, healthy, and massive boy.

He was a lion cub, a noble son,
Tall and handsome, lovely to look upon;
And all who saw this mammoth baby gazed
In wonder at him, murmuring and amazed.

They called him Rostam, and celebrations for his birth were held throughout Zabolestan and Kabolestan; gold and jewels and splendid gifts were distributed. Sam, Rostam's grandfather, was so pleased when he heard of the boy's birth that he almost smothered in coins the envoy who brought him the news.

From childhood Rostam was unlike all other children. Ten wet nurses gave him milk and even this was not enough for him. When he was weaned, he ate enough for five grown men. In a short time he was as tall as a man and he began to act and live as a warrior and hero. At the age of eight, he stood as tall and strong as a cypress tree, and he glowed with a starlike splendor. In stature, face, and behavior he reminded everyone of Sam. Sam was sent a portrait of the boy, and when he heard of Rostam's martial qualities, he came with his army and entourage from Mazanderan to see him. He embraced his grandson and called down God's blessings upon him and made

much of him; he was astonished by the boy's strength and splendor and stature. A few days were spent in festivities and wine-drinking until Sam took his leave of Rostam and once again set off for Mazanderan.

Rostam grew apace and became a young man without equal in bravery and strength. One night, after he had spent the day drinking wine with his friends, he was asleep in his bedchamber. Suddenly there was a loud commotion; Rostam started up from sleep and was told that Zal's white elephant had burst from its bonds and was threatening the lives of those nearby. Quickly he snatched up his grandfather's mace and set off to confront the beast. The castle guards tried to block his way, saying that his life would be in danger. Rostam flattened one with his fist and then turned on the others; they all fled in fear. Grasping his mace, he broke down the door and quickly made his way to the elephant.

> Raging, he rushed onward, wild as the sea.
> He looked, and saw the beast's immensity,
> As if it were a mountain roaring there,
> Pounding the quaking earth; its baleful glare
> Scattered all Rostam's friends—they ran to hide
> Like sheep that see a wolf at eventide.
> Rostam strode forward, yelled his battle cry,
> Intrepid and fearless, his head held high;
> Then, as the beast caught sight of him, it strove
> To trap him, like a mountain on the move.
> It lashed out with its trunk, but Rostam raised
> His mace and struck its head; trembling and dazed,
> The mammoth body toppled, fell full length,
> Harmless and helpless and bereft of strength.

The Fortress of the White Mountain

The next day, when Zal heard of Rostam's exploit he was astonished, since this elephant was hardened in battle and of great strength, and it had trampled to death many men who had attacked it on the battlefield. Zal realized that it was Rostam who should avenge the death of their ancestor Nariman.

Zal summoned Rostam and kissed him on the face and head and said, "O my brave son, although you are still a child in years, you have no equal as a man and a warrior. And therefore, before your fame spreads and you become a renowned warrior and enemies come of themselves, you must avenge the blood of Nariman, our ancestor, and take revenge on his behalf against his enemies. In the White Mountain there is a fortress whose walls are so high that not even the eagles of the air can overfly it. This fortress is

four leagues high and four leagues wide; within, there is water and vegetation and cultivated land and trees, as well as gold and money and every other kind of wealth. Its people are independent of the world and are a haughty race. In the time of Feraydun, Manuchehr's great-grandfather, they rebelled against the king, and Feraydun sent Nariman, who was a courageous chieftain, to take the fortress. For some years Nariman fought against them but was unable to gain entry to their fastness. At last they flung a rock from the fortress walls and it killed Nariman. The warlike Sam led an army to avenge his father's blood, and for many years besieged the fortress, but, since its inhabitants had no need of the outside world, Sam finally lost patience and abandoned the siege without having achieved his goal.

"Now, my son, before your fame spreads, it is time for you to think of some way to insinuate yourself into this fortress and so extirpate this race of malevolent rebels."

Rostam on the White Mountain

The brave Rostam said, "I shall do this." Zal said, "Be careful! One way to do it would be as follows: Disguise yourself as the leader of a camel caravan and load camels up with salt and take them to the fortress. There is no salt there, and they esteem salt above all other kinds of merchandise. In this way they will let you into the fortress."

Rostam put together a caravan of camels, loaded them up with salt (he had first hidden weapons beneath the bales), chose a few of his trusted companions to accompany him, and set off for the fortress.

The lookout saw them and informed the fortress chieftain. He sent someone out to them and learned that they were carrying salt. He was overjoyed and allowed Rostam and his companions to enter the fortress. Rostam spoke very persuasively and also presented the chieftain with some salt, so making him grateful to him. The people who lived in the fortress crowded around the caravan and were soon busy buying salt.

When night fell, Rostam and his companions made their way to the chieftain's quarters and attacked him.

> Rostam struck him so hard he seemed to thrust
> Half of him underground, beneath the dust.
> News of their chieftain's death spread far and wide
> And warriors rushed to fight from every side.
> Then such a tumult rose, such blood was shed,
> It seemed the sunset streamed there, wet and red,
> While Rostam with his sword and mace and bow
> Harried his enemies and laid them low.

By daybreak the castle's inhabitants had been defeated and all submitted to Rostam's authority. Rostam looked about himself and saw there a building made of granite, with a door of iron. With his mace he smashed the door open. Within the building he saw another building; hidden beneath its dome was a room filled with gold and coins and jewels. It was as though the gold from every mine and the jewels from every ocean were all gathered there. Immediately he wrote a letter to renowned Zal, his father.

> He greeted him as champion of Iran,
> The unmatched lord of wide Zabolestan,
> Who lifts the royal banner, and whose arm
> Preserves the Persian people from all harm.

Then he recounted his own victory: "I reached the White Mountain, entered the fortress, and made a night attack in which I defeated the enemy; the fortress is in my hands and I have taken possession of a great quantity of unworked silver and pure gold, as well as thousands of kinds of fine cloth. What is my father's command to me now?"

At the news of his son's victory, Zal seemed to grow young again. He wrote a letter congratulating Rostam: "Such a victory is worthy of you; you have destroyed our enemies and made the soul of Nariman glad. I have sent a camel train to you and you can load it with the choicest of the booty. When this letter arrives, mount your horse immediately and return to me, for I grow sad without you."

Rostam followed his instructions and set off for Sistan. The streets and buildings were decorated to honor his victory, and greeted by the din of drums and cymbals, Rostam dismounted and entered the castle.

> Rudabeh was the first he went to greet,
> Bowing his head before his mother's feet—
> She kissed his shoulders, his heroic chest,
> And praised the outcome of his martial quest.

Then a letter was written to Sam, telling him of his grandson's victory. He too rejoiced and gave the envoy a robe of honor, and sent a letter back to Rostam full of praise and congratulation,

> His letter said: "It's no surprise to hear
> A lion cub is brave and has no fear;
> Success is not unlooked-for from the son
> Of Zal, by whom great victories are won.

THE BEGINNING OF THE WAR BETWEEN IRAN AND TURAN

Nozar Is Crowned

Manuchehr had lived for a hundred and twenty years. His astrologers consulted his horoscope and saw that his life would soon draw to a close. They informed him of this and he summoned his nobles and courtiers. In their presence he turned to his son, Nozar, and said, "My life has lasted for a hundred and twenty years. I have lived happily in this world and achieved my heart's desires; I have conquered my enemies and, with the deaths of Salm and Tur, I have avenged my grandfather Iraj's death. I have rid the world of many evils and I have built cities and castles. Now it is time for my departure, and when I have departed, it will be as if I had never lived. It is true, the fickle world gives us no more than this, and it is unworthy of our trust and love. Now I pass to you, my son Nozar, the crown and throne that Feraydun passed to me. Rule in such a way that your good name will survive you.

"You should also know that the world will not remain at peace as it is now. The Turanians will not sit idly by; their evil influence will reach Iran, and you will have a hard and difficult time of it. When crisis threatens, ask for help from Sam, the son of Nariman, and from Zal-e Zar. Zal's young son, who is even now growing to manhood, will also be a prop to your kingdom and will fight on behalf of Iran and its people."

When Manuchehr stopped speaking, Nozar wept for him, and Manuchehr's eyes too were filled with tears. Then

> He closed his royal eyes, coldly he sighed;
> Thus Manuchehr, Iran's great sovereign, died.
> He left this world, but his achievements' fame
> Kept fresh throughout the world his royal name.

Pashang's Desire for Revenge

From the time that Tur had been killed by Manuchehr, during the war of vengeance for the death of Iraj, the Turanians had hated the people of Persia and watched for an opportunity to retaliate against them. But Manuchehr had been a strong, warlike, and courageous king, and while he lived they were unable to wage war against Iran.

When Manuchehr passed away and Pashang, the leader of Turan, learned of this, he remembered the defeat of his people, and thoughts of revenge stirred in his heart. He called together the nobles and great chiefs of his people, men like Garsivaz and Barman and Golbad and Viseh, as well as his own sons, Afrasyab and Aghriras, and spoke at length about Salm and Tur and the injustice that the Iranians had visited upon them. "You know," he said,

> "What these Iranians have done to us,
> How evil they have been, how infamous;
> But we must dry our eyes—it's time now for
> Revenge, rebellion, and relentless war!"

Afrasyab, with his noble stature, mighty arms, and fearless heart, was first among the champions of Turan. When he heard Pashang speak, his head spun with impatience and he stepped forward and said,

> "Against wild lions I can stand and fight,
> I am the match for Persia's monarch's might.

If my ancestor Zadsham had drawn his sword and fought for us as he should have, this humiliation would not have lasted so long, and we would not have remained slaves of these same Persians. Now is the time for insurrection, rebellion, and revenge!"

Pashang rejoiced to hear his son's words and forthwith prepared for war. He gave orders that a mighty army be assembled; he made Afrasyab its leader and commanded him to march on Iran.

Afrasyab's brother, Aghriras, was a wise and perspicacious man, and he was disturbed by this intemperate behavior. He came to Pashang and said, "My father, although Manuchehr is no longer there to lead the Iranians, Sam is still alive and they have other champions, such as warlike Qaren and renowned Keshvad, who are ready for battle. You yourself know how the Iranians dealt with Salm and Tur. For all the power and pomp at his disposal, our ancestor Zadsham never breathed a word about insurrection or revenge. Perhaps it would be better if we too did not risk rebellion and the danger and confusion it brings."

But Pashang's heart was set on war. He said, "It is not right for a man not to seek revenge on his ancestors' behalf. Afrasyab is a lion in battle and has readied himself to seek revenge for what was done to his forebears. You must accompany him and be his confidant in the vicissitudes of war. When spring comes, and the new grass sprouts on the plains and the world turns green again, lead an army out toward Amol. It was from there that Manuchehr led his army against us when he marched on Turan and overcame us. But now that Manuchehr is dead what have we to fear? Manuchehr's son, Nozar, is a person of no account, he's young and inexperienced. Go now and fight against Qaren and Garshasb, so that the souls of our forebears may be at peace."

Afrasyab Leads His Army against Iran

Afrasyab set off for Iran with a mighty army. News reached Nozar that Afrasyab's army had crossed the Oxus. The Persian army was made ready for battle and took the road for Dehestan. The warlike Qaren was in the vanguard, leading the army, and Nozar followed him in the center of their troops. Before he reached the vicinity of Dehestan, Afrasyab selected two of his chieftains, Shamasas and Khazarvan, and sent them at the head of thirty thousand Turanian troops toward Zabolestan. And just at this time news arrived that Sam, the renowned champion of Iran, had died. Afrasyab was overjoyed and immediately wrote a letter to his father saying that Nozar's army was theirs to hunt down at will, since Sam's death had followed so hard upon the heels of Manuchehr's, and he had been the only Iranian leader whom Afrasyab had feared. As Sam was no longer there, the rest of them could be dealt with easily enough.

The Combat between Barman and Qobad

As dawn broke, the vanguard of Afrasyab's army approached Dehestan. The two armies prepared for battle. Two parasangs, about eight miles, separated them. Barman, Viseh's son, rode forward and surveyed the Iranian army; he recognized Nozar's royal pavilion, which had been pitched beside Dehestan's fortified wall. He rode back to his own lines and said, "Now we must show our skill; it is no time to hide our light under a bushel. If the king gives me permission, I shall ride over to the Persian lines and challenge any comer to single combat, so that they shall have some taste of our prowess."

Aghriras said, "If Barman is killed by the Iranians, our chieftains will lose heart and this weakness will show when they have to fight. It might be better if we were to send some unknown warrior out for combat, instead of him." Afrasyab frowned and retorted, "That would be a shameful thing for us to do." Then he turned to Barman: "Put on your armor, notch an arrow to your bowstring, and get yourself out to the battlefield. There's no doubt at all that you will triumph over anyone in that army."

Barman set off for the Iranian lines, and when he drew near enough, he called out to Qaren, "Which famous warrior from your army will fight with me?"

Qaren looked at his warriors, but no one except his own brother, the aged Qobad, gave any response. Qaren was perturbed by this; he felt distressed that none of the young men in the army had opened their mouths to answer the challenge and that it had fallen to the white-haired Qobad to respond. He turned to his brother and said, "Qobad, you have reached the age when you should avoid fighting and warfare. Barman is a young, lion-hearted horseman. This is no time for you to engage in single combat. You are the wisest head in the army, and the king relies on your judgment and advice. If your white hair should turn red with blood, the brave warriors of our army will give up all hope."

Qobad was a brave, experienced fighter. He answered, "O my brother, a man's body is, finally, the prey of Death. But a man whose profession is warfare and combat, and who looks for fame and honor, is not disturbed by the thought of Death. Throughout all of Manuchehr's reign, I fought in his wars. One man will die by the sword while another completes his life at home in his own bed, according to the will of Fate. But since no man passes to heaven while he is alive, we must treat Death lightly and not concern ourselves about it unduly. And if I am to leave this ample world behind me now, I thank God that I leave here in my place a brother such as you. When I am gone, deal kindly with me; wash my head in musk and camphor and rosewater, and place my body on the Towers of Silence, according to our custom, and be at peace, having faith in God."

Having spoken, he turned his horse toward the battlefield. Barman, the warrior of Turan, galloped forward and called out, "Your life has reached its end, since you have come to fight with me. It's clear that Fate must bear some grudge against your soul." Qobad said, "To every man there is a time, and until that time is fulfilled, he will not look on Death." Having said this, he urged his horse forward and charged at Barman. Both warriors were strong and their combat was a lengthy one. From dawn until the setting of the sun, the champions roared their battle cries and fought with one another.

> But Barman was victorious at last;
> He sped onto the battlefield and cast
> A lance that struck Qobad, piercing his back;
> His spine was smashed. Slowly he toppled, slack
> And lifeless, from the saddle to the ground;
> Thus died the hero, aged and renowned.

When they brought the news to Qaren that his brother had been killed by Barman, blood swam before his eyes. He ordered the Persian army to advance toward the army of Turan. And on his side, Garsivaz led the Turanian army onto the battlefield.

> Two armies met like two great seas; you'd say
> A mighty earthquake shook the earth that day.
> The horses whinnied, and vast dust clouds soon
> Obscured the setting sun and rising moon;
> Then in the gloom, bright blades flashed here and there
> And bloodied spear points jabbed the darkened air.

When Afrasyab saw Qaren's martial prowess, he hurried to the battlefield and fought his way toward Qaren. From dawn to dusk the battle lasted, and Qaren and Afrasyab had almost reached one another when the darkness of night called the two armies back to rest and sleep.

The Battle of Nozar and Afrasyab

Both the death of Qobad and the valor of Afrasyab tormented Qaren. He said to Nozar, "Your ancestor Feraydun placed my war helmet on my head, commanding me to range the world and seek revenge for the death of Iraj. From that time till now, I have always lived face to face with Death; I have not removed my sword belt or let my sword slip from my hand. Now my brother is no more, and my end will be as his. But may you, my lord, live eternally in joy and glory." Then he drew up the army in its battleorder, and as the sun rose, the armies of Turan and Iran once again faced each other; to the din of drums battle was joined and blood flowed like a river from the forces of both sides. So much dust rose into the heavens that the sun was obscured. Wherever Qaren urged his horse, a river of blood was shed, and wherever Afrasyab turned his face, the slain fell heaped on the ground. Nozar, from the center of his troops, rode toward Afrasyab, and the two leaders

> Then flung such spears at one another, each
> Writhed like a snake in twisting out of reach.

The battle lasted until dusk, but finally Afrasyab began to gain on Nozar, and the Iranian forces fell back from the battlefield. Nozar's heart was heavy with pain and sorrow as he entered his royal pavilion; he summoned his sons Tus and Gostahom and wept before them, saying, "My father, Manuchehr, told me that armies would come to Iran from China and Turan and that Iran would suffer greatly from them. Now it is clear that the day my father foresaw has come and my heart grieves with anxiety for my women and young children in Pars. Without delay, you must set out for Isfahan and travel to Pars and take my family from there to the Alborz Mountains. Find some place of refuge for them in the mountains, so that they shall be safe from Afrasyab and the seed of Feraydun shall not be extirpated from the earth. We shall pit our strength against the enemy once more, and see what the outcome will be. If we do not meet again and no good news reaches you from our army, do not let your hearts grieve at this, since the way of Fate was ever thus, and in the final reckoning, he who is killed and he who dies naturally are as one."

Then the king embraced his two sons and tears fell from his eyes as he said farewell to them and dispatched them to Pars.

Both armies spent two days preparing for the coming conflict and refurbishing their weapons. On the third day they met in battle once again. Nozar and Qaren were in the center of their troops and Shapur and Taliman commanded the right and left flanks. From dawn until midday, the battle was hard fought and victory remained uncertain, but as the sun declined in the west, the army of Turan began to gain on its enemies. Shapur was overcome and lay dead on the ground, and his troops were routed, and many of the renowned warriors of Iran fell in that conflict. When Nozar and Qaren saw that Fortune did not favor the Persian army, they retreated and took refuge in the fortifications at Dehestan; by doing this, Nozar hampered the Persian army's ability to fight on the open plain and made it impossible for the cavalry to be effective.

Barman Is Killed

When Afrasyab saw this, he immediately made one Karukhan leader of a large detachment of horsemen and ordered him to travel by night to Pars and there take possession of the Iranian army's harem and impedimenta; he was to take all women and children prisoner and in this way deliver a crushing blow to Nozar's army.

Qaren realized what Afrasyab had done. Furious and distraught he went to Nozar and said, "This devious wretch Afrasyab has underhandedly sent an army in the darkness of the night to capture our women and children. If this comes to pass, our nobles will have no stomach for war and the incident will be a lasting shame to us. If the king so orders, I shall set off after this army and defeat them. Within these fortifications there is water and victuals and your army. You need have no worries and can remain here."

Nozar replied, "This would not be right. You are the leader of the army and the army derives its strength from you. I have already given thought to our women and children and have sent Tus and Gostahom to Pars, and they will soon arrive there. Set your mind at rest."

Then Nozar and his chieftains sat down to eat. But when Nozar had retired for the night, the chieftains and warriors of Iran went from his court to Qaren and, as with one voice, said, "We must have an army go to Pars. God forbid that our women and children should fall into the hands of Afrasyab." Finally Qaren, together with Keshvad and Shidush, decided to go ahead with his original plan and, around midnight, they set out for Pars with their own soldiers.

As dawn was breaking they reached the White Fortress, the keeper of which was Kazhdahom, a Persian nobleman. They saw that Barman had led his army against the fortress and was blocking the way forward. Longing for revenge raged in Qaren's heart, and he donned his armor and prepared to

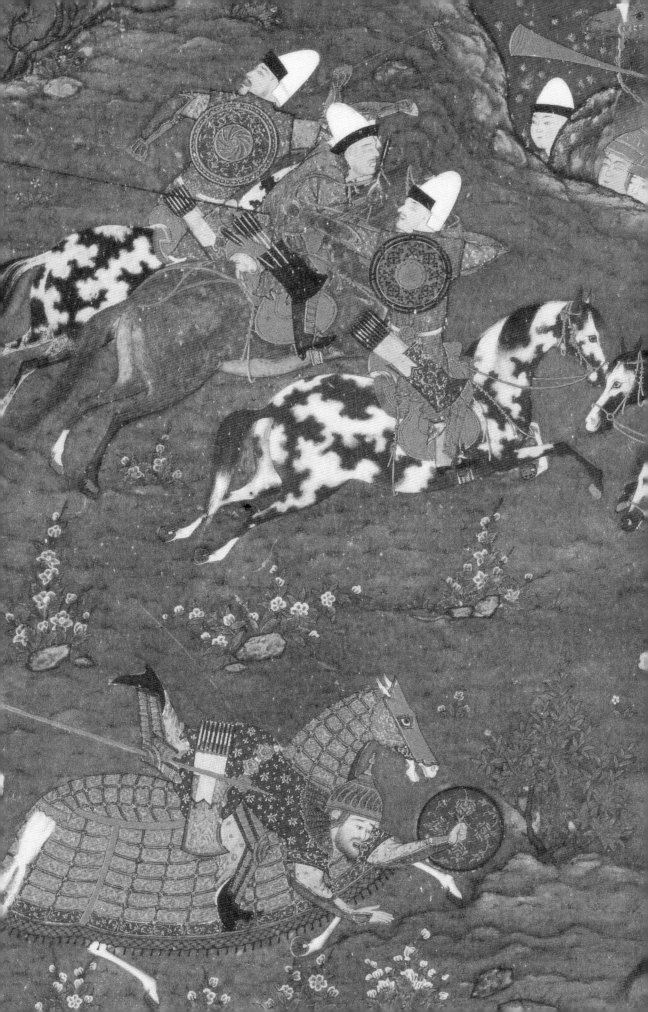

avenge his brother's death. Barman charged out like a lion and attacked Qaren. But Qaren gave him no chance to close with him; he invoked God and flung his spear, which penetrated so deeply into Barman's waist that his vital organs were pierced and torn and he fell headlong and dead in the dust. His army too was routed, and Qaren and his army continued on their way toward Pars.

Nozar Is Captured

When Nozar realized that Qaren had set out for Pars, fear gripped him and he decided to flee. He gathered his army together and left the fortifications and took the road for Pars. Afrasyab learned of this and quickly set off after him. Throughout the night a running battle went on between the two armies. Finally Nozar was captured, and he and twelve hundred of his entourage fell into Afrasyab's clutches. Afrasyab had them put in chains and brought before him, but however much he searched he could not find Qaren among the captives. They said that Qaren had taken the road to Pars. He gave orders that Barman was to follow Qaren and take him prisoner, but then he was told that Qaren had defeated Barman and left him dead in the dust.

Afrasyab's heart was distressed, and sleep and food became bitter to him. Finally he said to Viseh, Barman's father, "This is an undertaking for you; hurry after Qaren and avenge the blood of your son."

With a warlike detachment of soldiers Viseh set out toward Pars. He reached the place where Qaren had fought against his son, and he saw his own child sprawled in the dust, his banner torn beside him. His blood seethed with rage and he hastened after Qaren. Qaren was returning from Pars when he caught sight of a dust cloud in the distance, and then a little later, in the midst of the dust, he made out the banner of Turan's army. Viseh shouted from the army's center, "The wind has swept away your throne and crown, and all Iran is in our hands. When your king's been captured, where is there for you to flee to?" The answer came, "I am Qaren. I am not a man for either words or fear. I dealt with your son and now I shall deal with you." The armies urged their horses forward and the battle began. But it soon became clear that Qaren's forces had the upper hand and that Viseh was weakening. Viseh turned and fled with his men back toward Afrasyab, where he told him of Qaren's victory.

Afrasyab's Army in Zabolestan

The army that Afrasyab had sent to Zabolestan, under the command of Shamasas and Khazarvan, moved down toward Sistan and the River Hirmand. At this time Zal-e Zar was grieving for his father, and during the

formal period of mourning he had entrusted the country's affairs to Mehrab, Rudabeh's father and the lord of Kabol. Mehrab was a wise and perspicacious man. When he learned that Afrasyab's army was approaching, he sent an envoy bearing gold and coins to Shamasas, with the following message: "May Afrasyab, the king of Turan, live forever. As you know, I am of the family of Zahhak, and I have no love for kings from Feraydun's family. I made an alliance with Zal in order to remain safe, and because I had no other choice. I am pleased at this catastrophe that has befallen Zal, and my one hope is that I never see his face again. Now that he is in mourning, the whole of Zabolestan is under my command. Now I ask you to grant me time to dispatch a swift messenger to Afrasyab; I shall send him such presents as befit a king, and I shall open my heart to him. If Afrasyab commands my presence, I shall go to him as a suppliant and stand before his throne; there I shall hand over my kingdom to him and I shall send all my treasure to him, and in this way you champions will not have to put yourselves to any trouble."

Once he had interested the Turanian leaders by this ruse, he immediately sent a quick courier to Zal, saying, "Do not delay for one moment, because two champions from Turan, along with their army, are advancing on the River Hirmand like leopards of the plain. If you hesitate at all, our enemies will triumph."

Zal's Battle with the Forces of Turan

Zal lost no time in setting out with a fierce band of warriors for Mehrab's court. When he saw that Mehrab was still strong and in control of the country, he rejoiced and said, "Now there is no need for fear. Khazarvan is no more to me than a fistful of dirt. When evening comes, I shall show the forces of Turan just who it is they are dealing with."

And so at dusk he slung his bow over his shoulder and went close to the enemy encampment, and taking aim at places where their nobles and chieftains were gathered, he shot three huge arrows, each massive as the branch of a tree, into three places in the Turanian camp. A tumult ensued and, when dawn broke, they looked at the arrows' shafts.

> They said, "These arrows must be Zal's since no
> Brute force but his could notch them to the bow."

Shamasas said, "Khazarvan, we should have fought before and destroyed Mehrab and his army when we could. If we had fought then we would not have had to deal with Zal. Now we have a hard struggle ahead." Khazarvan replied, "And who is Zal? Zal is a person, he is not Ahriman and he is not invincible. Leave him to me and don't distress yourself."

The next day the din of drums and trumpets rang out and the two armies stood drawn up, facing one another. Khazarvan came forward before anyone else and, armed with his mace and shield, went for Zal. He struck out violently with his mace and Zal's breastplate split from the force of the blow and fell away uselessly. Zal retreated enraged. He replaced the breastplate with a cloth garment and, grasping his father Sam's mace, made furiously for the battleground. Khazarvan came out to meet him like an angry lion. Zal urged his horse forward; the dust went up and Zal raised his

mace and brought it down with such tremendous force on the Turanian champion's head that his spattered blood spotted the ground like a leopard's hide. Then Zal turned to search out Shamasas, but Shamasas was so afraid he had hidden himself away. Zal came on Golbad, another chieftain of Turan, but when Golbad saw Zal's mace and sword he tried to flee from the battlefield in fear for his life. Zal grasped his bow and notched an arrow to the string and aimed for Golbad's back. The arrow sped with such power that it pierced Golbad's armor and his trunk as well and pinned him to the pommel of his saddle.

When Khazarvan and Golbad had both been defeated and lay prone in the dirt, Shamasas fled in terror and the army of Turan was routed. Zal and Mehrab and their forces pursued them and laid many of them low in the dust. The remnant abandoned their weapons and fled toward Afrasyab. But they had the misfortune to meet up with Qaren, who had just routed Viseh's army. When Qaren saw the scattered Turkmen soldiers, he realized what had happened; he blocked their way and told his men to grasp their spears and swords and finish the fugitives off. Of all that mighty army only Shamasas and a few others escaped alive to tell the tale to Afrasyab.

Nozar Is Killed by Afrasyab

When Afrasyab learned that his chieftains had been killed in this way and that his army had been destroyed, anger overcame him and he said in rage, "How can I endure this, that Nozar, the king of Iran, is in my power while my lords and chieftains are killed by his army? I have no choice but to avenge the blood of Barman and the other lords with the death of Nozar."

He ordered his executioner to bring Nozar to him. While soldiers from the army watched, Nozar was dragged from his tent, bareheaded and humbled, his arms tightly bound behind him, and brought before Afrasyab. Nozar knew that his life had come to an end. As soon as Afrasyab saw Nozar he began to speak harshly to him, reminding him of the deaths of Salm and Tur at Manuchehr's hands. As he spoke, his rage increased and he called for a sword, and with his own hands he beheaded the king, so that Nozar's body sprawled in the dust.

In this way the scion of Manuchehr was thrust out of the world, and the crown and throne of Iran were left empty and ownerless.

Afrasyab Is Crowned

After Nozar had been killed, his companions and courtiers who had been taken prisoner were dragged out to be put to the sword. They pleaded for mercy and Aghriras interceded for them, saying, "These men are unarmed; they are bound and our prisoners, and it is not right to kill prisoners. It

would be more fitting if you handed them over to me; I shall keep them captive in a cave, and so they will die there, humiliated and comfortless."

Afrasyab agreed to this and handed the prisoners over to Aghriras and gave orders that they were to be taken in chains to Sari and kept captive there. Then he marched his army from Dehestan to Ray, where he placed the Kayanid crown on his own head and sat on the throne of Iran.

Zal Learns of the Death of Nozar

Tus and Gostahom heard the news that Nozar, their father, had been killed and that Afrasyab, the lord of Turan, had taken his place on the imperial throne of Iran. They rent their clothes in grief and wept bitter tears and went, wailing and lamenting, to Zabolestan. When they reached Zal's court, they cried out in lamentation:

> *"Alas for Nozar and his bravery,*
> *His might, his crown, his magnanimity;*
> *Protector of Iran, prop of the state,*
> *King of the world, most glorious of the great;*
> *Scion of Feraydun, of unmatched worth,*
> *Whose horse's hooves subdued the willing earth;*
> *We'll dip our swords in poison and avenge*
> *His unjust death, relentless in revenge."*

Zal wept to hear them and rent his clothes and said, "May the king's soul dwell in light, for we are all at last the prey of Death. But now that his head has been severed and injustice flourishes, I shall not sheathe my sword nor take my foot from the stirrup till I have avenged Nozar's death and freed his companions from their captivity." He spoke and, with his army, took the road for war.

The End of Aghriras

News reached the Iranian captives that Zal and other warriors had risen against Afrasyab's rule and were preparing for war. Their hearts were filled with fear of Afrasyab and they secretly sent a message to Aghriras, saying, "O great lord, of beloved name, your chivalry has given us our lives and we are all grateful to you for this. You know that Zal and Mehrab hold Zabolestan and Kabolestan, and that chieftains like Qaren, Barzin, Kherrad, and Keshvad will not abandon Iran, and that they have risen, seeking revenge for Nozar's death. Since this is how they tug at their reins, Afrasyab's anger will increase; he will not hesitate to kill us and we shall be destroyed. If Aghriras can find it in his heart to release us, we shall scatter to the earth's four corners and remain ever grateful to him."

Aghriras answered them, "This is not possible. If I do this I will have made my enmity to Afrasyab plain and he will be angry with me. But I shall do something else for you. If Zal-e Zar sends troops to Sari and Amol, I shall lead my army out from Amol and leave you to him; I am prepared to accept this disgrace to help you."

The lords of Iran praised him and sent a swift courier to Zal, saying, "Aghriras is our friend and he has promised that if you send an army to Mazanderan, he will lead his army out to Ray and so leave us to you, in this way sparing our lives."

When Zal heard the captives' message, he gathered his chieftains and nobles about him and asked for a warrior to undertake this mission. Keshvad volunteered and set out with an army from Zabol, taking the road for Amol. As he had promised, Aghriras led his troops out toward Ray, leaving the Persian prisoners at Sari. Keshvad soon freed Nozar's companions and returned safely with them to Zal. Everyone rejoiced and made much of the former captives, giving them splendid apartments in palaces and castles.

But when Aghriras led his army out from Mazanderan to Ray and Afrasyab heard that the Persian captives had been freed, he turned on Aghriras in fury: "I told you to kill them. Was this a time for delay and caution? Revenge and judicious behavior cannot be mixed together. What business has a warrior got being judicious?" Mildly, Aghriras replied, "A man should consider what is right and what is shameful. Many crowns and thrones may come to a man, but for no man do they last forever. And those to whom they come by evil means should be mindful of God and evil's consequences."

When he saw that Aghriras was talking about shame and wisdom while he himself was overcome by anger and the longing for revenge, Afrasyab was at a loss for words. His blood seethed within him and he started up like a maddened elephant; he drew his sword and sprang at his brother, cleaving him in two.

The Reigns of Zav and Garshasb

After Nozar had been killed by Afrasyab, Tus and Gostahom went to Zabol, to Zal's court. Other chieftains and nobles, such as Qaren, Barzin, and Keshvad, also arrived there, so that they could discuss how best to help Iran.

When Zal learned that Aghriras too had been slain by Afrasyab, he took this as a sign that Afrasyab's fortunes were on the wane; he therefore gathered a mighty army and set off from Zabolestan, accompanied by the other chieftains and nobles. As soon as Afrasyab learned of this, he marched toward them with his forces. Skirmishes between the two armies went on indecisively for two weeks.

One evening Zal and the Iranian nobles were discussing what to do about Afrasyab. Zal said, "However much victory in war depends on tested and experienced warriors and champions, the army and the country need someone more than this. They need someone who is wise and farsighted, who can set our people's affairs in order. If Tus and Gostahom possessed the imperial *farr* and were worthy of the throne, there would be no one more suitable than one of them. But we need a king from the clan of Feraydun who is protected by the divine *farr*, and whose words radiate wisdom."

After lengthy discussion, the council finally agreed to choose Zav as the king of Iran. Zav was the son of Tahmasb, of the clan of Feraydun; he was an old, experienced man, benevolent and God fearing.

During the long, uncertain war between Iran and Turan, a severe drought struck the land, and both the people and their armies suffered greatly. The drought lasted for five months. Both armies were gravely weakened and cried out in distress, believing that the heavens withheld their bounty because of the continuing warfare between the two peoples. Warriors from both armies sent messengers to Zav, saying, "We are sated with war. Our sufferings and sorrows have brought us to the brink of death; all of us feel this distress and seek relief from it. Let us now cleanse this ancient grudge from our hearts and establish a border between our two countries and give no more thought to the past."

Zav agreed to this. The River Oxus was established as the border between the two lands; warfare between them was laid aside and Zal returned to

Zabolestan. Then the clouds cast their shadows over the earth and the thunder roared in the heavens and rain descended; mountains and plains flowed with water once more and the earth shone with green splendor.

Five years of peace and prosperity followed. And then it was as if the world was sated with tranquillity; death came to Zav, and his son Garshasb was crowned.

As soon as Afrasyab learned of Zav's death, he renewed the ancient grudge and, contemplating new plans of conquest, marched on Ray. Throughout Garshasb's reign there was continuous warfare between the two countries. After reigning for nine years, Garshasb, too, died.

During all this period Pashang was angry with his son Afrasyab, refusing to receive his messengers or to have anything to do with him, because his heart was filled with grief at the death of his other son, Aghriras, whom Afrasyab had killed.

And then unexpectedly a letter arrived from Pashang to Afrasyab: "Now is the time to wage war; the throne of Iran is empty. Cross the Oxus before anyone is crowned and seize the crown and throne of Iran."

◃ ROSTAM AND HIS HORSE RAKHSH ▹

A New Champion

Afrasyab crossed the Oxus with a mighty army, and fear gripped the nobles of Iran, because Garshasb had died without an heir and the land of Persia had no lord. In their distress a number of the country's chieftains turned to Zabolestan and went to Zal asking for help. Their terror made them reproach him harshly: "You have neglected your responsibilities, and since you have been the foremost champion of the world, after Sam's death, we have not passed one day free of fear and distress. But at least while Zav and Garshasb reigned, the country had a lord and guardian. Now they too are gone and the army is left leaderless. It is time you bestirred yourself to think of some remedy."

Zal answered, "My lords, since I have prepared myself for war, no horseman like me has sat in the saddle, and no one has been able to defeat me in combat. In war, day and night to me were as one, and none of my enemies were safe from my sword's edge. Now I am no longer young and the passing years have bent my back double. But I thank God that, though I have grown old, a young man sprung from my loins has grown to manhood. My son, Rostam, is now like a cypress tree in stature. He has a lion's courage and is ready to be tested in war. I must choose him a horse that will be worthy of him; I shall recount to him the story of Afrasyab's evil and the harm this malevolent monarch has done to Iran, and then I shall send Rostam out to do battle with him."

At these words the nobles all rejoiced and felt hope renew within them.

Rakhsh Is Chosen

Zal sent out a swift courier to sound the call to arms far and wide, while he himself went to Rostam and said, "My son, although you are still young and should be passing your time in pleasure and feasting rather than in combat and warfare, a desperate situation has arisen and your presence on the battlefield is necessary. But, I am unsure as to how you will answer me, my child."

Rostam said, "O my famous father, you seem to have forgotten my feats of courage. You seem to have no recollection of the fact that I killed the white elephant and sacked the fortress on the White Mountain. Now is the time for me to be tested in battle, not for feasting and idleness. Where is the enemy who can make me turn tail and run?"

Zal replied, "O my brave son, I had not forgotten about the white elephant or about the fortress on the White Mountain, but being tested in battle against Afrasyab is quite another story. Afrasyab is a strong, courageous, and warlike king. Thinking of him has robbed me of rest and sleep. I don't know how I can send you out to fight against him."

> And Rostam answered Zal: "Pleasure and wine,
> Feasting and rest, are no concern of mine—
> My long-fought battles and my martial might
> Know nothing of such comfort or delight,
> Hard-pressed in war, or on the battlefield,
> With God to aid me, I shall never yield.
> I need to capture with my noose a horse
> Of mountain size and weight, of mammoth force;
> I need a craglike mace if I'm to stand
> Against Turan, defending Persia's land.
> I'll crush their heads with that tremendous mace
> And none shall dare oppose me face to face—
> Its weight will break an elephant, one blow
> From it will make a bloody river flow."

Zal rejoiced to hear Rostam's words and said, "The mace that is worthy of you is my father Sam's mace; Sam was the son of Nariman, and Nariman had this mace from his father Garshasb. It was this mace which the famous Sam used in his wars in Mazanderan, when he defeated the demons of that area. And this is the mace I shall pass on to you."

Rostam was overjoyed and thanked his father, and said: "Now I need a horse, one that can bear me, as well as my mace and armor, and that will not falter in the heat of battle." Zal gave orders that all the herds of horses that roamed in Zabolestan or Kabolestan were to be driven past Rostam so that he could select a horse that pleased him.

This was done. But whenever Rostam picked out a horse and placed his hand on its back, the back would buckle from Rostam's strength and its belly would touch the ground. At last a mare was found that was strong and had a body like that of a lioness:

> Full-maned, her waist was elegantly lean,
> She'd ears like pointed daggers, pricked and keen.

Behind the mare there followed a foal, black-eyed, slender-waisted, elegantly and nimbly stepping,

> *Its body was a wonder to behold,*
> *Like saffron petals, mottled red and gold;*
> *Brave as a lion, a camel for its height,*
> *An elephant in massive strength and might.*

When Rostam caught sight of this foal he looped his royal lariat to throw it and so snare the animal. An old man who guarded the herd called out, "Heh, young warrior, you can't noose others' horses!" Rostam asked, "Whose horse is this then, since there's no brand on its rump to show who owns it?" The herdsman answered, "No one knows who owns this horse, and there are many tales told about it. Its name is Rakhsh, and it's like spring water for its goodness and like fire for its fleetness. For three years now Rakhsh has been ready to be saddled, and the nobles have all had their eye on him. But every time its mother sees some horseman after her foal, she comes out and fights like a lion. Why is a secret, but you be wise now and forget about this horse,

> *Because, when this mare fights, a lion's heart,*
> *A leopard's hide, will both be torn apart."*

When Rostam heard these words, he whirled his rope and flung it, looping the noose over the foal's head. The mare turned and charged Rostam like a maddened elephant, snapping at him with her teeth. Rostam roared like an angry lion and brought his fist down on the mare's neck. She swayed and trembled and fell to the ground, then scrambled up and galloped over to the rest of the herd. Rostam looped his lariat and drew Rakhsh toward him; when he was close enough, he stretched out his hand and placed it on Rakhsh's back, and pushed down. But Rakhsh's back did not buckle and he seemed unaware of Rostam's hand and strength. Rostam was overjoyed, and in his heart he said: "This is my horse, and now I am ready for whatever Fate may bring." Like the wind, he leaped on Rakhsh's back and urged him forward.

Then he asked the herdsman, "What is the price of this horse?" The herdsman answered, "The price of this horse is the land of Iran. If you are Rostam, he is your horse, and with him you will put Iran's affairs in order again." Rostam laughed and gave thanks to God. Preparing his heart for battle, he began to train and nourish Rakhsh. Little by little, the horse became so swift and powerful that, to keep the evil eye from him, men sprinkled fires with wild rue.

> *Rakhsh and his noble rider seemed to bring*
> *To Zal's reviving heart the joy of spring.*

⇛ ROSTAM AND KAY QOBAD ⇚

Zal and Rostam Prepare for War

When Rostam was ready to make war on Afrasyab, Zal assembled an army of stout-hearted warriors and marched out from Zabolestan to confront Afrasyab. Rostam led the army while the older heroes came after him. The din of war drums, the neighing of horses, and the soldiers' cries resounded like the noise of the Last Judgment.

News reached Afrasyab that Zal was moving toward him with an army eager for battle. He grew anxious and immediately led his own forces toward Ray. The army from Zabolestan approached, until there remained no more than a few miles between them.

Then Zal summoned the nobles and councillors of his army and said, "My councillors, my lords, who are experienced in the ways of the world, we have put together a mighty army. We have always striven for justice and righteousness, but, alas for us, the throne of Iran remains unoccupied, and the land remains without a head or leader. This will make it impossible for us to complete our task. You remember how after the murder of Nozar, Zav occupied the throne, and how splendid his reign was and how the world rested from warfare. Now we need just such a monarch, one who is wise and possesses the royal *farr*. There is such a one, worthy of sovereignty, a champion who is just and wise and endowed with the royal *farr*, and this is Kay Qobad, who is of the family of Feraydun."

Rostam's Journey to Kay Qobad

Zal turned to Rostam and said, "My son, you must hurry to the Alborz Mountains, where Kay Qobad resides. Take him a message from the lords and champions of Iran, saying, 'The imperial throne is ownerless; the army know's of none but you who is worthy to occupy it, and they have prepared the crown and throne in your name. You must come to us without delay, and assume lordship over us.'"

Immediately Rostam set out for the Alborz Mountains. Scouts from the army of Turan blocked his way. Rostam hoisted his ox-headed mace onto his shoulders and charged against his enemies; in no time the Turanians saw that they were powerless against him and turned tail and fled, carrying the news to Afrasyab and whining in fear about Rostam. Afrasyab was enraged and summoned a courageous, clever warrior named Qalun and said to him, "I entrust this task to you; block the Persians' way forward and destroy this young upstart of a champion they've sent out. But be on the watch, for these Iranians are cunning and sly and have many tricks up their sleeves. Be careful not to fall for some sudden deceitful ploy of theirs."

Meanwhile, after Rostam had put the Turanian scouts to flight, he set off once again for the Alborz Mountains. He came to a hilly place that was green with vegetation, beautiful and splendid to look upon, and there he saw a magnificent throne on which sat a young man handsome as the shining moon, while all around him stood warriors ranged in martial order.

When they saw Rostam, they rushed forward, greeting him warmly and saying: "Young hero, as you are passing through this area, you are our guest; we can't let you leave until you drink with us." Rostam replied, "My lords, I have business in hand which is urgent, and I have to make my way to the Alborz Mountains without delay. I cannot linger here.

> Our borders swarm with vengeful enemies,
> Death and loud mourning haunt our families;
> Iran is leaderless—it is a crime
> For me to drink your wine at such a time."

They said, "If you're in such a hurry to get to the Alborz Mountains, at least tell us who you are looking for so that we can guide and help you, since we are horsemen from the marches of the Alborz."

Rostam said, "I am searching for a prince, a scion of Feraydun, whose name is Kay Qobad. If you can guide me to him, I shall be grateful to you." When the noble youth who was the horsemen's chief heard this, he said, "I have news of Kay Qobad. If you dismount from your horse and do us the honor of sitting with us for a while, I shall pass on this news to you."

When Rostam heard the name Kay Qobad he quickly dismounted from Rakhsh and joined the group. In a spot shaded by trees and next to a river he sat on a golden throne beside the young chieftain. The youth took his wine cup in his hand and said, "You asked me for news of Kay Qobad. Tell me where you learned this name."

Rostam said, "I bear a message from the warriors and chieftains of Iran. The nobles of Iran have prepared a royal throne for Kay Qobad, and my father, Zal-e Zar, who is the leader of Iran's warriors, told me to hurry to the Alborz

Mountains to find Kay Qobad and give him the Persian nobles' message. Now, if you can, give me the news of Kay Qobad which you mentioned."

The young chieftain was very pleased to hear what Rostam said, and laughed and said, "Young warrior, I am this Kay Qobad, the scion of Feraydun, whom you seek." Rostam descended from the golden throne and bowed his head and made his obeisance:

> *"O king of kings, protector of our land,*
> *May Persia live beneath your guiding hand."*

Then he delivered Zal's greetings and repeated the message from the Persian nobles. Kay Qobad drank to Rostam's good fortune, and Rostam in his turn lifted his wine cup and drank to Kay Qobad, and a shout of congratulation went up.

Kay Qobad said, "Last night I dreamed that two white hawks flew slowly toward me and placed a crown that shone like the sun upon my head. When I woke, my heart was filled with hope. I gave orders for the celebration which you see here because of that dream." Rostam said, "Your dream bears witness to God's will:

> *Now rise, we'll travel to Iran and there*
> *We'll aid our heroes in their deep despair."*

Kay Qobad leapt up like fire and mounted his horse, and Rostam too, like the wind, mounted Rakhsh, and they made all speed toward Iran.

The End of Qalun

Qalun learned that Rostam was passing through the foothills of the Alborz. With his army he blocked the hero's way. Kay Qobad paused, ready to fight with Qalun. Rostam said, "My king, this combat is unworthy of you. While I and Rakhsh and my mace are here, there is no one who can withstand us in battle." He urged Rakhsh forward against the vanguard of the Turanians. Everywhere his mace descended, a horseman toppled to the dust:

> *There one by one he charged them and they fell*
> *Down in the dust, thrown headlong and pell-mell—*
> *His strength subdued them and his fierce attacks*
> *Left broken necks and heads and broken backs.*

Qalun saw that Rostam was like a devil that had burst from its bonds and fallen among his army. He grasped his lance, bore down on Rostam like the wind, and, with a thrust, severed the fastenings of his opponent's breastplate.

Rostam gripped the lance's shaft, and, roaring like thunder, he wrenched it from Qalun's grasp. With that same lance, he jabbed at Qalun and pierced him and lifted him up from the saddle; then he struck the base of the spear into the ground and Qalun writhed on it like a spitted hen.

The Turanian soldiers were astonished and terrified; they abandoned Qalun to his fate and fled.

Rostam took Kay Qobad down into the plains and they rode on toward Zal throughout the night. When they arrived, Zal and Kay Qobad and Rostam and the other nobles gave themselves up to feasting and rejoicing for a week. On the eighth day, they prepared the imperial throne according to ancient custom and placed the royal crown on Kay Qobad's head.

⊰ KAY QOBAD AND AFRASYAB ⊱

Iran and Turan Renew the War

When Kay Qobad felt that he was secure on the Persian throne he prepared to make war on Afrasyab, drawing up a great army of Persian warriors. He entrusted command of the right flank to Mehrab, the king of Kabol, and of the left flank to brave Gostaham. The center was commanded by Qaren and Keshvad.

The young champion Rostam rode ahead of the army, and behind him rode Zal and Kay Qobad. The Kaviani banner, memento of the Persians' victory over Zahhak, fluttered in front of the troops.

For his part, Afrasyab had put together a huge army of Turanian warriors. He had entrusted the right flank to Viseh and Ajnas, and the left to Garsivaz and Shamasas. Afrasyab himself, together with a group of valiant warriors, was in the center of their battle order.

When the two armies met, the din of drums and fifes rang out, the horses reared and charged, and the troops from each side sprang to the attack. Qaren, who was still tormented by his brother's death, roared his battle cry like a raging lion and, with his sword drawn, plunged into the Turanian ranks. Everywhere he turned the dead sank to the ground. Suddenly he caught sight of the Turanian commander, Shamasas. He tugged at his horse's reins;

> Quickly he reached the proud Turanian lord,
> And cried out as he raised his glittering sword,
> "I am Qaren, whom all Turanians dread."
> The sword stroke severed Shamasas's head;
> Down slipped the hero from his horse's side
> And in that moment, as he fell, he died.

Afrasyab Is Thrown Down by Rostam

Rostam could not take his eyes from Qaren, and when he saw how he fought and how he wielded his sword he went to his father Zal and said, "Great hero, tell me, which is Afrasyab, the leader of the forces of Turan?

Where is his banner displayed and what is he wearing and where is his place in their ranks? I long to grasp him by his waist and drag him before our new king, the lord of all Iran."

Zal said, "My son, be sensible and think of what it is you are doing, Afrasyab is like a dragon in battle. His banner is black, and he wears an iron helmet on his head, and his armor is of black iron fretted with gold inlay. Beware of him, for Afrasyab is a valiant and cunning warrior." Rostam replied, "Father, do not be anxious on my behalf;

> God is my friend and he will not neglect me,
> My heart and sword and strength will all protect me."

And so saying, he urged Rakhsh forward, yelled his battle cry, and approached the Turanian lines. Afrasyab saw a warrior like a dragon that has broken its bonds and ravages the land. He paused in astonishment and asked, "Who is this, for I have never seen him in the Iranian ranks before?" They answered, "This is Rostam, the son of Dastan, who is Sam's son. Can you not see that he carries Sam's mace in his hand?" Shouting his war cry, Afrasyab rode to the front of his troops. When Rostam caught sight of Afrasyab he lifted his mace to his shoulder and pressed his thighs hard against Rakhsh:

> And, seeing Rostam, Afrasyab wheeled round,
> Unsheathed his flashing sword and stood his ground,
> Eager to overcome Zal's warlike son,
> Whose mighty prowess vanquished everyone.

Throwing his mace aside, Rostam urged his horse against Afrasyab; he stretched out his hands and grasped Afrasyab by the belt and lifted him lightly from the saddle and pulled him toward himself. But Afrasyab struggled so violently that his belt broke apart as Rostam held it in his grasp, and Afrasyab fell headlong, sprawling on the ground.

Turanian horsemen crowded around him and hurriedly bore him from the battlefield. And Rostam, who had nothing to show for his encounter but Afrasyab's belt, bit the back of his hand, regretting that he had not grasped at Afrasyab's trunk.

Quickly the good news reached Kay Qobad that Rostam had broken the center of Turan's army and fought with Afrasyab, dragging him from his saddle and sending him sprawling in the dust; the banner of Turan had disappeared from sight and the king of Turan had been hustled from the battlefield on a swift horse, surrounded by his warriors, so that their army was left leaderless.

When Kay Qobad learned of this he ordered his army to charge forward as one man. The army of Iran moved against their enemies like a mighty ocean:

The din of battle rose into the skies—
The clash of weapons and the wounded's cries.
The two sides fought so closely none could say
Which side was which on that decisive day,
Young Rostam with his mace piled up such dead,
The ground beneath his feet was stained blood red,
And where he rode, men's heads lay scattered round
As thick as autumn leaves that hide the ground.
All day the hero fought with sword and mace—
With every weapon and in every place
He left the heads and limbs and trunks of those
He fought, hacked, hewn, and shattered by his blows.

Zal observed his great son's strength and *farr*, and his heart beat faster within him. Eleven hundred and sixty warriors were overthrown by Rostam. Turan's army was broken, and those who were left turned tail and were routed, fleeing toward the River Oxus. Their treasury and wealth all fell to the Persian army as booty, and the Persian warriors returned in triumph to their camp, where they made their obeisance to Kay Qobad and congratulated him on his victory.

Proud and satisfied with his day's work, Rostam also came before Kay Qobad. The king rose and took Rostam's hand in his and sat him beside him on a throne, and he sat Zal down on his other side, as a demonstration of his gratitude to them.

Pashang Asks for a Truce

Meanwhile Afrasyab fled precipitately till he reached the shores of the Oxus. There he rested for seven days. On the eighth day he set out for his father Pashang's court. When he arrived he said, "O my father, king of all Turan, it was wrong to break our oath with Iran and go to war again; we have gained nothing from this war and the house of Feraydun still flourishes. Each time a king of theirs has died, another has replaced him. And now Kay Qobad is their king, and he has answered our attack with a new war against us. Worse than this is that a horseman has appeared who is of the seed of the great champion Sam; his father is Dastan and he himself is called Rostam. He appeared before us like some monster of the deep and scattered our army by the force of his attacks. When he saw my banner and recognized me, he threw his mace aside and, with his bare hands, lifted me from the saddle as if I were a mere fly. Our horsemen saved me from his clutches. You know the power of my hand and heart in war; but for this mammoth, lionhearted warrior, war is a mere sport, a joke, and when he fights, it's as if both the sea and the mountains are as nothing to him. You'd say he was fashioned from stone and iron and brass. More than a thousand maces struck his helmet and he made no move. If Sam had had Rostam's prowess, too, he would not have left a single warrior from Turan alive.

"Now we have no choice but to ask for a truce, since I am the mainstay of your army and its leader, and I am no match for this new warrior. It would be best if we declared ourselves satisfied with the portion that Feraydun allowed us. We should remember too how much wealth we have lost in this war, in the form of helmets and golden shields and swords from India and Arab horses, and also how many of our chieftains lie dead in the dust, great men like Barman and Golbad and Shamasas, who were killed by Qaren, and Khazarvan, who was slaughtered by Zal's mace. We should let the past go and seek for peace."

Pashang was astonished at Afrasyab's wisdom and moderation, and he immediately wrote a conciliatory letter to Kay Qobad, greeting him warmly, congratulating him on his throne and crown, and saying, "It is true that, in the beginning, Iraj, the king of Iran, suffered because of Tur. But Manuchehr avenged him by destroying Tur and Salm. Now it is fitting that we should wash all thoughts of vengeance from our hearts and refrain from war and be satisfied with the division of his kingdom which Feraydun made between his sons, keeping the River Oxus as the border between our countries and not crossing it. Consider that in this constant war of revenge, Zal has lived from his youth to old age, and the black earth is red with the blood of our two countries' heroes. None of us live eternally in this world, and therefore how much better it would be if we could pass in peace our few days in this vale of dust and sorrow. If now the lord of all Iran agrees to a truce, and if the Iranians agree not to cross the River Oxus, even in their dreams the men of Turan will not consider crossing the river again."

Then Pashang sealed the letter and sent it to Kay Qobad by a messenger, who also bore as gifts golden thrones and jewel-studded crowns and Indian swords and Arab horses and beautiful slaves bedecked with golden belts.

Kay Qobad Agrees to Peace

Kay Qobad's answer was as follows: "This feud began with you; it was your people who spilt the blood of Iraj, the king of Iran. And in our day it was Afrasyab who first crossed the water that separates us and looked for war. Likewise it was Afrasyab who put his wise and just brother Aghriras to the sword—Aghriras who always looked for peace and kept his word. For all this, I am not a vengeful man, and if you desire that there be peace between us, then I agree to it."

Not long afterward news reached the court that the army of Turan had retired beyond the Oxus; and so the fire of vengeance died down once again, and the two lands rested from warfare.

In recognition of his prowess and the help that he had given, Kay Qobad confirmed Rostam as lord of the land of Zabolestan as far as the Sea of Send, and the throne and crown of Nimruz were granted him, the grant being written on silk and handed over together with much treasure and wealth. Mehrab was confirmed as the lord of Kabolestan. Next Kay Qobad sent his greetings and thanks to Zal, ordering that five elephants caparisoned in gold-embroidered cloth should bear to him a throne inlaid with shining turquoise, together with bales of gold-worked cloth and crowns and belts studded with rubies and turquoise and other precious gifts.

Kay Qobad also honored other nobles and heroes who had taken part in the war, such as Qaren, Keshvad, Kherrad, Barzin, and Pulad, giving each of them treasure and a fitting robe of honor. He distributed a great many gold and silver coins among the soldiery, rewarding each man according to his rank, while he himself took his place on the throne and ruled with dignity and kingly *farr*. In this fashion Kay Qobad lived for one hundred years.

⋙ THE SEVEN TRIALS OF ROSTAM ⋘

The First Trial: The Lion's Thicket

Rostam quickly mounted Rakhsh and set off to free Kay Kavus from captivity among the demons. Day and night Rakhsh galloped forward, covering two days' travel in one, until Rostam grew hungry and began to look for something to eat. A plain, on which a herd of wild asses roamed, came into view. Gripping Rakhsh with his thighs, Rostam flung his lariat and lassoed a wild ass. He lit a fire, using his arrowheads to produce the spark, and roasted the animal and ate it. Then he lifted the bridle from Rakhsh's head and let him forage for fodder, while he himself went to a nearby reed bed and made himself a bolster to sleep against, and, believing that there was no danger there, he stretched out and was soon asleep.

But this reed bed was inhabited by a lion. When one watch of the night had gone by the lion appeared, returning to its lair. It saw the massive hero stretched out asleep against the bundle of reeds and Rakhsh nearby, cropping the grass. The lion thought, "First I must bring down the horse, and then I'll tear its rider apart." And so it sprang at Rakhsh. Rakhsh reared up like leaping fire and brought its two front hooves down on the lion's head and sunk its teeth into the beast's hide. He flung the lion against the ground so hard that it was rendered helpless, and then Rakhsh tore it apart.

Rostam awoke and saw that Rakhsh had destroyed a savage lion. He said, "Rakhsh, this was very inadvisable; who told you to fight with lions? If you had been killed by the lion, how could I have taken this helmet and lariat and bow and mace and sword and tigerskin to Mazanderan on foot?" And having said this, he lay back and slept until dawn.

The Second Trial: The Waterless Desert

When the sun lifted its head above the mountains, Rostam rose and groomed Rakhsh and placed the saddle on his back and set off once more. After a while he found himself in a burning, waterless desert. The heat was such that, if a bird had passed that way, it would have been burned alive. Rostam's tongue became dry and cracked, and Rakhsh's strength began to fail. Rostam dismounted and, with his lance in his hand, stumbled forward like a drunkard. The desert seemed endless and the heat was intense, and no help appeared. Rostam felt he had reached the limit of his endurance, and he turned his face to the heavens and cried, "O just Lord of all the world, all men's pain and pleasure come from you. If my suffering is your will, then know that my sufferings have been great. I took this pain upon myself so that God would save Kavus and free the Persians from the demons' clutches, for they are all God fearing and God's slaves. I have offered up my body and soul for their freedom. You are just and a present help to those who are oppressed, and I ask you to recognize what I have done and not to render my sufferings worthless. Save me now, and do not make the aged Zal's heart grieve for me."

So he went forward with prayers on his lips, but no ray of hope appeared and his strength drained away from moment to moment. He saw Death before him and, with sorrow and regret, he said to himself, "If I had faced an army, I would have fallen on them like a lion and routed them with one attack. If I had faced a mountain I would have leveled it with my mace, and if the waters of the Oxus had thundered before me, I would have diverted them in their course with my God-given strength. But what use are courage and strength against a long, weary road and no water and pitiless heat; and when death comes in such a fashion, how can it be opposed?"

And as he spoke his mammoth body, weakened by suffering and thirst, fell helplessly and sprawled on the burning ground. And then he caught sight of a sheep that was passing by. Rostam's heart swelled with hope, since he thought there must be a water hole not far away. He gathered his remaining strength and forced himself to his feet and began to follow the sheep, which led him to the edge of a stream. Rostam realized that this help had come to him from God; he greeted the sheep respectfully and drank deep of the pure, fresh water. Then he lifted the saddle from Rakhsh and washed and groomed him in the stream, and, when their thirst had been slaked, he went in search of a wild ass to eat. Having found and killed one, he roasted it and ate it and prepared himself for sleep. Before he slept, he turned to Rakhsh and said, "While I'm asleep you're not to quarrel with anyone, and there's to be no fighting with lions or demons! If an enemy turns up, come and tell me about it."

The Third Trial: Combat with a Dragon

For half the night Rakhsh cropped grass contentedly. But the plain where Rostam had chosen to sleep was the dwelling place of a dragon of such ferocity that no lion or elephant or demon dared trespass there. When the dragon was returning to its lair, it saw Rostam asleep on the ground and Rakhsh cropping grass nearby. It was astonished that anyone should have the courage to show his face there; snorting with indignation, it turned toward Rakhsh.

Rakhsh immediately galloped to Rostam's side and neighed and struck the earth with his mighty hoof. Rostam started up from sleep, and thoughts of battle coursed through his head. But the dragon used sorcery and suddenly disappeared from sight. Rostam looked around and saw nothing. He angrily reproached Rakhsh for waking him in this way, then once more lay down his head and went off to sleep. Again, the dragon emerged from the darkness. Once again Rakhsh stood by Rostam and struck his mighty hoof against the ground, making the earth spurt up. Rostam awoke and stared around at the empty plain and once more saw nothing. He became angry and said to Rakhsh, "On such a dark night you've no thoughts of sleep, and you want me to be awake too, do you? If you wake me once more, I shall cut off your head with my sharp sword and walk to Mazanderan. I said, if an enemy appears don't confront him but let me know. I didn't say that you were to keep me awake all night. Now, let this be the last time you wake me!"

The dragon appeared for a third time, roaring and spewing fire from its mouth. Rakhsh galloped from the pasture but, caught between fear of Rostam and fear of the dragon, was uncertain what he should do, since the dragon was powerful and Rostam was terrible in his rage.

But at last his love for Rostam drew him to the sleeping hero. Like the wind he flew to his side, neighing and whinnying and pawing violently against the ground. Rostam started up from a deep sleep and flew at Rakhsh in fury, but this time the world's Creator prevented the dragon's sorcery and it was unable to hide itself. In the darkness Rostam caught sight of the dragon's form. He drew his sword from its sheath and thundered like a cloud in springtime and rushed at the monster, crying out, "What is your name? For your days on earth have come to an end and I've no wish to kill you without knowing who and what you are."

The dragon roared and said, "The eagles of the air dare not overfly this plain, and the very stars do not shine here for fear of me. When you set foot on this plain, you delivered your own soul over to Death. What is your name? Because it is time for your mother to weep for your fate."

The hero cried, "I am Rostam, the son of Dastan, of the clan of Nariman, and single-handed I can break an army's strength. Stand, and see how a man can fight." He attacked, but the dragon was mighty and powerful and flew at Rostam with such force that it seemed as if victory would be his. When Rakhsh saw this, he reared and sank his teeth into the dragon's side, and tore at his skin like a ravening lion. Rostam was astonished by Rakhsh's devotion and courage. He whirled his sword around and severed the dragon's head. A river of blood spewed out across the ground, and the dragon's lifeless body fell like a boulder. Rostam gave thanks to God and waded into the nearby stream, washing his head and body. Then he mounted Rakhsh and set off on his journey again.

The Fourth Trial: The Sorceress

Rostam rode ever forward, until he came to a delightful landscape through which a gentle stream flowed. Plants and flowers grew in abundance at the stream's edge, and among them there was a cloth laid out for a banquet. On the cloth lay a roasted lamb and other fine foods and next to the cloth there was a golden goblet filled with wine. Rostam rejoiced to see all this and, not realizing that this banquet was the work of demons, dismounted and sat beside the cloth and drank from the goblet. There was a lutelike instrument next to the goblet; Rostam picked this up and began to improvise a charming song describing his own life:

> "This is the song of Rostam, who's been given
> Few days of happiness by Fate or heaven.
> He fights in every war, in every land;
> His bed's a hillside, or the desert sand;
> Demons and dragons are his daily prey,
> Devils and deserts block his weary way.
> Fate sees to it that perfumed flowers and wine
> And pleasant vistas, are but rarely mine—
> I'm always grappling with an enemy,
> Some ghoul or leopard's always fighting me."

The sound of Rostam's voice and instrument reached the ears of an old sorceress. At once she changed her shape to that of a young and beautiful woman; coquettishly, her form a paradise of tints and scents, she walked toward Rostam. Rostam was overjoyed to see this vision and greeted her respectfully and praised God that he had been vouchsafed the sight of her. But as soon as the name of God passed Rostam's lips, the sorceress's appearance suddenly changed and she became as ugly and deformed as Ahriman. Rostam stared at her, realizing she was a witch. She made to flee, but Rostam deftly threw his lariat over her head. As he came near her, he saw that she was a monstrous wrinkled hag, full of evil wiles and deceit. He drew his dagger from his belt and cut her in two.

The Fifth Trial: Combat with Ulad

Once again Rostam set off on his long journey, traveling until night fell and then through the darkness. At dawn he reached a green and pleasant land, filled with murmuring streams. He was sorely in need of rest, and the difficulties of the way had left his clothes soaked with sweat. He took off the tigerskin he wore, and his helmet too, and laid them in the sun. When they were dry, he put them on again and removed Rakhsh's bridle and let him wander in the green pasture. He made himself a bolster of plants and then, placing his shield beneath his head and his sword beside him, he sank into sleep.

There was a peasant who cultivated the plain there, and when he saw Rakhsh wandering through the young growth, he ran after him and struck him smartly on the legs with a stick. Rostam meanwhile had woken up and the peasant said to him, "Hey, you devil, why have you let your horse graze in my fields, taking advantage of all my labors?" Rostam was enraged by his words and jumped up and grabbed him by the ears, and without saying a word, tore them off and flung them aside.

The peasant screamed with pain and retrieved his ears and, with his hands and head covered in blood, went off to find Ulad, who was the local landowner and champion. He raised a great clamor, saying: "There was a man like a ghoul asleep in the pasture; his armor's of leopard skin and he has an iron helmet and a monstrous body, and he'd let his horse roam in the new growth. When I went to drive his horse away, he jumped up and tore my ears off, as you can see." Ulad and his companions decided to hunt this man down; they mounted their horses and set off to find Rostam and punish him.

Ulad and his band reached the place where Rostam had been resting. Rostam mounted Rakhsh, ready to encounter Ulad; grasping his sword he roared like a thunder cloud. When they came closer to one another, Ulad shouted out, "Who are you, and what is your name, and who is your king? Why did you tear this farmer's ears off and let your horse roam in his pastures? This very moment I shall make the world dark before your eyes and bring your helmet down into the dust."

Rostam said, "My name is Cloud; imagine that a cloud has lion claws and pours down swords and spears instead of rain. If my true name reaches your ears, your blood will freeze in your veins. Your mother bore you so that you would be covered in a shroud, and it's clear that today your fate will be fulfilled." He drew his sword from its sheath and fell on Ulad and his followers as a lion falls on a flock of sheep. With each flourish of his sword two heads were severed, and in a short time Ulad's army was routed and fled. Rostam sped after them like a maddened elephant, his lariat looped over his arm. When Rakhsh brought him close enough to Ulad, Rostam whirled the lariat and noosed the champion's head. He pulled him down from his horse and bound his two arms tightly behind him. Then, remounting Rakhsh, Rostam addressed Ulad: "Your life is in my hands. If you tell the truth and show me where the White Demon and Pulad Ghondi are, and tell me where King Kavus lies in chains, you will be well-treated by me, and when I have secured the crown and throne of Mazanderan by means of my massive mace, I shall make you king of that province. But if you lie and try to deceive me, I shall make two rivers of blood flow from your eyes."

Ulad said, "O brave warrior, lay aside your anger and spare my life. I shall be your guide and, one by one, I shall show you the demons' lairs and where Kavus is. From here to where Kavus is held is a hundred leagues, and from there to where the demons are is another hundred, and the whole way is hard and difficult. Twelve thousand demons guard the Persian prisoners. Bid and Sanjeh are the demons' lords, and Pulad Ghondi is their commander in battle. The chief of all these demons is the White Demon, whose body is like a mountain and before whom all tremble in fear. Even with your stature and strength and mount, and with your mace and spear and sword, it would not be right for you to fight with the White Demon and so place your life in danger. When you pass the demons' lair you reach the Plain of Sanglakh, where not even the deer can run. After that you reach a mighty river two leagues in width, and this is guarded by a demon called Kanarang. On the other side of the river lies the land of the Bozgushan (Goat-eared) and the Narmpayan (Soft-footed), which is three hundred leagues across. From there to the seat of the king of Mazanderan there are still many long, hard leagues to travel. The king of Mazanderan commands the allegiance of thousands upon thousands of horsemen, all well-armed and equipped. He has twelve hundred war elephants alone. You have no companions and, even if you are made of steel, that steel will be worn away against such opponents."

Rostam laughed and said, "You need not concern yourself with that, simply show me the way:

> And then you'll see what this one man can do
> Against their king's demonic retinue;
> Protected by the world Creator's will,
> Helped by my sword and arrows and my skill.
> When they first glimpse my body's strength and might,
> And see the massive mace with which I fight
> Their skins will split with fear; headlong they'll ride,
> Routed, with tangled reins, and terrified.

Now, hurry and guide me to where Kavus is being held."

Rostam and Ulad rode that day and into the night, until they reached the foothills of Mount Asporuz, not far from where Kavus had fought against the demons and suffered defeat at their hands.

The Sixth Trial: Combat with the Demon Arzhang

Halfway through the night they could see ahead where torches and candles and fires were lit on all sides, and a confused noise came from the direction of Mazanderan. Rostam asked Ulad, "What place is that, where fires are lit on every side?" Ulad said, "That is the marches of the country of Mazanderan; demons keep watch there, and in that spot where a tree rises almost to the heavens, the demon Arzhang has pitched his tent, and there is always a noise of rumbling and roaring rising up from that place."

Having learned where the demon Arzhang was, Rostam leaned back contentedly and fell asleep. When dawn broke, he tied Ulad to a tree; he then mounted Rakhsh, placed his royal helmet on his head, grasped the mace that had belonged to Sam, his grandfather, and set out for Arzhang's tent. Soon he found himself in the midst of the demon's army and as he came closer to Arzhang's tent, he gave an earsplitting roar, which brought Arzhang hurrying out. Catching sight of him, Rostam urged Rakhsh forward and descended on the demon like lightning, grappling with his head and trunk; then with one mighty blow he severed the demon's head from his body and flung him, bleeding and lifeless, into the midst of his soldiers. When the demons saw their leader's head severed in this way, and their eyes fell on Rostam's massive body and mace, their hearts quaked within them; fear invaded their souls, and they turned and fled. Rostam drew his sword and fell among the demons, cleansing the earth of them; when the sun stood at its highest in the heavens, he returned in triumph to Mount Asporuz.

Rostam Reaches Kavus

Rostam untied Ulad from the tree and said, "Now show me where Kavus is." Ulad ran ahead of Rakhsh and Rostam, as they made their way to where the Persian prisoners were being held.

When they drew near the place, Rakhsh gave a tremendous neigh, which was heard by Kavus. The king's heart took hope; he realized what was afoot, and, turning to his men, he said, "I have heard Rakhsh's neigh, and my heart rejoices at this. This is the same neigh I heard from Rakhsh during my father's wars with the Turkmen peoples." But the Iranian army was in such despair that they murmured among themselves, saying that Kavus was talking foolishly, that the sorrows of his captivity had affected his mind, and that he was like one who prattles randomly in his sleep. They were certain that Fortune had forsaken them, and that they would never be free again.

They were talking thus when Rostam appeared. A great cry went up from the Persians, and the nobles and chieftains like Tus, Gudarz, Giv, Gostaham, Shidush, and Bahram crowded round him. Rostam made his obeisance to Kavus and asked him of the sufferings he had endured. Kavus embraced him and enquired after Zal-e Zar, and the hardships of the way.

Then Kavus said to Rostam, "We must proceed with caution, and we must hide Rakhsh from the demons. If the White Demon learns that you have slain Arzhang and have reached us, he will gather all the demons together and your trials and sufferings will go for nothing. You must trust to your strength and sword and bow once again, and set out to confront the White Demon. If, with God's help, you can overcome him you will free us from our sufferings, for he is the pillar and prop of all the demons. To reach where he lives, you must cross seven mountains. At every pass there wait malignant demons, ready for war. The demons' seat, the pivot of their power, lies within a cave, and if you destroy that, you have broken their might. Our army has suffered greatly in these chains, and I have been brought to the point of death by the darkness of my eyes. Physicians say that the cure for this darkness is the White Demon's blood, and a wise doctor has told me that if I drop but three drops of that blood in my eyes, this darkness will disappear and my sight will be restored."

Rostam said, "I shall travel to the White Demon's lair. Be on the watch, for this demon is strong, and a mighty sorcerer, and he has a great army of lesser demons at his beck and call. If he bends me to his will, you will remain in these chains for many a long day. But if God aids me and I destroy him, we shall once again reach the marches of Iran and return to our own people."

The Seventh Trial: Combat with the White Demon

Then Rostam mounted Rakhsh and, taking Ulad with him, he set off like the wind for the mountain where the White Demon lived. Quickly he crossed the seven mountains that lay between him and his goal, and at last he came near to the White Demon's cave. He saw a huge mob of demons standing on watch there and said to Ulad, "So far I have seen nothing from you but honesty and fair dealing, and you have guided me everywhere as you promised. Now you must tell me the secret of how the White Demon can be overcome."

Ulad said: "First you must wait till the sun rises. When the sun is up and the air grows warmer, the demons are overcome by sleep, and you will see that all these demons, except for a couple of guards, will sink into a deep slumber. This is the time for you to attack the White Demon. If God is with you, you will be victorious in your combat with him."

Rostam followed his advice and waited until the sun had risen and the demons had lain back limp and listless, overcome with sleep. Then once

again he tied Ulad up with his lariat and drew his monstrous sword; invoking God, and roaring his war cry in a voice like thunder, he fell upon the demons. Left and right he slashed off demons' heads and none of them could withstand the onslaught. Finally he fought his way to the mouth of the White Demon's cave. He saw that it was as dark as the mouth of hell, and that its interior was all but filled with the mountainous bulk of a huge sleeping ghoul, as pale and pasty as white milk. When Rostam found the White Demon asleep, he was in no hurry to kill him. He roared like a leopard, and the White Demon started up from sleep and seized a huge millstone that lay near him and, like a moving mountain, sprang to the attack. Rostam leaped forward like a ravening lion and smote with his sword against the Demon's trunk, slashing away one of his arms and one of his legs. The White Demon roared in anguish and like a maddened elephant flung his mutilated, bleeding carcass against the hero.

The cave was filled with the confused din of their combat. The two massive fighters grappled with one another, tearing chunks of flesh from each other's bodies while the cave floor swam with their blood. Rostam said to himself that if he escaped alive from this combat, Death would hold no further fears for him, and the Demon said to himself that if, mutilated and limbless, he were to escape from this dragon's clutches, he would never show his face in the world again. And so they fought, with blood streaming from them like a river. At last Rostam gathered all his might together and, like a lion, grappled with the Demon and lifted him high in the air, then hurled him to the ground and immediately plunged a dagger into his side and hacked out his liver. The White Demon lay on the ground like a lifeless mountain.

Besmeared with blood, Rostam emerged from the cave, released Ulad, and handed the Demon's liver to him, and then the two of them set off on the return journey to Kavus.

Ulad was astonished by Rostam's victory and by his courage, and said, "O lion warrior, you have conquered all the world by your sword and have destroyed these demons' power. Do you remember that you promised me that when you were victorious you would give Mazanderan to me? Now it is time that you fulfilled your promise, as is fitting for a chivalrous warrior."

Rostam said, "So be it, I shall give all of Mazanderan to you. But there is still hard work to be done. The king of Mazanderan still sits on his throne and thousands upon thousands of demons still guard him and do his bidding. First I must drag him down from his throne and bind him in chains, and then I shall hand Mazanderan over to you and make you rich and prosperous."

Kay Kavus's Sight Is Restored

Meanwhile Kay Kavus and the Persian nobles were eagerly waiting Rostam's return, and wondering whether he had emerged victorious from his encounter with the White Demon. Finally news arrived that Rostam was returning in triumph; a great shout of joy went up from the Persians, and they streamed out to welcome him, praising him to the skies. Rostam said to Kay Kavus, "O king, now you can rejoice and put your heart at rest, for I split open the White Demon's trunk and cut out his liver and have brought it to you."

Kay Kavus rejoiced and praised his champion and said, "God be thanked for your mother, that she bore such a son, and for your father that he reared such a warrior. That I have a champion like you as my subject makes me more fortunate than any other king. Now you must pour drops of blood from this demon's liver into my eyes, and then we shall know whether my eyes will clear and whether I shall ever see you again."

They poured the drops into his eyes, and immediately Kavus's sight was restored. A cry of joy rose into the heavens. Kay Kavus sat upon the ivory throne again and placed the Kayanid crown on his head; then he passed a week feasting and drinking wine with his nobles and chieftains—Tus, Gudarz, Giv, Fariborz, Raham, Gorgin, Bahram, and the rest.

On the eighth day all prepared themselves for battle and, under Kay Kavus's command, they attacked Mazanderan; they fought all day with the demons and sorcerers who opposed them, and by nightfall they had laid many of them low in the dust.

The War between Kay Kavus and the King of Mazanderan

Night came, and the Persian army rested from the slaughter. Kavus said, "The demons of Mazanderan have received their punishment and it would be wrong to shed any more of their blood. Now we must send a wise, cautious man to the king of Mazanderan, inviting him to submit to us."

Kavus ordered a scribe to write an eloquent letter, filled with both threats and promises, to the king: "O king, you are the prisoner of arrogance and pride, you have allied yourself with demons and sorcerers and turned to evil and an evil faith. You should realize that if you act with evil, you shall suffer evil; but if you act justly and follow wise, religious precepts, your reward will be a good one and men will praise you and your memory. You can see how God has dealt with your demons and sorcerers. Now, if wisdom guides you and you desire to live securely and safely, descend from the throne of Mazanderan and come to my court as a subject and pay tribute to me, and I shall confirm you in your sovereignty over Mazanderan. And if you do otherwise, you will suffer the same fate as Arzhang and the White Demon."

Then Kay Kavus chose Farhad, one of the renowned warriors of Iran, and handed him the letter and bade him take it to the king of Mazanderan.

When Farhad reached the city of the Narmpayan, he sent news ahead to the king of Mazanderan that he was bringing a message from Kavus. The king of Mazanderan chose a group of haughty champions and sent them out with a large army to greet Farhad. They stood before him with frowning faces, in silence. When they approached, one of the champions grasped Farhad's hand and tried to crush it in his fist, but Farhad showed no response and made light of the pain. They took him to the court of Mazanderan. When the king there read Kavus's letter and learned of Rostam's exploits, and of how Pulad Ghondi and Bid and Arzhang and the White Demon had been killed, his heart failed within him and he fell to brooding and said to himself, "This Rostam is like a pestilence; nowhere in the world is safe from him."

He kept Farhad with him for three days. On the fourth he rose brusquely and said, "Tell Kavus my answer is as follows: 'O young and foolish king, your impatience and inexperience will not let you recognize your own equals and superiors, since, if this were not the case, how could you have asked someone like me, with the vast country over which I rule and with all my power and wealth, to come and submit to you at your court? I command thousands upon thousands of fierce warriors, and I have twelve hundred war elephants, and you have not a single one in your army. Prepare to fight, for I am about to march on your forces, and with my army I shall soon drive these foolish dreams out of your and your soldiers' heads.'"

Rostam Takes a Message to the King of Mazanderan

When this message reached Kavus and Rostam, and the messenger had told them of the king of Mazanderan's power and of the splendor of his court, Rostam said, "I should be the one to take a message to this king. A letter like a slashing sword is what we need; I shall take it to him and add my own words and then we'll see how he reacts."

Kavus was pleased by this suggestion and had another letter written: "O arrogant king, you have spoken foolishly, uttering words without wisdom. Either rid your mind of this extravagant pride and come to me as a slave, or I shall unleash upon Mazanderan an army like a mighty sea, and make blood flow there like a river, and feed your brains to the vultures."

Rostam mounted Rakhsh and set off with Kavus's letter. Once again a band of soldiers rode out to strike fear into the heart of Kavus's courier. When Rostam came within sight of the group, there was a tree with many branches growing by the wayside; Rostam reached out, grasped two of its branches, and wrenched the tree up by its roots. Then he hefted it like a huge javelin and flung it at the Mazanderani soldiers; it struck a number of their horsemen, unseating them. The leader of the band, who was a renowned champion, came forward, and, to show his strength, grasped Rostam's hand and squeezed it with all his might. Rostam laughed, then suddenly crushed the other's fist in his own. The champion's face turned pale; his hand was broken and he fell from his horse, insensible with pain. The soldiers of Mazanderan were astonished by Rostam's behavior and sent a horseman to inform their king. The king of Mazanderan summoned one of his warriors, called Kolahvar, a warlike, courageous man, who delighted in combat as a leopard delights in the chase. The king said, "You must go to this messenger and show him your skill, and make him weep with fear and tremble with shame." Kolahvar rode out like a lion; frowning, he took Rostam's hand in his and wrung it so hard that the whole hand was bruised. But Rostam showed no reaction; he simply crushed Kolahvar's hand with such force that the fingernails fell out. His hand crushed and aching with pain, Kolahvar returned to his king and said, "I couldn't hide such pain, and I cannot fight with such a warrior. It would be better for you to make peace with these people and to agree to pay tribute, and so avoid future trouble."

When Rostam reached the court, the king of Mazanderan assigned him a worthy place and enquired after Kavus and the Persian army and the vicissitudes of the journey. Then he asked, "Are you, with this mighty chest and arm of yours, Rostam?" Rostam replied, "I am the servant of Rostam's servant, if indeed I am even worthy of that. What am I compared to Rostam? Rostam is a matchless hero:

Since God first made the world, no man's appeared
Like him, no man is feared as he is feared;
In battle he's a mountain; Rakhsh, his horse,
And his huge mace, are both of matchless force;
His strength can raise the sea above the land,
Or level mountains with the desert sand—
He is an army in himself, and he's
Too great a man to carry messages.

But he gave me a message for you, which was that if you have any wisdom you will not sow the evil seeds of rebellion; instead you should be obedient, because once I have permission from the Persian king I won't leave a single soldier of yours alive." Then he handed over Kavus's letter.

When the king of Mazanderan heard the message and saw the letter, he was taken aback and burst out in rage to Rostam, "What foolish, idle chatter is this, for King Kavus to compare himself with me? Tell Kavus, 'You may be king of the Persians, but I am the king of Mazanderan, and my army and power and gold and wealth far exceed yours. Put these ridiculous thoughts out of your head, and cease to covet other kings' thrones. Turn your horses' heads and go back to your own land, for if I stir from here and lead my army against you, I shall annihilate you in an instant.' And you can also give Rostam a message from me; say to him, 'Great hero, what good has Kavus ever done for you that you should be so eager to serve him? If you come to serve me, I shall reward you in a hundred ways and make you first among my chieftains, and you shall never want for gold or wealth.'"

Rostam was enraged and said, "O witless king, if Fortune had not turned her back on you, you would not have spoken in this way. Do you imagine that the great Rostam has any need for your wealth and army? Rostam is the son of Dastan and the king of Zabolestan and has no equal in all the world. If you speak like this again, Rostam will tear your tongue from your mouth."

These words only increased the king of Mazanderan's fury and, turning to his executioner, he roared: "Take this messenger and cut off his head immediately!" When the executioner stepped toward him Rostam grasped him by the arm and pulled him forward; then taking one leg in his hand and locking the other under his own leg, he ripped the man in half. Then he turned to the king of Mazanderan and said: "If I had my king's permission, I would have utterly destroyed your army and dealt with you as you deserve. But wait, and you will see the punishment for your impertinent, malicious ways." And having said this, he stormed from the court, leaving the king of Mazanderan astonished and afraid.

Rostam's Combat with Juya

As soon as Rostam left Mazanderan, its king began to prepare for war; he gathered a huge army and had his royal pavilion taken out of the city, and with his demons and a host of war elephants, he bore down on the Persian army like a mighty wind.

Meanwhile Rostam had reached Kavus's court and informed him of what had happened. He said, "There is no need for fear. We must be courageous and go forward to this war with the demons, and when the day of battle comes, my mace will utterly destroy them."

Before long, news came that the army of Mazanderan was approaching. Kay Kavus ordered Rostam to prepare for war. Then he called the army's chieftains to him and commanded them to draw up the army in battle order. Tus was given command of the right flank, Gudarz of the left, while Keshvad and the king himself were to command the center. The mighty Rostam went ahead of the whole army.

When the two armies drew near one another, a renowned warrior of Mazanderan, called Juya, lifted his heavy mace to his shoulders and, like a ravening lion, galloped toward the Iranian lines, roaring in such a tremendous voice that the very mountains and plain trembled, and fear found its way into the Persians' hearts. He cried out, "Who will do battle with me?" His breastplate glittered in the sun, and his conquering sword menaced all who watched. From Kavus's army not a single voice rose in response. Kavus turned toward his champions and warriors and said, "What has happened to you all, that you wait there silent at the sound of this demon's voice, with the color fled from your cheeks?" But still no response came; fear of Juya seemed to have melted away the army's courage. Then Rostam tugged at his reins and came close to Kavus and said, "Great king, leave this demon to me." Kavus said, "So be it, as the rest are silent. May you deliver me from this demon; God be with you."

Dust billowed up as Rostam urged Rakhsh forward; he roared his war cry, couched his lance, and, like a maddened elephant, charged toward his opponent. Juya said, "Prepare to die, for even now I'll make your mother mourn for you." When Rostam heard this, he roared in response, calling on God for aid, and charged like a moving mountain. Fear of Rostam gripped Juya's heart and he tugged at the reins and galloped aside. Rostam came after him like the wind and thrust his lance into Juya's back. The blow severed the fastenings of Juya's breastplate, which fell away useless. Juya was spitted like a chicken on the lance and Rostam plucked him from the saddle and hurled him to the ground. The army of Mazanderan watched in astonishment, and when they saw the greatest of their heroes dead in the dust, fear filled their hearts.

Rostam's Victory over the King of Mazanderan

When the king saw this, he ordered his men to draw their swords and charge the watching Persians. The din of drums rang out, and the two armies charged toward one another. The horses sent up so much dust that the air was thick and dark, and swords and lances flashed and glittered in the murk.

> *The demons' cries, the darkened atmosphere,*
> *The din of drums, the horses' neighs of fear*
> *Shook the firm land—no man had seen before*
> *Such fury or such violence or such war;*
> *The clash of weapons filled the air, and blood*
> *Flowed from the heroes like a monstrous flood—*
> *The earth became a lake, a battleground*
> *Where waves of warriors broke and fell and drowned;*
> *Blows rained on helmets, shields, and shattered mail*
> *Like leaves whirled downward in an autumn gale.*

The battle between the two armies went on for seven days, and although Rostam slew many of the demons, neither side gained final victory.

On the eighth day Kay Kavus removed the Kayanid crown from his head and stood in prayer; he bent his head to the ground and begged before the throne of God that the world's Creator would grant him victory over these audacious demons and preserve him in his reign as lord of all Iran. Then he returned to his troops and placed his war helmet on his head and, gathering his warriors and chieftains about, inspired them with new heart for the fight. When he gave orders that the war drums be sounded, the fire of battle was rekindled in the Persians' hearts, and together they charged the enemy lines. Like a maddened elephant Rostam turned on their center and let loose a flood of blood; Gudarz and Keshvad attacked on the right, and Giv was victorious on the left.

The encounter lasted from dawn until dusk. With his men Rostam fought toward the king of Mazanderan's position, but the king held his ground and, surrounded by his demons, did not flinch before Rostam's onslaught. Rostam fell upon the demons with his mace and laid many of them low in the dust. When the king of Mazanderan was almost face to face with the hero, he roared his war cry and, lifting his mace from the pommel of his saddle, cried out, "Evil and worthless wretch, stand and see how a man can fight!" Enraged, Rostam laid his mace aside and, grasping his lance, he gave a great bellow of fury and charged at the king. The king of Mazanderan saw a maddened elephant bearing down on him, bringing tidings of death. His soul failed within him, and his courage melted away; but Rostam gave him no quarter and plunged his lance into the king's waist. The king's belt and armor split apart and the lance came to rest deep in the king's gut.

But suddenly Rostam saw that through magic and sorcery the king had been able to slip from his human form and had become a mountain crag. Rostam and the Persian army stared in wonder. At this moment Kay Kavus rode forward with his entourage, asking how the tide of battle flowed. Rostam told him what had happened, saying in conclusion, "I plunged my lance into their king's gut, and I expected him to fall lifeless from his saddle; but suddenly he turned to stone before my eyes and held his place there like a mighty mountain. But I will not leave him thus; I will drag him to our camp and hack him from the rock."

Kay Kavus gave orders that the massive rock was to be taken to the Persian army's encampment, but, however much they struggled, the soldiers were unable to shift it. Finally Rostam himself came forward and stretched out his hand, and with one tug he lifted the rock from the ground and placed it on his shoulders; he carried it back to the Persian camp and flung it on the ground. Then he faced the rock and said, "Leave your magic and come out of the rock, and if you don't, I shall hack the rock to pieces with iron and steel and so destroy you." As soon as he had said this, the rock dispersed, as insubstantial as a cloud; in its place stood the Demon-King, tall and ugly of face, with a wild boar's tusks, and wearing his helmet and breastplate. Rostam laughed to see him and took his arm and dragged him before Kay Kavus.

Kay Kavus stared at him and saw that he deserved to die. And so he handed the Demon King over to the executioner, and his heart was cleansed of all anxiety.

A vast amount of booty, in the form of treasure and gold and jewels, was collected from the army of Mazanderan. Kay Kavus stood in prayer for a week, and expressed his gratitude to God for his victory. Then he opened the gates of the treasury and for another week distributed wealth, giving the needy the means to live and bestowing gold and precious goods on the deserving. And for the third week he feasted, at ease with his wine and musicians.

Now that the monarchy was secure again, Kay Kavus congratulated Rostam and thanked him, saying, "O greatest of heroes, it is due to your chivalry

toward Turan, heartsick and with two parts of his army destroyed. Seeking sweetness and pleasure from the world, he had found only bitter poison.

For his part, Kavus returned in triumph to Pars; he reigned in splendor, giving himself up to the pleasures of court life. He sent out great warriors, wise and just men, to confirm his rule in his possessions, in Merv and Nayshapur and Balkh and Herat; the world was filled with justice and the wolf turned harmlessly from the lamb. On Rostam, Kavus bestowed the title of Champion of all the World.

Kavus Is Tempted by Eblis

Then one morning the devil Eblis addressed a convocation of demons, in secret and unbeknownst to the king: "Under this king our lives are miserable and wretched: I need a nimble demon, one who knows court etiquette, who can deceive the king and wrench his mind away from God and bring his royal glory down into the dust; in this way the burdens he has placed upon us will be lightened." The demons heard him, but none at first responded, out of fear of Kavus. Then an ugly demon spoke up, "I'm wily enough for this." And so saying, he transformed himself into a handsome, eloquent youth, one who would grace any court.

It happened that the king went out hunting, and the youth saw his opportunity. He came forward and kissed the ground; handing Kavus a bouquet of wild flowers, he said, "Your royal *farr* is of such splendor that the heavens themselves should be your throne. The surface of the earth is yours to command; you are the shepherd and the world's nobles are your flock. There is but one thing remaining to you, and when this is accomplished your glory will never fade. The sun still keeps its secrets from you; how it turns in the heavens, and who it is that controls the journeys of the moon and the succession of night and day, these are as yet unknown to you."

The king's mind was led astray by this demon's talk, and his mind forsook the ways of wisdom: He did not know that the heavens are immeasurable, that the stars are many but that God is one, and that all are powerless beneath his law. The king was troubled in his mind, wondering how he could fly into the heavens without wings. He asked learned men how far it was from the earth to the heavens; he consulted astronomers and set his mind on a foolish enterprise.

He gave orders that men were to go at night and rob eagles' nests of their young; these squabs were to be placed in houses in pairs and reared on fowl and occasional lamb's meat. When the eagles had grown as strong as lions and were each able to subdue a mountain goat, Kavus had a throne constructed of aloe wood and gold, and at each corner he had a lance attached. From the lances he suspended lamb's meat; next he bound four eagles tightly to the structure. Then King Kavus sat on the throne, his mind deceived by the wiles of Ahriman. When the eagles grew hungry they flew up toward the suspended meat and the throne was lifted above the ground, rising up from the level plain into the clouds. The eagles strained toward the meat to the utmost of their capacity, and I have heard that Kavus was carried into the heavens as far as the sphere of the angels. Others say that he fought with his arrows against the sky itself, but God alone knows if these and other such stories are true. The eagles flew for a great while, but finally their strength gave out and their wings began to tire; they tumbled down from the dark clouds, and the king's throne plummeted toward the ground. It finally came to rest in a thicket near Amol and, miraculously, the king was not killed. Hungry and humiliated, Kavus was filled with regret at his foolishness; he waited forlornly in the thicket, praying to God for help.

Once Again King Kavus Is Rescued

While he was begging forgiveness for his sins, the army was searching for some trace of him. Rostam, Giv, and Tus received news of his whereabouts and set off with a band of soldiers to rescue him. Gudarz said to Rostam:

> "Since I was weaned of mother's milk I've known
> The ways of kings and served the royal throne;
> I've seen the world's great monarchs and their glory,
> But never have I heard so mad a story
> As this we hear now of Kavus, this fool
> Who's so unwise he's hardly fit to rule."

The heroes reached Kavus and furiously reproached him. Gudarz said:

> "A hospital is where you need to be,
> Forget your palaces and sovereignty;
> You throw away your power, you don't discuss
> Your plans and foolish fantasies with us.
> Three times disaster's struck you down, but still
> You haven't learned to curb your headstrong will:
> First you attacked Mazanderan, and there
> Captivity reduced you to despair;
> Then, trusting to your enemies, you gave
> Your heart away and so became their slave;
> And now your latest folly is to try
> Your strength against the ever-turning sky."

Shamefaced and humble, Kavus replied, "All that you say is true and just." He was placed in a litter, and on his journey home humiliation and regret were his companions. When he reached his palace again, his heart remained wrung with sorrow, and for forty days he waited as a suppliant before God, his head bowed in the dust. His pride was humbled, and shame kept him locked within his palace. Weeping and praying, he neither granted audience nor feasted, but in sorrow and regret had wealth distributed to the poor.

But when Kavus had wept in this way for a while, God forgave him. King Kavus reestablished justice in the world, and it shone equally on nobles and commoners alike. Justice made the world as rich and splendid as a fine brocade, and over all the king presided, majestic and magnificent.

❧ THE TALE OF SOHRAB ❧

Rostam Loses Rakhsh

At dawn one day Rostam decided to go hunting, to drive away the sadness he felt in his heart. Filling his quiver with arrows, he set off for the border with Turan, and when he arrived in the marches he saw a plain filled with wild asses; laughing, his face flushed with pleasure, he urged Rakhsh forward. With his bow, his mace, and his noose he brought down his prey and then lit a fire of brushwood and dead branches; next he selected a tree and spitted one of the slaughtered asses on it. The spit was as light as a feather to him, and when the animal was roasted he tore the meat apart and ate it, sucking the marrow from its bones. He sank back contentedly and slept. Cropping the grass, his horse Rakhsh wandered off and was spotted by seven or eight Turkish horsemen. They galloped after Rakhsh and caught him and bore him off to the city, each of them claiming him as his own prize.

Rostam woke from his sweet sleep and looked round for his horse. He was very distressed not to see Rakhsh there and set off on foot toward the closest town, which was Samangan. To himself he said, "How can I escape from such mortifying shame? What will our great warriors say, 'His horse was taken from him while he slept?' Now I must wander wretched and sick at heart, and bear my armor as I do so; perhaps I shall find some trace of him as I go forward."

Samangan

The king of Samangan was told that the Crown Bestower, Rostam, had had his horse Rakhsh stolen from him and was approaching the town on foot. The king and his nobles welcomed him and enquired as to what had happened, adding, "In this town we all wish you well and stand ready to serve you in any way we can." Rostam's suspicions were laid to rest and he said, "In the pastures, Rakhsh wandered off from me; he had no bridle or reins. His tracks come as far as Samangan and then peter out into reeds and the

river. If you can find him, I shall be grateful, but if he remains lost to me, some of your nobility will lose their heads."

The king responded, "No one would dare to have done this to you deliberately. Stay as my guest and calm yourself; tonight we can drink and rejoice, and drown our worries with wine. Rakhsh is such a world-renowned horse, he will not stay lost for long."

Mollified by his words, Rostam agreed to stay as the king's guest. He was given a chamber in the palace and the king himself waited on him. The chieftains of the army and the city's nobility were summoned to the feast; stewards brought wine, and dark-eyed, rosy-cheeked girls sought to calm Rostam's fretfulness with their music. After a while Rostam became drunk and felt that the time to sleep had come; his chamber had been sweetened with the scents of musk and rosewater, and he retired there for the night.

Tahmineh

When one watch of the night had passed, and Venus rose into the darkened sky, a sound of muffled whispering came to Rostam's ears; gently his chamber door was pushed open. A slave entered, a scented candle in her hand, and approached the hero's pillow; like a splendid sun, a paradise of tints and scents, her mistress followed her. This beauty's eyebrows curved like an archer's bow, and her ringlets hung like nooses to snare the unwary; in stature she was as elegant as a cypress tree. Her mind and body were pure, and she seemed not to partake of earthly existence at all. The lionhearted Rostam gazed at her in astonishment; he asked her what her name was and what it was that she sought on so dark a night. She said:

> "My name is Tahmineh; longing has torn
> My wretched life in two, though I was born
> The daughter of the king of Samangan,
> And am descended from a warrior clan.
> But like a legend I have heard the story
> Of your heroic battles and your glory,
> Of how you have no fear, and face alone
> Dragons and demons and the dark unknown,
> Of how you sneak into Turan at night
> And prowl the borders to provoke a fight,
> Of how, when warriors see your mace, they quail
> And feel their lionhearts within them fail.
> I bit my lip to hear such talk, and knew
> I longed to see you, to catch sight of you,
> To glimpse your martial chest and mighty face—

211

And now God brings you to this lowly place.
If you desire me, I am yours, and none
Shall see or hear of me from this day on;
Desire destroys my mind, I long to bear
Within my woman's womb your son and heir;
I promise you your horse if you agree
Since all of Samangan must yield to me."

When Rostam saw how lovely she was, and moreover heard that she promised to find Rakhsh for him, he felt that nothing but good could come of the encounter; and so in secret the two passed the long hours of night together.

As the sun cast its noose in the eastern sky, Rostam gave Tahmineh a clasp which he wore on his upper arm and said to her, "Take this, and if you should bear a daughter, braid her hair about it as an omen of good fortune; but if the heavens give you a son, have him wear it on his upper arm, as a sign of who his father is. He'll be a boy like Sam, the son of Nariman, noble and chivalrous; one who'll bring down eagles from their cloudy heights, a man on whom the sun will not shine harshly."

Then the king came to Rostam and asked how he had slept, and brought news that Rakhsh had been found. Rostam rushed out and stroked and petted his horse, overjoyed to have found him; he saddled him and rode on his way, content with the king's hospitality and to have found his horse again.

Sohrab Is Born

Nine months passed, and the princess Tahmineh gave birth to a son as splendid as the shining moon. He seemed another Rostam, Sam, or Nariman, and since his face shone bright with laughter, Tahmineh named him Sohrab (Bright-visaged). When a month had gone, he seemed a year old; at three, he played polo; and at five, he took up archery and practiced with a javelin. By the time he was ten, no one dared compete with him and he said to his mother, "Tell me truly now, why is it I'm so much taller than other boys of my age? Whose child am I, and what should I answer when people ask about my father? If you keep all this hidden from me, I won't let you live a moment longer." His mother answered, "Hear what I have to say, and be pleased at it, and control your temper. You are the son of the mammoth-bodied hero Rostam and are descended from Dastan, Sam, and Nariman. This is why your head reaches to the heavens; since the Creator made this world, there never has been such a knight as Rostam." Secretly she showed him a letter that Rostam had sent, together with three rubies set in gold; then she said, "Afrasyab must know nothing of this, and if Rostam hears of how you've grown, he'll summon you to his side and break your mother's heart." Sohrab answered, "This is not something to be kept secret; the world's chieftains tell tales of Rostam's prowess; how can it be right for me to hide such a splendid lineage? I'll gather a boundless force of fighting Turks and drive Kavus from his throne; then I'll eradicate all trace of Tus from Iran and give the royal mace and crown to Rostam, I'll place him on Kavus's throne. Next I'll march on Turan and fight with Afrasyab and seize his throne too. If Rostam is my father and I am his son, then no one else in all the world should wear the crown; when the sun and moon shine out in splendor, what should lesser stars do, boasting of their glory?" From every quarter swordsmen and chieftains flocked to the youth.

War Breaks Out Again

Afrasyab was told that Sohrab had launched his boat upon the waters and that, although his mouth still smelled of mother's milk, his thoughts were all of swords and arrows. The informants said that he was threatening war against Kavus, that a mighty force had flocked to him, and that in his self-confidence he took no account of anyone. Afrasyab laughed with delight; he chose twelve thousand warriors, placed them under the command of Barman and Human, and addressed his two chieftains thus: "This secret must remain hidden. When these two face each other on the battlefield, Rostam will surely be at a disadvantage. The father must not know his son, because he will try to win him over; but, knowing nothing, the ancient warrior filled with years will be slain by our young lion. Later you can deal with Sohrab and dispatch him to his endless sleep." Afrasyab sent the two to Sohrab, and he entrusted them with a letter encouraging the young warrior in his ambitions and promising support.

The White Fortress

There was an armed outpost of Iran called the White Fortress; its keeper was an experienced warrior named Hejir. Sohrab led his army toward the fortress, and, when Hejir saw this, he mounted his horse and rode out to confront him. Sohrab rode in front of the army, then drew his sword and taunted Hejir, "What are you dreaming of, coming to fight alone against me? Who are you, what is your name and lineage? Your mother will weep over your corpse today." Hejir replied, "There are not many Turks who can match themselves against me. I am Hejir, the army's brave commander, and I shall tear your head off and send it to Kavus, the king of all the world; your body I shall thrust beneath the dirt." Sohrab laughed to hear such talk; the two attacked each other furiously with lances. Hejir's lance struck at Sohrab's waist but did no harm, but when Sohrab returned the blow, he sent Hejir sprawling from his saddle to the ground. Sohrab leapt down from his horse, intending to sever his enemy's head, but Hejir twisted away to the right and begged for quarter. Sohrab spared him, and in triumph preached submission to his captive. Then he had him bound and sent to Human. When those in the fortress realized that their leader had been captured, both men and women wailed aloud with grief, crying out, "Hejir is taken from us."

Gordafarid

But one of those within the fortress was a woman, daughter of the warrior Gazhdaham, named Gordafarid. When she learned that their leader had allowed himself to be taken, she found his behavior so shameful that her rosy cheeks became as black as pitch with rage. With not a moment's delay she dressed herself in a knight's armor, gathered her hair beneath a Rumi helmet, and rode out from the fortress, a lion eager for battle. She roared at the enemy's ranks, "Where are your heroes, your warriors, your tried and tested chieftains?"

When Sohrab saw this new combatant, he laughed and bit his lip and said to himself, "Another victim has stepped into the hero's trap." Quickly he donned his armor and a Chinese helmet and galloped out to face Gordafarid. When she saw him, she took aim with her bow (no bird could escape her well-aimed arrows) and let loose a hail of arrows, weaving to left and right like an experienced horseman as she did so. Shame urged Sohrab forward, his shield held before his head to deflect her arrows. Seeing him approach, she laid aside her bow and snatched up a lance and, as her horse reared toward the clouds, she hurled it at her opponent. Sohrab wheeled round and his lance struck Gordafarid in the waist; her armor's fastenings were severed, but she unsheathed her sword and hacked at his lance, splitting it in two. Sohrab bore down on her again and snatched her helmet from her head; her hair streamed out, and her face shone like a splendid sun. He saw that his opponent was a woman, one whose hair was worthy of a diadem. He was amazed and said, "How is it that a woman should ride out from the Persian army and send the dust up from her horse's hooves into the heavens?" He unhitched his lariat from the saddle and flung it, catching her by the waist, then said: "Don't try to escape from me; now, my beauty, what do you mean by coming out to fight? I've never captured prey like you before, and I won't let you go in a hurry." Gordafarid saw that she could only get away by a ruse of some kind, and, showing her face to him, she said, "O lionhearted warrior, two armies are watching us and, if I let them see my face and hair, your troops will be very amused by the notion of your fighting with a mere girl; we'd better draw aside somewhere, that's what a wise man would do, so that you won't be a laughing stock before these two armies. Now our army, our wealth, our fortress, and the fortress's commander will all be in your hands to do with as you wish; I'll hand them over to you, so there's no need for you to pursue this war any further." As she spoke, her shining teeth and bright red lips and heavenly face were like a paradise to Sohrab; no gardener ever grew so straight and tall a cypress as she seemed to be; her eyes were liquid as a deer's, her brows were two bent bows, you'd say her body was a bud about to blossom.

Sohrab said, "Don't go back on your word; you've seen me on the battlefield; don't think you'll be safe from me once you're behind the fortress walls again. They don't reach higher than the clouds and my mace will bring them down if need be." Gordafarid tugged at her horse's reins and wheeled round toward the fortress; Sohrab rode beside her to the gates, which opened and let in the weary, wounded, woman warrior.

The defenders closed the gates, and young and old alike wept for Gordafarid and Hejir. They said, "O brave lioness, we all grieve for you, but you fought well and your ruse worked and you brought no shame on your people." Then Gordafarid laughed long and heartily and climbed up on the fortress walls and looked out over the army. When she saw Sohrab perched on his saddle, she shouted down to him:

> "O king of all the Asian hordes, turn back,
> Forget your fighting and your planned attack."
> She laughed; and then, more gently, almost sighed:
> "No Turk will bear away a Persian bride;
> But do not chafe at Fate's necessity—
> Fate did not mean that you should conquer me.
> Besides, you're not a Turk, I know you trace
> Your lineage from a far more splendid race;
> Put any of your heroes to the test—
> None has your massive arm and mighty chest.
> But news will spread that Turan's army's here,
> Led by a stripling chief who knows no fear;

Kavus will send for noble Rostam then
And neither you nor any of your men
Will live for long: I should be sad to see
This lion destroy you here—turn now and flee,
Don't trust your strength, strength will not save your life;
The fatted calf knows nothing of the knife."

Hearing her, Sohrab felt a fool, realizing how easily he could have taken the fortress. He plundered the surrounding settlements and sulkily said: "It's too late for battle now, but when dawn comes, I'll raze this fortress's walls, and its inhabitants will know the meaning of defeat."

But that night Gazhdaham, Gordafarid's aged father, sent a letter to Kavus telling him of Sohrab's prowess, and secretly, before dawn, most of the Persian troops evacuated the fortress, traveling toward Iran and safety.

When the sun rose above the mountains, the Turks prepared to fight; Sohrab mounted his horse, couched his lance, and advanced on the fortress. But as he and his men reached the walls, they saw very few defenders; they pushed open the gates and saw within no preparations for battle. A straggle of soldiers came forward, begging for quarter.

Kavus Summons Rostam

When King Kavus received Gazhdaham's message, he was deeply troubled; he summoned his chieftains and put the matter before them. After he had read the letter to his warrior lords—men like Tus, Gudarz (the son of Keshvad), Giv, Gorgin, Bahram, and Farhad—Kavus said, "According to Gazhdaham, this is going to be lengthy business. His letter has put all other thoughts from my mind; now, what should we do to remedy this situation, and who is there in Iran who can stand up to this new warrior?" All agreed that Giv should go to Zabol and tell Rostam of the danger threatening Iran and the Persian throne.

Kavus wrote to Rostam, praising his prowess and appealing to him to come to the aid of the throne. Then he said to Giv, "Gallop as quickly as wind-borne smoke and take this letter to Rostam. Don't delay in Zabol; if you arrive at night, set off on the return journey the next morning. Tell Rostam that matters are urgent." Giv took the letter and traveled quickly to Zabol, without resting along the way. Rostam came out with a contingent of his nobles to welcome him; Giv and Rostam's group dismounted together, and Rostam questioned him closely about the king and events in Iran. After they had returned to Rostam's palace and rested a while, Giv repeated what he had heard, handed over the letter, and gave what news he could of Sohrab.

When Rostam had listened to him and read the letter, he laughed aloud and said in astonishment, "So it seems that a second Sam is loose in the world; this would be no surprise if he were a Persian, but from the Turks it's unprecedented. I myself have a son over there, by the princess of Samangan, but he's still a boy and doesn't yet realize that war is the way to glory. I sent his mother gold and jewels, and she sent me back an answer saying that he'd soon be a tall young fellow; his mouth still smells of mother's milk,

but he drinks his wine, and no doubt he'll be a fighter soon enough. Now, you and I should rest for a day and moisten our dry lips with wine, then we can make our way to the king and lead Persia's warriors out to war. It's possible that Fortune's turned against us, but if not, this campaign will not prove difficult; when the sea's waves inundate the land, the fiercest fire won't stay alight for long. And when this young warrior sees my banner, his heart will know his revels are all ended; he won't be in such a hurry to fight anymore. This is not something we should worry ourselves about."

They sat to their wine and, forgetting all about the king, passed the night in idle chatter. The next morning Rostam woke with a hangover and called again for wine; this day too was passed in drinking and no one thought about setting out on the journey to Kavus. And once again on the third day Rostam ignored the king's summons and had wine brought. On the fourth day Giv bestirred himself and said, "Kavus is a headstrong man and not at all intelligent; he's very upset about this business and he can neither eat nor sleep properly. If we stay much longer here in Zabolestan, he will be extremely angry." Rostam replied, "Don't worry about that; there's not a man alive who can meddle with me." He gave orders that Rakhsh be saddled and that the tucket for departure be sounded. Zabol's knights heard the trumpets and, armed and helmeted, they gathered about their leader.

Rostam and Kavus

They arrived at the king's court in high spirits and ready to serve him. But when they bowed before the king, he at first made them no answer, and then, addressing Giv, he burst out in fury, "Who is Rostam that he should ignore me, that he should flout my orders in this way? Take him and string him up alive on the gallows and never mention his name to me again." Giv was horrified at Kavus's words and remonstrated, "You would treat Rostam in this way?" The courtiers stared, struck dumb, as Kavus then roared to Tus, "Take both of them and hang them both." And, wildly as a fire that burns dry reeds, he sprang up from the throne. Tus took Rostam by the arm to lead him from Kavus's presence and the warriors there watched in wonder, but Rostam too burst out in fury and addressed the king:

> "Smother your rage; each act of yours is more
> Contemptible than every act before.
> You're not fit to be king; it's Sohrab you
> Should hang alive, but you're unable to."
> Tus he sent sprawling with a single blow
> Then strode toward the door as if to go
> But turned back in his rage and said, "I am
> The Crown Bestower, the renowned Rostam,
> When I am angry, who is Kay Kavus?
> Who dares to threaten me? And who is Tus?
> My helmet is my crown, Rakhsh is my throne,
> And I am slave to none but God alone.
> If Sohrab should attack, who will survive?
> No child or warrior will be left alive
> In all Iran—too late, and desperately,
> You'll seek for some escape or remedy;

This is your land where you reside and reign—
Henceforth you'll not see Rostam here again."

The courtiers were deeply alarmed, since they regarded Rostam as a shepherd and themselves as his flock. They turned to Gudarz and said, "You must heal this breach, the king will listen to no one but you; go to this crazy monarch and speak to him mildly and at length, and with luck we'll be able to restore our fortunes again." Gudarz went to Kavus and reminded him of Rostam's past service and of the threat that Sohrab was to Iran, and when he had heard him out, Kavus repented of his anger and said to Gudarz, "Your words are just, and nothing becomes an old man's lips like wisdom. A king should be wise and cautious; anger and impetuous behavior bring no good to anyone. Go to Rostam and remind him of our former friendship; make him forget my outburst." Gudarz and the army's chieftains went in search of Rostam; finally they saw the dust raised by Rakhsh and caught up with him. They praised the hero and then said, "You know that Kavus is a brainless fool, that he is subject to these outbursts of temper, that he erupts in rage and is immediately sorry and swears to mend his ways. If you are furious with the king, the people of Iran are not at fault; already he regrets his rage and bites the back of his hand in repentance."

Rostam replied, "I have no need of Kay Kavus: My saddle's my throne, my helmet's my crown, this stout armor's my robes of state, and my heart's prepared for Death. Why should I fear Kavus's rage; he's no more to me

than a fistful of dirt. My mind is weary of all this, my heart is full, and I fear no one but God himself." Gudarz replied, "Iran and her chieftains and the army will see this in another way; they'll say that the great hero was afraid of the Turk and that he sneaked away in fear; they'll say that if Rostam has fled, we should all flee. I saw the court in an uproar over Kavus's rage, but I also saw the stir that Sohrab has created. Don't turn your back on the king of Iran; your name's renowned throughout the world, don't dim its luster by this flight. And consider: The army is hard pressed, this is no time to abandon the throne and crown."

Rostam stared at him and said, "If there's any fear in my heart I tear it from me now." Shamefaced, he rode back to the king's court, and when he entered, the king stood and asked his forgiveness for what had passed between them, saying, "Impetuous rage is part of my nature; we have to live as God has fashioned us. This new and unexpected enemy had made my heart grow faint as the new moon; I looked to you for help and when you delayed your coming, I became angry. But seeing you affronted by my words, I regretted what I had said." Rostam replied, "The world is yours; we are all your subjects. I have come to hear your orders." Kavus said, "Tonight we feast, tomorrow we fight." Entertained by musicians and served by pale young slaves, the two then sat to their wine and drank till half the night had passed.

The Persian Army Sets Out against Sohrab

At dawn the next day the king ordered Giv and Tus to prepare the army; drums were bound on elephants, the treasury doors were opened, and war supplies were handed out. A hundred thousand warriors gathered and the air was darkened by their dust. Stage by stage they marched till nightfall, and their glittering weapons shone like points of fire seen through a dark curtain. So day by day they went on until at last they reached the fortress's gates, and their number was so great that not a stone or speck of earth was visible before the walls.

A shout from the lookouts told Sohrab that the enemy's army had come. Sohrab went up onto the city walls and then summoned Human; when Human saw the mighty force opposing them, he gasped and his heart quailed. Sohrab told him to be of good cheer, saying, "In all this limitless army, you'll not see one warrior who'll be willing to face me in combat, no, not if the sun and moon themselves came down to aid him. There's a great deal of armor here and many men, but I know of none among them who's a warrior to reckon with. And now in Afrasyab's name I shall make this plain a sea of blood." Cheerful and fearless, Sohrab descended from the walls. For their part the Persians pitched camp, and so vast was the number of tents and pavilions that the plain and surrounding foothills disappeared from view.

In all the world there's none can equal me."
Then Sohrab said, "I'm going to question you.
Your answer must be honest, straight, and true:
I think that you're Rostam, and from the clan
Of warlike Sam and noble Nariman."
Rostam replied, "I'm not Rostam, I claim
No kinship with that clan or noble name:
Rostam's a champion, I'm a slave—I own
No royal wealth or crown or kingly throne."
And Sohrab's hopes were changed then to despair,
Darkening before his gaze the sunlit air.

The First Combat between Rostam and Sohrab

Sohrab rode to the space allotted for combat, and his mother's words rang in
his ears. At first they fought with short javelins, then attacked one another
with Indian swords, and sparks sprang forth from the clash of iron against
iron. The mighty blows left both swords shattered, and they grasped their
ponderous maces, and a weariness began to weigh their arms down. Their
horses too began to tire, and the blows the heroes dealt shattered both the
horse armor and their own cuirasses. Finally, both the horses and their rid-
ers paused, exhausted by the battle, and neither hero could summon the
strength to deliver another blow. The two stood facing one another at a dis-
tance, the father filled with pain, the son with sorrow, their bodies soaked
with sweat, their mouths caked with dirt, their tongues cracked with thirst.
How strange the world's ways are! All beasts will recognize their young—the
fish in the sea, the wild asses on the plain—but suffering and pride will make
a man unable to distinguish his son from his enemy.

Rostam said to himself, "I've never seen a monster fight like this; my
combat with the White Demon was as nothing to this and I can feel my
heart's courage begin to fail. A young, unknown warrior who's seen noth-
ing of the world has brought me to this desperate pass, and in the sight of
both our armies."

When their horses had rested from the combat, both warriors—he who was old in years and he who was still a stripling—strung their bows, but their remaining armor rendered the arrows harmless. In fury then the two closed, grasping at one another's belts, each struggling to throw the other. Rostam, who on the day of battle could tear rock from the mountain crags, seized Sohrab's belt and strove to drag him from his saddle, but it was as if the boy were untouched and all Rostam's efforts were useless. Again these mighty lions withdrew from one another, wounded and exhausted.

Then once more Sohrab lifted his massive mace from the saddle and bore down on Rostam; his mace struck Rostam's shoulder and the hero writhed in pain. Sohrab laughed and cried, "You can't stand up to blows, it seems; you might be cypress-tall, but an old man who acts like a youth is a fool."

Both now felt weakened by their battle, and sick at heart they turned aside from one another. Rostam rode toward the Turkish ranks like a leopard who sights his prey; like a wolf he fell on them, and their great army scattered before him. For his part Sohrab attacked the Persian host, striking down warriors with his mace. Rostam feared that some harm would come to Kavus from this young warrior, and he hurried back to his own lines. He saw Sohrab in the midst of the Persian ranks, the ground beneath his feet awash with wine-red blood; his spear, armor, and hands were smeared with blood and he seemed drunk with slaughter. Like a raging lion Rostam burst out in fury, "Bloodthirsty Turk, who challenged you from the Persian ranks? Why have you attacked them like a wolf run wild in a flock of sheep?" Sohrab replied, "And Turan's army had no part in this battle either, but you attacked them first even though none of them had challenged you." Rostam said, "Evening draws on, but, when the sun unsheathes its sword again, on this plain we shall see who will die and who will triumph. Let us return at dawn with swords ready for combat; go now, and await God's will!"

Sohrab and Rostam in Camp at Night

They parted and the air grew dark. Wounded and weary, Sohrab arrived at his own lines and questioned Human about Rostam's attack. Human answered, "The king's command was that we not stir from our camp; and so we were quite unprepared when a fearsome warrior bore down on us, as wild as if he were drunk or had come from single combat." Sohrab answered, "He didn't destroy one warrior from this host, while I, for my part, killed many Persians and soaked the ground with their blood. Now we must eat, and with wine drive sorrow from our hearts."

And on the other side, Rostam questioned Giv, "How did this Sohrab fight today?" Giv replied, "I have never seen a warrior like him. He rushed into the center of our lines intending to attack Tus, but Tus fled before him, and there was none among us who could withstand his onslaught." Rostam grew downcast at his words and went to King Kavus, who motioned him to his side. Rostam described Sohrab's massive body to him and said that no one had ever seen such valor from so young a warrior. Then he went on, "We fought with mace and sword and bow, and finally, remembering that I had often enough pulled heroes down from the saddle, I seized him by the belt and tried to drag him from his horse and fling him to the ground. But a wind could shake a mountainside before it would shift that hero. When he comes to the combat ground tomorrow, I must find some way to overcome him hand to hand; I shall do my best, but I don't know who will win; we must wait and see what God wills, for he it is, the Creator of the sun and moon, who gives victory and glory." Kavus replied, "And may he lacerate the hearts of those who wish you ill. I shall spend the night in prayer to him for your success."

Rostam returned to his own men, preoccupied with thoughts of the coming combat. Anxiously, his brother Zavareh came forward, questioning him as to how he had fared that day. Rostam asked him first for food, and then shared his heart's forebodings. He said, "Be vigilant, and do nothing rashly. When I face that Turk on the battlefield at dawn, gather together our army and accoutrements—our banner, throne, the golden boots our guards wear—and wait at sunrise before our pavilion. If I'm victorious I shan't linger on the battlefield, but if things turn out otherwise, don't mourn for me or act impetuously; don't go forward offering to fight. Instead, return to Zabolestan and go to our father, Dastan; comfort my mother's heart, and make her see that this fate was willed for me by God. Tell her not to give herself up to grief, for no good will come of it. No one lives forever in this world, and I have no complaint against the turns of Fate. So many lions and demons and leopards and monsters have been destroyed by my strength, and so many fortresses and castles have been razed by my might; no one has ever overcome me. Whoever mounts his horse and rides out for battle is knocking at the door of Death, and if we live a thousand years or more, Death is our destiny at last. When she is comforted, tell Dastan not to turn his back on the world's king, Kavus. If Kavus makes war, Dastan is not to tarry, but to obey his every command. Young and old, we are all bound for Death; on this earth no one lives forever." For half the night they talked of Sohrab, and the other half was spent in rest and sleep.

Sohrab Overcomes Rostam

When the shining sun spread its plumes and night's dark raven folded its wings, Rostam donned his tigerskin and mounted Rakhsh. His iron helmet on his head, he hitched the sixty loops of his lariat to his saddle, grasped his Indian sword in his hand, and rode out to the combat ground.

Sohrab had spent the night entertained by musicians and drinking wine with his companions. To Human he had confided his suspicions that his opponent was none other than Rostam, for he felt himself drawn to him, and besides, he resembled his mother's description of Rostam. When dawn came, he buckled on his armor and grasped his huge mace; with his head filled with battle and his heart in high spirits, he came onto the field shouting his war cry. He greeted Rostam with a smile on his lips, for all the world as if they had spent the night in revelry together:

> *"When did you wake? How did you pass the night?*
> *And are you still determined we should fight?*
> *But throw your mace and sword down, put aside*
> *These thoughts of war, this truculence and pride.*
> *Let's sit and drink together, and the wine*
> *Will smooth away our frowns—both yours and mine.*
> *Come, swear an oath before our God that we*
> *Renounce all thoughts of war and enmity.*
> *Let's make a truce, and feast as allies here*
> *At least until new enemies appear.*
> *The tears that stain my face are tokens of*
> *My heart's affection for you, and my love;*
> *I know that you're of noble ancestry—*
> *Recite your lordly lineage to me."*

Rostam replied, "This was not what we talked of last night; our talk was of hand-to-hand combat. I won't fall for these tricks, so don't try them. You might be still a child, but I am not, and I have bound my belt on ready for our combat. Now, let us fight, and the outcome will be as God wishes. I've seen much of good and evil in my life, and I'm not a man for talk or tricks or treachery." Sohrab replied, "Talk like this is not fitting from an old man. I would have wished that your days would come to an end peacefully, in your bed, and that your survivors would build a tomb to hold your body while your soul flew on its way. But if your life is to be in my hands, so be it; let us fight and the outcome will be as God wills."

They dismounted, tethered their horses, and warily came forward, each clad in mail and helmeted. They closed in combat, wrestling hand to hand, and mingled blood and sweat poured from their bodies. Then Sohrab, like a maddened elephant, struck Rostam a violent blow and felled him; like a lion leaping to bring down a wild ass, he flung himself on Rostam's chest, whose mouth and fist and face were grimed with dust. He drew a glittering dagger to sever the hero's head from his body, and Rostam spoke:

"O hero, lion destroyer, mighty lord,
Master of mace and lariat and sword,
Our customs do not count this course as right;
According to our laws, when warriors fight,
A hero may not strike the fatal blow
The first time his opponent is laid low;
He does this, and he's called a lion, when
He's thrown his rival twice—and only then."

By this trick he sought to escape death at Sohrab's hands. The brave youth bowed his head at the old man's words, believing what he was told. He released his opponent and withdrew to the plains where, unconcernedly, he spent some time hunting. After a while Human sought him out and asked him about the day's combat thus far. Sohrab told Human what had happened and what Rostam had said to him. Human responded, "Young man, you've had enough of life, it seems! Alas for this chest, for these arms and shoulders of yours; alas for your fist, for the mace that it holds; you'd trapped the tiger and you let him go, which was the act of a simpleton! Now, watch for the consequences of this foolishness of yours when you face Rostam again."

Sohrab returned to camp, sick at heart and furious with himself. A prince once made a remark for just such a situation:

"Do not make light of any enemy
No matter how unworthy he may be."

For his part, when Rostam had escaped from Sohrab, he sprang up like a man who has come back from the dead and strode to a nearby stream where he drank and washed the grime from his face and body. Next he prayed, asking for God's help and for victory, unaware of the fate the sun and moon held in store for him. Then, anxious and pale, he made his way from the stream back to the battlefield.

And there he saw Sohrab mounted on his rearing horse, charging after wild asses like a maddened elephant, whirling his lariat, his bow on his arm. Rostam stared at him in astonishment, trying to calculate his chances against him in single combat. When Sohrab caught sight of him, all the arrogance of youth was in his voice as he taunted Rostam, "So you escaped the lion's claws, old man, and crept away from the wounds he dealt you!"

Sohrab Is Mortally Wounded by Rostam

Once again they tethered their horses, and once again they grappled in single combat, each grasping the other's belt and straining to overthrow him. But, for all his great strength, Sohrab seemed as though he were hindered by the heavens, and Rostam seized him by the shoulders and finally forced him to the ground; the brave youth's back was bent, his time had come, his strength deserted him. Like a lion Rostam laid him low, but, knowing that the youth would not lie there for long, he quickly drew his dagger and plunged it in the lionhearted hero's chest. Sohrab writhed, then gasped for breath, and knew he'd passed beyond concerns of worldly good and evil. He said:

> "I brought this on myself, this is from me,
> And Fate has merely handed you the key
> To my brief life: not you but heaven's vault—
> Which raised me and then killed me—is at fault.
> Love for my father led me here to die.
> My mother gave me signs to know him by,
> And you could be a fish within the sea,
> Or pitch black, lost in night's obscurity,
> Or be a star in heaven's endless space,
> Or vanish from the earth and leave no trace,
> But still my father, when he knows I'm dead,
> Will bring down condign vengeance on your head.
> One from this noble band will take this sign
> To Rostam's hands, and tell him it was mine,
> And say I sought him always, far and wide,
> And that, at last, in seeking him, I died."

When Rostam heard the warrior's words, his head whirled and the earth turned dark before his eyes, and when he came back to himself, he roared in an agony of anguish and asked what it was that the youth had which was a sign from Rostam, the most cursed of all heroes.

"If then you are Rostam," said the youth, "and you killed me, your wits were dimmed by an evil nature. I tried in every way to guide you, but no love of yours responded. Open the straps that bind my armor and look on my naked body. When the battle drums sounded before my door, my mother came to me, her eyes awash with tears, her soul in torment to see me leave. She bound a clasp on my arm and said, 'Take this in memory of your father, and watch for when it will be useful to you'; but now it shows its power too late, and the son is laid low before his father." And when Rostam opened the boy's armor and saw the clasp he tore at his own clothes in grief, saying, "All men praised your bravery, and I have killed you with my own hands." Violently he wept and tore his hair and heaped dust on his head. Sohrab said, "By this you make things worse. You must not weep; what point is there in wounding yourself like this? What happened is what had to happen."

The shining sun descended from the sky and still Rostam had not returned to his encampment. Twenty warriors came riding to see the battlefield and found two muddied horses but no sign of Rostam. Assuming he had been killed, they sent a message to Kavus saying, "Rostam's royal throne lies desolate." A wail of mourning went up from the army, and Kavus gave orders that the drums and trumpets be sounded. Tus hurried forward and Kavus told him to have someone survey the battlefield and find out what it was that Sohrab had done and whether they were indeed to weep for the fortunes of Iran, since if Rostam had been killed, no one would be able to oppose Sohrab and they would have to retreat without giving battle.

As the noise of mourning rose from the army, Sohrab said to Rostam, "Now that my days are ended, the Turks' fortunes too have changed. Be merciful to them, and do not let the king make war on them; it was at my instigation they attacked Iran. What promises I made, what hopes I held out to them! They should not be the ones to suffer; see you look kindly on them."

Cold sighs on his lips, his face besmeared with blood and tears, Rostam mounted Rakhsh and rode to the Persian camp, lamenting aloud, tormented by the thought of what he had done. When they caught sight of him, the Persian warriors fell to the ground, praising God that he was alive, but when they saw his ripped clothes and dust-besmeared head and face, they asked him what had happened and what distressed him. He told them of the strange deed he had done, of how he had slaughtered the person who was dearer to him than all others, and all who heard lamented aloud with him.

Then he said to the chieftains, "I've no courage left now, no strength or sense; go no further with this war against the Turks, the evil that I have done today is sufficient." Rostam returned to where his son lay wounded, and the nobles—men like Tus, Gudarz, and Gostaham—accompanied him, crowding round and saying, "It's God who will heal this wound, it's he who will lighten your sorrows." But Rostam drew a dagger, intending to slash his own neck with it; weeping with grief, they flung themselves on him and Gudarz said, "What point is there in spreading fire and sword throughout the world by your death, and if you wound yourself a thousand times, how will that help this noble youth? If there is any time left to him on this earth, then stay with him and ease his hours here; and if he is to die, then look at all the world and say, 'Who is immortal?' We are all Death's prey, both he who wears a helmet and he who wears the crown."

Rostam replied, "Go quickly and take a message from me to Kavus and tell him what has befallen me; say that I have rent my own son's vitals with

a dagger, and that I curse my life and long for death. Tell him, if he has any regard for all I have done in his service, to have pity on my suffering and to send me the elixir he keeps in his treasury, the medicine that will heal all wounds. If he will send it, together with a goblet of wine, it may be that, by his grace, Sohrab will survive and serve Kavus's throne as I have done."

Like wind the chieftain bore this message to Kavus, who said in reply, "Which warrior, of all this company, is of more repute than Rostam? And are we to make him even greater? Then, surely he will turn on me and kill me. How will the wide world contain his glory and might? How will he remain the servant to my throne? If, some day, evil's to come to me from him, I will respond with evil. You heard how he referred to me:

> 'When I am angry, who is Kay Kavus?
> Who dares to threaten me? And who is Tus?'"

When Gudarz heard these words, he hurried back to Rostam and said:

> "This king's malicious nature is a tree
> That grows new, bitter fruit perpetually;

You must go to him and try to enlighten his benighted soul." Rostam gave orders that a rich cloth be spread beside the stream; gently he laid his wounded son there and set out to where Kavus held court. But he was overtaken on the way by one who told him that Sohrab had departed this world; he had looked round for his father, then heaved an icy sigh, and groaned, and closed his eyes forever. It was not a castle the boy needed his father to provide for him now, but a coffin.

Rostam dismounted and removed his helmet and smeared dust on his head.

> Weeping, he cried: "Dauntless and brave young man,
> Intrepid warrior of a warlike clan,
> Not sun, nor moon, nor armor, nor the throne
> Will see your like again! O who has known
> A grief like mine, or done what I have done?
> Old now, and full of years, I've killed my son,
> The scion of great Sam, and of the fame
> His mother gave him by her royal name.
> Would that these hands were severed, that I lay
> Deep in earth's dark! What will his mother say?
> Who can I send to her? What shall I plead
> When all men curse me for my monstrous deed,

When Zal reproaches me, and my disgrace
Brings ignominy on Sam's noble race?
Who would have thought so young a child could be
So stout and strong, tall as a cypress tree,
That he could lead an army out to fight
And turn my shining days to darkest night?"

Then he commanded that the boy's body be covered in royal brocade—the youth who had longed for fame and conquest, and whose destiny was a narrow bier borne from the battlefield. Rostam returned to his royal pavilion and had it set ablaze; his warriors smeared their heads with dust, and in the midst of their lamentations they fed the flames with his throne, his saddlecloth of leopardskin, his silken tent of many colors. Rostam wept and ripped his royal clothes, and all the heroes of the Persian army sat in the wayside dust with him and tried to comfort him, but to no avail.

Kavus said to Rostam, "The heavens bear all before them, from the mighty Alborz Mountains to the lightest reed; man must not love this earth too much. For one it comes early and for another late, but Death comes to all. Accept this loss, pay heed to wisdom's ways, and know that if you bow the heavens to the ground or set the seas aflame, you cannot bring back him who's gone; his soul grows old, but in another place. I saw him in the distance once, I saw his height and stature and the massive mace he held; Fate drove him here to perish by your hand. What is it you would do? What remedy exists for this? How long will you mourn in this way?"

Rostam replied, "Yes, he is gone. But Human still camps here on the plains, along with chieftains from Turan and China. Have no rancor in your heart against them. Give the command, and let my brother Zavareh lead off our armies." The king said, "This sadness clouds your soul, great hero. Well, they have done me evil enough, and they have wreaked havoc in Iran, but my heart feels the pain you feel, and for your sake I'll think no more of them."

Rostam Returns to Zabolestan

Rostam returned then to his home, Zabolestan, and when news of his coming reached his father, Zal-Dastan, the people of Sistan came out to meet him, mourning and grieving for his loss. When Dastan saw the bier, he dismounted from his horse, and Rostam came forward on foot, his clothes torn, with anguish in his heart. The chieftains took off their armor and stood before the coffin and smeared their heads with dust. When Rostam reached his palace, he cried aloud and had the coffin set before him; then he ripped out the nails and pulled back the shroud and showed the nobles gathered there the body of his son. A tumult of mourning swept the palace, which seemed a vast tomb where a lion lay; the youth resembled Sam, as if that hero slept, worn out by battle. Then Rostam covered him in cloth of gold and nailed the coffin shut and said, "If I construct a golden tomb for him and fill it with black musk, it will not last for long when I am gone; but I see nothing else that I can do."

> This tale is full of tears, and Rostam leaves
> The tender heart indignant as it grieves:
> I turn now from this story to relate
> The tale of Seyavash and his sad fate.

⁂ APPENDICES ⁂

He civilized the world and all its ways
The world remembered him with grateful praise

GLOSSARY OF NAMES AND THEIR PRONUNCIATION

The following is a list of the names which appear in the stories included in this volume, together with a brief description of who or what they designate.

Persian names are pronounced with a more even stress than is common in English, and to an English speaker's ear this often sounds as if the last syllable is being stressed. A slight extra stress on the last syllable of names will bring the reader closer to a Persian pronunciation.

Persian has two distinct sounds indicated in English by the letter "a." One is a long sound (as in "father") and this has been indicated here by the accent "ā" (e.g., Zāl). The other is a short sound (as in "cat") and this has been indicated by the standard "a" (e.g., Zav). The vowel given as "i" is a long vowel, like the second vowel in "police." The vowel given as "u" is also a long vowel, like the first vowel in "super." "Q" and "gh" are pronounced approximately as a guttural hard "g," far back in the throat. "Zh" is pronounced like the sound represented by the "s" in "pleasure." "Kh" is pronounced like the Scottish "ch" in "loch."

AFRĀSYĀB: a king of Turān, the brother of Aghriras and Garsivaz.

AGHRIRAS: the brother of Afrāsyāb and Garsivaz.

AHRIMAN: the evil god of the universe.

AJNĀS: a warrior of Turān.

ALĀNĀN: a fortress of Turān.

ALBORZ: the mountains to the south of the Caspian Sea.

ĀMOL: a town near the Caspian.

ĀREZU: the bride of Salm.

ARNAVĀZ: the daughter of Jamshid.

ARVAND: the name of a river.

ARZHANG: a demon of Māzanderān.

ASPORUZ: a mountain in Māzanderān.

ĀTEBIN: the father of Feraydun.

BAHRĀM: a warrior of Irān.

BALKH: a town in northern Afghānistān.

BĀRMĀN: two warriors of Turan go by this name; one is a son of Viseh and is killed by Qāren, the other accompanies Sohrāb on his expedition against Irān.

BARMĀYEH: the ox that nourishes the young Feraydun.

BARZIN: a warrior of Irān.

BID: a demon of Māzanderān.

DAMĀVAND: an extinct volcanic peak; the highest mountain in Irān.

DASTĀN: another name given to Zāl, the son of Sām and father of Rostam.

DEHESTĀN: an area to the east of the Caspian.

DEZHKHIM: a warrior of Māzanderān.

DILMĀN: a province south of the Caspian.

EBLIS: the devil.

FARĀNAK: the mother of Feraydun.

FARHĀD: a warrior of Irān.

FARIBORZ: a Persian prince, the son of Kay Kāvus.

FARVARDIN: the first month of the Persian year, which begins at the spring equinox in late March.

FERAYDUN: a Persian king.

GARSHĀSB: a Persian king, Zav's son; the Persian army commander of the same name seems to be a different person and the father of Nariman is yet another bearer of the same name.

GARSIVAZ: a warrior of Turān, the brother of Afrāsyāb and Aghriras.

GAZHDAHAM: a warrior of Irān, the father of Gordāfarid.

GIV: a warrior of Irān, the son of Gudarz.

GOLBĀD: a warrior of Turān.

GORĀZ: a warrior of Irān.

GORDĀFARID: a female warrior of Irān.

GORGĀN: an area to the east of the Caspian.

GORGIN: a warrior of Irān.

GOSTAHAM: a warrior of Irān.

GOSTAHOM: a Persian prince, the son of Nozar.

GUDARZ: a warrior of Irān, the father of Giv, the son of Keshvād.

HĀMĀVERĀN: the name of a country; its whereabouts are vague, but it is placed near the Barbary Coast (North Africa) and not far from Syria.

HEJIR: a warrior of Irān.

HERĀT: a town in western Afghānistān.

HIRMAND: a river that marks one boundary of Zābolestān; its modern name is the River Helmand.

HORMOZD: the good god of the universe.

HUMĀN: a warrior of Turān.

HUSHANG: a Persian king, the grandson of Kayumars.

IRAJ: the youngest son of Feraydun.

ISFAHĀN: one of the chief cities in central Irān.

JAMSHID: a Persian king.

JANDAL: King Feraydun's councillor.

JUYĀ: a warrior of Māzanderān.

KĀBOL, KĀBOLESTĀN: eastern Afghānistān and its chief city.

KĀKUI: a champion of Turān.

KANĀRANG: a demon of Māzanderān.

KARUKHĀN: a warrior of Turān.

KĀVEH: a blacksmith who leads the insurrection against the demon-king Zahhāk.

KĀVIANI: an adjective from Kāveh, applied particularly to the banner made from Kāveh's leather apron.

KAY ĀRASH: a Persian prince, son of Kay Qobād.

KAY ĀRMIN: a Persian prince, son of Kay Qobād.

KAY KĀVUS: a Persian king, son of Kay Qobād.

KAY PASHIN: a Persian prince, son of Kay Qobād.

KAY QOBĀD: a Persian king.

KAYĀNID: the name of the Persian royal house.

KAYUMARS: the first Persian king.

KAZHDAHOM: a Persian nobleman.

KESHVĀD: a warrior of Irān, the father of Gudarz.

KHĀQĀN: the title of the emperor of China.

KHAZARVAN: a warrior of Turān.

KHERRĀD: a warrior of Irān.

KOLĀHVAR: a warrior of Māzanderān.

KONDROW: Zahhāk's treasurer.

MĀH: the bride of Tur.

MĀH-ĀFARID: the wife of Iraj.

MAKRĀN: southern Afghānistān and the south of what is now Pakistan.

MANUCHEHR: a Persian king, the grandson of Iraj.

MĀZANDERĀN: modern Māzanderān is the area to the south of the Caspian Sea. Various locations for Ferdowsi's Māzanderān have been suggested.

MEHRĀB: the king of Kābol, Rudābeh's father.

MEHREGĀN: a festival celebrating the autumnal equinox.

MERDĀS: the father of Zahhāk.

MILĀD: a warrior of Irān.

NARIMĀN: the founder of the royal house of Sistān, to which belong Sām, Zāl, and Rostam.

NIMRUZ: the ancestral homeland of Sām, Zāl, and Rostam; also called Zābol, Zābolestān, Zāvol, Zāvolestān, and Sistān.

NOZAR: the son of Manuchehr, the king of Irān.

PĀRS: a province in central southern Irān, and the homeland of the country's two most important pre-Islamic dynasties, the Achaemenids and the Sasanians.

PASHANG: two men bear this name; one is a king of Turān, and the father of Afrāsyāb, the other is a Persian, the nephew of Feraydun and the father of Manuchehr.

PULĀD: a warrior of Irān.

PULĀD GHONDI: a demon of Māzanderān.

QALUN: a warrior of Turān.

QĀREN: a Persian army commander, also called Qāren-e Kāvus.

QOBĀD: two men bear this name; one is a Persian warrior, the other a Persian king.

RAKHSH: Rostam's horse.

RAY: a town south of modern Tehran.

ROSTAM: the preeminent hero of the epic; the son of Zāl and Rudābeh and father of Sohrāb.

RUDĀBEH: a princess of Kābol; Zāl's wife and Rostam's mother.

RUM: the West.

RUMI: of the West.

SADEH: a festival commemorating the discovery of fire.

SAHI: the bride of Iraj.

SALM: Feraydun's eldest son.

SĀM: the father of Zāl.

SAMANGĀN: a border town, between Irān and Turān.

SANGLAKH, PLAIN OF: a mythical area, "sanglakh" means "stony."

SANJEH: a demon of Māzanderān.

SĀRI: a town to the southeast of the Caspian.

SEND: approximately modern Pakistan; the sea adjacent to it.

SHĀHEH: a mythical city in Hāmāverān.

SHAHRNAVĀZ: a daughter of Jamshid.

SHAMĀSĀS: a warrior of Turān.

SHĀPUR: a warrior of Irān.

SHIDĀSB: the chief minister of King Tahmures.

SHIDUSH: a Persian warrior.

SHIRUI: a warrior of Turān.

SIĀMAK: the son of King Kayumars.

SIMORGH: the fabulous bird which rears Zāl.

SINDOKHT: the wife of Mehrāb and the mother of Rudābeh.

SISTĀN: the ancestral homeland of Sām, Zāl, and Rostam; also called Zābol, Zābolestān, Zāvol, Zāvolestān, and Nimruz.

SOGHDIA: Transoxiana generally, and in particular the area around Samarkand.

SOHRĀB: the son of Rostam.

SORUSH: an angel.

SUDĀBEH: the daughter of the king of Hāmāverān.

TAHMINEH: the daughter of the king of Samangān; Sohrāb's mother.

TAHMURES: a Persian king, the son of Hushang known as the Binder of Demons.

Talimān: a warrior of Irān.

TUR: Feraydun's second son.

TURĀN: the country to the north of the Oxus.

TUS: a Persian prince, the son of Nozar.

ULĀD: a landowner and warrior of Māzanderān.

VISEH: a warrior of Turān.

ZĀBOL/ZĀBOLESTĀN: another name for Sistān, the homeland of Sām, Zāl, and Rostam.

ZĀDSHAM: an ancestor of Afrāsyāb.

ZAHHĀK: a demon-king brought down by Kāveh and Feraydun.

ZĀL: also called Zāl-e Zar and Zāl-Dastān, Sām's son, the father of Rostam.

ZAREH: a country and sea near North Africa.

ZAV: a Persian king.

ZAVĀREH: a warrior of Irān, the brother of Rostam.

ZĀVOL/ZĀVOLESTĀN: another name for Sistān, the homeland of Sām, Zāl, and Rostam.

ZHENDEH-RAZM: a warrior of Turān.

Ferdowsi, painted by Aqa Mirak c. 1520–30

⇥ A SUMMARY OF THE COMPLETE *SHAHNAMEH* ⇤

The poem opens with an invocation to God, followed by a passage in praise of wisdom; then come short descriptions of the creation of the world, mankind, and the sun and the moon. Praise of the prophet Mohammad is next. An interesting passage follows, perhaps including some literal fact but certainly also a measure of poetic formula, describing how the sources for the poem were gathered; after this there is a brief notice on Daqiqi (Ferdowsi took over the writing of the poem after Daqiqi, having written about one thousand lines of it, was murdered by a slave) and the circumstances in which Ferdowsi assumed responsibility for completing the poem. A passage in praise of Sultan Mahmud of Ghazni, from whom the poet clearly hoped for patronage, concludes the exordium.

The first king is Kayumars; his reign is largely concerned with battling against demons. His son Siamak is killed by a demon, and Siamak's son Hushang temporarily defeats the demons. Kayumars dies and Hushang becomes king. After Hushang's death his son Tahmures, known as "the Binder of Demons," continues the war against evil, and he is succeeded on the throne by his son Jamshid.

Jamshid is presented as a mighty king who introduces the arts of civilization to mankind, but his ambition leads him to think of himself as the rival of God. During his reign, human beings, rather than demons, become the source of evil—though they are as yet human beings with fabulous attributes. One Zahhak, an Arab, is seduced by the devil (Ahriman) and covets his father's position; he kills him while he is praying. Ahriman disguises himself as a cook and as a sign of submission kisses Zahhak on the shoulders; immediately two snakes, which can only be nourished by human brains, grow there. Zahhak gathers the nobility of Iran, who have become disaffected from Jamshid due to his arrogance, into an army. They defeat Jamshid who is killed.

Zahhak's reign is marked by cruelty and oppression; young Iranian men are fed to the snakes on his shoulders. A blacksmith named Kaveh, joined by a scion of the former royal family, Feraydun, leads a popular revolt against Zahhak and defeats him. Zahhak is imprisoned beneath Mount Damavand—the highest mountain in Iran—and Feraydun becomes king.

Feraydun rules wisely but decides to divide his kingdom, which comprises all the known world, between his three sons Salm, Tur, and Iraj. To Salm he gives the West, to Tur central Asia and China, to the youngest, Iraj, the land of Iran. From this moment on central Asia is known in the poem as Turan. Salm and Tur conspire against Iraj and kill him in order to appropriate his share. Feraydun brings up a grandson of Iraj, Manuchehr, who is sent to war against Salm and Tur. Manuchehr kills the two brothers and becomes king of his grandfather's inheritance, Iran. Enmity between Turan and Iran is virtually constant from this point on, until it is eclipsed by the enmity with the West (Greece and "Rum," i.e., Byzantium).

Manuchehr is a just king. At his coronation a vassal pledges allegiance. This vassal is Sam, the son of Nariman; he and his family rule in Sistan, a quasi-independent fiefdom of Iran. The narrative turns now to the fortunes of Sam's family.

Sam has a son named Zal, who is born with white hair. Taking this as an adverse sign from God, Sam has the baby exposed on a mountainside. Here it is found by a fabulous bird, the Simorgh. Zal is carried off to the Simorgh's nest and there reared. From now on Zal and his descendants are under the protection of the Simorgh. Zal and his father, Sam, are reunited; after initial opposition from his father and King Manuchehr, Zal marries Rudabeh, daughter of the king of Kabol and a descendant of Zahhak. Their son is Rostam, the preeminent hero of Iranian folklore.

Manuchehr is succeeded on the Iranian throne by his son Nozar, an incompetent and unscrupulous king during whose reign Iran is overrun by the forces of Turan under their king, Afrasyab. Nozar is killed by Afrasyab, and Iran is pillaged. Zal and Rostam rally the Iranian forces while two relatively weak kings, Zav-e Tahmasb and Garshasb, attempt to hold Iran together. Zal and a council of nobles nominate Kay-Qobad as king.

Qobad drives out the invaders and rules justly. He is succeeded by his son Kay-Kavus. Kavus's reign is one of the most thoroughly explored of the whole poem; in particular, it is during this reign that the theme of the relations between the king and his champions is first fully developed.

Kavus's reign is punctuated by a series of near-disasters. He makes war on Mazanderan and is imprisoned by the Demon-King there; he goes courting to Hamaveran and is imprisoned by his father-in-law; he attempts to build a flying machine drawn aloft by eagles and crashes in enemy territory. In each case he is rescued by Rostam. While Rostam is traveling to Mazanderan to rescue Kavus from the Demon-King he performs his *haft kh'an* or "seven heroic trials." It is also during Kavus's reign that the single most famous episode of the poem occurs. Rostam sires a son, Sohrab, while on a hunting foray in the marches of Turan. Sohrab grows up to become the champion of the Turanian army; unbeknownst to one another father and son meet in combat, and Sohrab is killed. During this episode the uneasy relations between Rostam and Kavus come to a head, and at one point Rostam curses Kavus for a fool.

The present selection of stories from the legendary and mythological sections of the *Shahnameh* ends with the death of Sohrab.

Kavus has a son, Seyavash. Kavus's wife Sudabeh, Seyavash's stepmother, tries to seduce the youth, and when he refuses her advances she accuses him before Kavus of having tried to rape her. He passes through a hill of fire to prove his innocence and then leaves the court in order to lead the armies of Iran against Afrasyab, who has again attacked. After a successful campaign he concludes a peace treaty with Afrasyab, asking for hostages as a guarantee of the Turanian king's good behavior. Kavus is enraged that his son has made peace and demands that the hostages be sent to his court where they will be killed. Seyavash, rather than comply with this order, goes over to Turan. He is welcomed at first but finally killed due to a plot hatched by Garsivaz, the brother of Afrasyab and the commander of the forces Seyavash had defeated on the battlefield. Seyavash's wife, Farigis, the daughter of Afrasyab, is saved from death by Piran, Afrasyab's councillor. She is pregnant with Khosrow who as a young man escapes to Iran.

Khosrow takes over the reins of power from Kavus, and a long war of vengeance for the death of Seyavash, against Turan and conducted by Rostam and Khosrow, begins. A particularly tragic casualty of the war is Forud (Seyavash's son by another wife, Jarireh, daughter of Afrasyab's councillor, Piran), who is killed despite Khosrow's express orders to the contrary. This is the most combat-filled section of the *Shahnameh* and includes stories of der-ring-do by Rostam against various central Asian heroes (and against a demon, the Akvan Div, who almost defeats him), as well as lengthy descriptions of single combat between warriors drawn from the armies of Turan and Iran.

During the course of the warfare there is a romance-like interlude, the story of Bizhan and Manizheh. A Persian warrior, Bizhan, falls in love with a daughter of Afrasyab, Manizheh, and is imprisoned by Afrasyab in a dark well. Manizheh looks after him while he is a prisoner, and he is eventually rescued by Rostam. The war ends with the defeat and execution of Afrasyab, and it is only at this point that Kavus, Khosrow's grandfather, dies.

Khosrow, fearing the hubris that absolute power brings, decides to abdi-cate. Zal and the other Iranian nobles attempt to dissuade him, but he retires to a mountaintop where he disappears from his retinue's view in a snowstorm. Being without sons, he had nominated Lohrasp as his succes-sor. Lohrasp does not have the Iranians' confidence, and Rostam and Zal in particular distance themselves from the new court.

Lohrasp's son, Goshtasp, becomes king. The prophet Zoroaster appears and proclaims the Zoroastrian faith, which is accepted by Goshtasp and his court. (This section is the one thousand or so lines written by Daqiqi and incorporated by Ferdowsi into his poem.) Goshtasp's son, Esfandyar, becomes a warrior-proselytizer for the new faith. Esfandyar and his father quarrel, and Esfandyar is imprisoned. A new hero of Turan, Arjasp, attacks Iran, and Goshtasp is forced to free Esfandyar so that he can fight the new menace. While traveling to free his sisters who have been imprisoned by Arjasp, Esfandyar performs seven heroic trials (his *haft kh'an*) which closely parallel Rostam's *haft kh'an*, except that Esfandyar kills a Simorgh in the course of his labors whereas Rostam and his family live under the Simorgh's protection. Esfandyar defeats and kills Arjasp.

Goshtasp is troubled by Esfandyar's ambitions and by Rostam's indiffer-ence to the new dynasty; he decides to send Esfandyar to Rostam in order to bring him to the Persian court in chains. Esfandyar is reluctant to carry out this order, but his notion of religious duty involves absolute submission to his father's wishes, and he sets out. Rostam unsuccessfully tries to dissuade him from his mission; the two fight, and Esfandyar is killed.

Shortly after this Rostam is himself killed as a result of a plot by his brother Shaghad. Esfandyar's son, Bahman, decides to take revenge for his father's death and destroys Rostam's remaining family members, including Rostam's still-living father, Zal. Rostam's son, Faramarz, rises in rebellion but is defeated and killed.

Bahman marries his own daughter Homai and dies shortly afterward; she bears his son Darab who is entrusted to the River Euphrates in a basket. Darab grows up, is recognized by his mother who has been ruling Iran in the meantime, and is made king by her. Darab marries a daughter of Filqus (Philip), the king of Greece. He is, however, offended by her bad breath (sic!) and sends her back to her father, where she bears Darab's son, Eskandar. Darab marries another princess who bears him a second son, Dara, who on the death of his father becomes king of Iran.

Eskandar (Alexander the Great) attacks, defeats Dara, and becomes the king of Iran. In the *Shahnameh*, as in other Islamic literature, Eskandar is a figure of fable and romance, with something of the aura of a wonder-worker and sage as well as a warrior. After his death, his empire breaks up into petty princedoms, and Ferdowsi remarks that it was as if there were no king for two hundred years. At the end of this interlude a new king emerges, Ardavan. Ardavan is killed by his ward, Ardeshir, who is the founder of the Sasanian dynasty.

Ardeshir's reign is presented as a refurbishing and revivification of the Iranian nation, and a new legal code is promulgated. Ardeshir is followed by a series of Sasanian monarchs, who can be identified with historical kings, and about many of whom Ferdowsi has very little to say. The tone of the poem throughout much of the Sasanian period is more like that of romance than epic, and there are frequent love stories and folktalelike interludes in the narrative. The most interesting Sasanian kings, as they appear in the poem, are Shapur Zu'l Aktaf, Yazdegerd the Unjust, Bahram Gur, Kasra Anushirvan, Hormozd, Khosrow Parviz, and Yazdegerd, the last Sasanian monarch. (Ferdowsi's, or his source's, notion of the importance of many of these monarchs often differs considerably from a modern historian's; for example, Shapur, Ardeshir's son, who defeated the Romans and captured the Roman emperor Valerian and under whom Sasanian power can be said to have reached its apogee, is very summarily treated by Ferdowsi.)

Shapur Zu'l Aktaf is noticeable chiefly as the king within whose reign the prophet Mani appears. In Ferdowsi's poem he comes from China and is a painter as well as a religious leader (his reputation in Persian culture generally is as an almost supernaturally gifted painter and wonder-worker). Shapur orders him killed as a heretic. Yazdegerd the Unjust's reign is briefly treated; it is presented as a paradigm of injustice and cruelty, and

Yazdegerd's memory is cursed by his son, Bahram Gur, when he ascends the throne. Bahram Gur's reign is largely given over to stories of amours and folktalelike anecdotes. By contrast, the reign of Kasra Anushirvan is discussed in great detail and with considerable seriousness. Anushirvan's title is "the Just"; while he is still crown prince, he uproots the heresy of Mazdakism embraced by his father. He is helped by his councillor Bozorjmehr ("Great Light"), who is presented as a paragon of wisdom. At one point, the two quarrel and Bozorjmehr is imprisoned, but later released.

The reigns of Hormozd and his son, Khosrow Parviz, are largely taken up with the rebellion of Bahram Chubineh, the champion of both kings and later their opponent in the struggle for the throne. Bahram Chubineh is finally defeated and then assassinated while a refugee at the Chinese court. A particularly fascinating character in this section of the narrative is Gordyeh, Bahram Chubineh's sister, who becomes the representative of the old heroic and loyal spirit which had informed the earlier pages of the poem and which is now seen to be almost completely absent from Iranian political life. After the death of Bahram Chubineh, Khosrow Parviz's reign becomes very similar to that of Bahram Gur—i.e., largely a record of amours and domestic rather than heroic incidents. Included in these is the famous story of Khosrow's love for Shirin, later reworked by Nezami (who also utilized Ferdowsi's treatments of Bahram Gur and Eskandar as sources for other poems). Khosrow Parviz is finally killed by a slave suborned by his disaffected nobles.

A number of brief reigns lead into the final reign, that of Yazdegerd. This is memorable chiefly for its portrait of Rostam pur-e Hormozd (son of Hormozd), the commander of Yazdegerd's armies. He is an astrologer as well as a soldier and foresees the destruction that is about to overwhelm Iran at the hands of the Arab armies of Islam. He sets out his prophecy of the disasters to come in a letter he writes to his brother warning him to escape while there is time. Nevertheless, a last avatar of that earlier loyalty invoked and despaired of by Bahram Chubineh's sister, Gordyeh, Rostam himself stays to lead the imperial army. The army is defeated, Rostam is killed, and the fleeing Yazdegerd is ignominiously murdered by a miller. Ferdowsi concludes with the statement that, though the poem has cost him his life to write and he has been scantly rewarded for his pains, he is now assured of fame:

> From now on I shall not die; I live;
> For I have broadcast the seed of my speech;
> Whoever has sense and understanding and righteousness
> Shall praise me after my death.
>
> (IX, 382, 864-865)

DICK DAVIS

ILLUSTRATING A *SHAHNAMEH*

Countless illustrated manuscripts of the *Shahnameh*, or "The Book of Kings," have survived; few are exciting works of art. Indo-Turko-Iranian rulers customarily commissioned illustrated copies of this important text. Partly legend, it is also history, a manual on kingship, a compendium of royal and heroic tales, a dissertation on wisdom, statesmanship, cleverness, love, passion, friendship, warfare, on the pursuit of beasts (and of enemies), on magic, and humor. Firing up pride in lands and people, it is also a joy to read, to hear recited, and to see. Shahs, and those aspiring to rule, needed one. And the greater the shah, the more ambitious would be his version of this Iranian epic and imperial symbol. Royal copies—as opposed to the more modest manuscripts produced by commercial workshops for lesser patrons—were commissioned from masters in the patron's own ateliers. Major *Shahnameh* manuscripts not only delighted every eye that beheld and read them but also proclaimed their owners' power, prestige, and aesthetic standards. In addition, they underscored his wealth. Maintaining the small army of craftsmen and painters and supplying materials was costly.

Whatever the artistic level, each *Shahnameh* manuscript possesses its own character. Even if the names of the scribe, artists, and illuminators were omitted or had been expunged, manuscripts can be ascribed both provenance and date on purely visual grounds. Occasionally, the names of the calligraphers, artists, and illuminators of arabesque ornamentation can be identified.

Commissioning a great manuscript was a major undertaking, comparable to planning an architectural complex or launching a military campaign. Many decisions had to be made, ranging from such technical essentials as paper, pigments, and scale to more creative topics. The manifold challenge of creating a great manuscript is evident when we consider the so-called *Houghton Shahnameh*, probably the most lavishly ambitious of all, and the source of most of the illustrations in this volume.[1] Shah Isma'il, the first Safavid shah (r. 1502-24), must have met lengthily, enjoyably, and often with his enormously talented senior artist, Soltan Mohammad. After these consultations and meetings with other bibliophiles, a program of subjects was conceived and assigned to members of the imperial workshop. Inasmuch as the early section of this *Shahnameh* is unprecedented in being so fully illustrated—ultimately comprising 258 paintings, vastly more than in most versions—Soltan Mohammad and his fellow court artists could look ahead to decades of hard work.

Because of its projected magnificence, Shah Isma'il's *Shahnameh* was far from complete when he died prematurely at Tabriz in 1524. By then, however, his even more ardently art-loving son, high-strung Prince Tahmasb (b.

Shah Tahmasb, painted by Aqa Mirak c. 1520–30

1514; r. 1524-76), had begun to share its patronage. His active involvement also strongly influenced the artistic development of early Safavid painting, which can be traced through the *Shahnameh's* cycle of illustrations. The young shah's artistic background and predilections differed greatly from his father's. While Isma'il grew up in western Iran, centered at Tabriz, within the orbit of the Aq-Qoyunlu (White Sheep Turkman) royal family to whom he was related, the crown prince was nurtured in a quite different cultural tradition. As an infant he had been sent eastward by his father to serve as nominal governor of Herat. There he was closely supervised by Qadi-ye Jahan, a *laleh*, or "regent," who later became his prime minister. This congenial, highly cultivated father figure arranged for his royal charge to meet and learn from Herat's impressive poets, thinkers, musicians, and artists. Individually and collectively remarkable, they had been brought together by the last Timurid ruler of Herat, Sultan Husayn Bayqara ("The Eagle"; r. 1469-1506), who was renowned as a brilliant patron of poetry and painting. Whereas Shah Isma'il rejoiced in the rich artistic legacy of Turkman Tabriz, a major center of trade, whose powerful, visionary artistic style incorporated dragonish motifs from China and central Asia as well as naturalistic elements from Europe, the extremely young, precocious, and impressionable Tahmasb had grown to admire the more refined and restrained idiom of Timurid Herat. As a young boy, Prince Tahmasb sat at the feet of one of Iran's major artists, Master Behzad, whose illustrations for a *Bustan* of Sa'di, dated 1488, represent the peak of classical Iranian painting.[2] Characteristic of the eastern wing of Iranian art, Behzad's work differs profoundly from that of Shah Isma'il's major artist, Soltan Mohammad—ranked with Behzad as one of Iran's legendarily great masters—who had espoused the tradition of Turkman Tabriz. Infinitely fine in scale and workmanship, Behzad's paintings contain myriads of accurately observed, naturalistically proportioned people and animals, and offer nuances of personality rarely expressed in the bolder, earthier, art of Tabriz. In his jewellike miniatures, still life, costumes, and architecture are handled in such palpably convincing detail that from them craftsmen could replicate Sultan Husayn's elegant possessions.

By 1524, when Prince Tahmasb inherited the throne, the western Iranian style of Tabriz had begun to blend with the eastern style of Herat in a vivid new artistic synthesis. Soltan Mohammad's otherworldly vision progressively melded with Behzad's sensitive interpretation of the real world. The young shah now assumed full direction of his father's ateliers and of its foremost project, the great *Shahnameh*. If the dynamically direct and outspoken father was an effective patron, the quiet, thoughtful, complex son was even more so. Fascinated by art, Shah Tahmasb ranks high among history's kings not only for his innovative and inspiring guidance of artists, but for his gift as a practicing painter. Few royal hands ever surpassed his two lively portrayals, preserved in the Topkapu Palace Museum Library of Istanbul, of members of the royal household.[3] Although Shah Tahmasb's two surviving pictures were influenced by Behzad's psychological concerns, their comedy, breadth of handling, and vivacity reflect his admiration for earthier, funnier Soltan Mohammad, who demonstrated this side in such paintings as *Hushang Slays the Black Div* [see p. 260]. Propitiously, young Shah Tahmasb's openness to the pleasures of art and life enabled him to appreciate both Behzad and Soltan Mohammad. It also fueled the devotion and energy needed to bring together their two very different styles.

Although the scenario of the creation of Shah Isma'il's and Shah Tahmasb's *Shahnameh* is probably the most complicated in the history of Iranian book illustration, it enables us to trace the development of early Safavid painting between about 1515 and the early 1540s. But because its miniatures are so rooted in both the western and eastern traditions, it is also relevant in many ways to Iranian painting in general. In Soltan Mohammad's earlier work for this watershed of a manuscript, during Shah Isma'il's patronage, he remained within the traditional pan-Iranian mode, enriching it with his vital humor, his dashing line, and a broad vision universal in its appeal. To maintain a practical pace without sacrificing artistic standards, Soltan Mohammad initiated practices at once effective, appropriate, and visually exciting. He painted a series of miniatures in a simplified idiom that recalls Rubens's dashing oil sketches. Abundant in gusto, such pictures as *Hushang Slays the Black Div*, *The Feast of Sadeh*, and *Tahmures Defeats the Divs* hark back to Iranian popular art, while elevating it to a truly royal level. Both Mir Mosavvar and Aqa Mirak, the other senior artists, did likewise. Each of this trio also sketched designs to be colored by apprentices (aspiring junior masters) and by a corps of lesser painters. The great work progressed, gradually incorporating Behzadian characteristics. But for the time being, as in virtually all of the earlier illustrations to the *Shahnameh*, there are few indications in the paintings by the less innovative hands of specific times, locales, or personalities. In these—the majority of the paintings—action takes place, not in a particular setting, but in picturesque epic land, and except for the characteristically Safavid baton-turbans, costumes belong to no specific tribe or court. None of the players, however lively, could be mistaken for true portraits. As before, the plots are carefully based upon Ferdowsi's text.

Young Shah Tahmasb, however, admiring Master Behzad, preferred true-to-life Iranian settings over conventionalized, imaginary ones intended to heighten the moods of their episodes. He urged his artists to use familiar locales, and to render the mere human ciphers of tradition as identifiable personalities of the court. When Mir Mosavvar, master of color and gloriously lucid arabesques, painted *The Nightmare of Zahhak*—his visual reply to Soltan Mohammad's *Court of Kayumars*—he beguilingly included servants of the ilk of "Melon-Sultan." In rendering the tyrant's palace, he itemized every inlaid door, sumptuously ornamented ceramic tile, and polychromed wooden balcony, thus creating an idealized but credible view of a great Safavid building. Tyrannical Zahhak, its owner, is a tormented villain attired in Safavid court costume of circa 1525; his wives are elegant Safavid princesses, wearing chic ensembles of the moment.

While his *Shahnameh* progressed, the art-inspired young shah also painted. One admires his enthusiastic perseverance as well as talent in mastering a deceptively simple, but in fact very difficult, technique. Like any boy or girl aspiring to paint, he apprenticed himself to an admired master, probably Behzad or Soltan Mohammad. But he was also encouraged and advised by courtier-artist Aqa Mirak, described in contemporary chronicles as "boon companion" of his aesthetically inclined patron. From them, the young shah learned how to sort and grind pigments, how to make brushes by tying hairs from the chests of small squirrels or kittens into bird quills. He mastered pounding nuggets of gold, silver, and copper between sheets of parchment into paper-thin sheets which were later ground in a mortar with coarse salt. The resulting powder could be mixed with a gummy binding medium before being burnished from dull tan into refulgent gold or silver. He also learned about fine papers, how to stretch them out atop a large flat, smooth stone, and how to burnish them with smooth agate or crystal tools.

Seated on the ground, surrounded by clamshells of pigment and binding medium, a jar of water, brushes, and burnishers, he studied drawing. Although his own pictures show that he enjoyed sketching from life, his training included copying the atelier's generous archive of standard motifs: a varied world of human types, animals, birds, trees, flowers, architecture, and almost anything else he might need. Inasmuch as artists often composed by assembling single elements from earlier paintings and drawings, he was taught how to trace them onto sheets of transparent gazelleskin, to prick along the outlines, and to transfer them to the work in progress by rubbing powdered charcoal through the pinholes.

Finally, he was instructed to prepare creamy-white paint for raised passages, such as turbans, jewelry, or flowers, and to brush on gold pigment, before touching it with a pointed burnishing stone, or lending it glitter with strokes of a not-too-sharp steel needle. Learning all of this required patience, dedication, more than a measure of humility, and the encouragement of devoted teachers.

Like Sultan Husayn Bayqara, who was portrayed by Behzad as royal host in his copy of Sa'di's *Bustan*, Shah Tahmasb appears in the very first miniature in the sequence of his *Shahnameh* [see p. 260]. His very presence, added almost a decade after his father's death, marks the volume as his own, rather than one shared with his father. On the basis of many other likenesses, his somewhat wanly sensitive countenance and spindly anatomy are identifiable, standing somewhat removed and beyond Ferdowsi, who is seen encountering the leading poets of Ghazna. As might be expected, this is the work of his close friend Aqa Mirak, who was older than he but considerably younger than Soltan Mohammad. Although royal personages also appear in Turkman Tabriz manuscripts, such as the great *Quintet* of Nezami partially illustrated for the Aq-Qoyunlu patron, Sultan Yaqub Beq, and his brother, Sultan-Khalil,[4] Aqa Mirak's likeness of his patron is remarkable in Iranian art for its degree of psychological revelation. Figure and face sensitively convey a complex temperament, at once charming and melancholic, already hinting of proneness to the sequence of troubling nightmares that eventually turned Shah Tahmasb against most pleasures, including painting. Few Safavid portraits reach so deeply and candidly into individual character, which suggests that only members of the shah's innermost circle were privileged to see this extraordinarily personal *Shahnameh*. Although Shah Tahmasb's exhilarating patronage of painting ended in about 1544, and he released from service most of his artists, Aqa Mirak—along with 'Abd ul-Aziz—remained active in the diminished imperial workshop.

Few ateliers in world history have equaled Shah Tahmasb's in expressing the moods, thoughts, and activities of their patrons. If Aqa Mirak was the leading vehicle for these personal revelations, Soltan Mohammad was equally understanding and communicative of the shah's usually sympathetic complexities. Encouraged to do so, these artists infused their pictures for the *Shahnameh* with anecdotal passages that are now only partially understood but shed light upon the life of the shah and of his court. This *Shahnameh*, therefore, not only recounts and illustrates Ferdowsi's Iranian epic, but it also provides vivid glimpses into the thought and activities of a particular court over a period of more than two decades.

Once familiar with this *Shahnameh*'s packed imagery and with the stylistic development of Safavid painting, we can see that the patron and his community of artists tinkered frequently with their project. Although the manuscript was initiated before 1520, Aqa Mirak's portrait of his still beardless friend was commissioned and inserted as the prestigious first miniature in the volume years later, probably between 1525 and 1530. Presumably because it was deemed to be old fashioned, Soltan Mohammad's superb *Sleeping Rostam*—painted for the earlier, mostly discarded "prelude" to the manuscript as we know it—was left unfinished and never placed in the manuscript.[5] As the work went forward, paintings were inserted. One of these is Soltan Mohammad's *Feraydun Crosses the River Arvand*, in which Behzadian characteristics are woven seamlessly into the master's Turkman-inspired, infectious comedy. As the first entirely successful attempt to bridge the two styles, it must have been especially welcome. [see p. 262]. Faces and figures that would once have been painted as lively but generic types have become benevolent but identifiable caricatures of members of the shah's circle. One senses the bursts of laughter at the first viewing. Although two pictures were added to Shah Tahmasb's *Shahnameh* as late as 1540, most of its paintings had been completed by 1535.

The *Shahnameh*'s pictures often suggest lively interplay between patron and painters, as well as between individual artists and families of artists. Soltan Mohammad's *Court of Kayumars* not only inspired Mir Mosavvar to paint his noblest picture, *The Nightmare of Zahhak* [see p. 261], but caused Aqa Mirak to produce his glorious *Feraydun, in the Guise of a Dragon, Tests His Sons* [see p. 263]. Perhaps the most inventively composed and most painterly picture in the volume, Aqa Mirak's work effectively challenges Soltan Mohammad's supremacy as painter of dragons, those enormously appealing creatures known so well to Turkman artists—and through their work to Soltan Mohammad—from Chinese art imported to Tabriz.

Not even a Soltan Mohammad, Mir Mosavvar, or Aqa Mirak could maintain uniformly high standards, however encouraging and devoted their patrons. The wonder and power, therefore, of this compact, portable art gallery rests not upon its sustained artistic importance, nor even upon its dozens of pictures of transcendental beauty, but upon its extraordinary evidence of a continuum of Safavid artistic life on the highest level. Close study of the paintings themselves and of surviving documents reveals a colorful community of notable personalities. Historical eminences such as Shah Tahmasb and his father, several artists of world rank, a dozen or so lesser ones, and a few virtually amateur hangers-on and servants all spring to life from the folios of this monumental *Shahnameh*, vivid as when they were created. From its paintings and from scanty biographical references, an inspired, busy nucleus of associates emerges with refreshing immediacy. We can share their delights and satisfactions, empathize with their rivalries, comaraderie, and changing moods, even be diverted by their foibles and scandals. How enlivening it is to learn that Shah Tahmasb's less sympathetic critics poked fun at his preoccupation with painting and noted his eccentricity in riding muleback to his studios. In the late twentieth century, are we shocked to discover that one of the artists, 'Abd ul-Aziz, absconded with Shah Tahmasb's favorite page boy, the son of a distinguished court physician? Probably not; and when we learn that for his crime the artist's nose was bobbed, and that he replaced it with a carved and polychromed wooden one, of his own manufacture—considered to be an improvement—we are amused.

By pooling their talents over more than two decades, two shahs and their artists and craftsmen, each stimulating the others, created a magnificent work of art. Avant garde not only in Iran but in the entire Indo-Turko-Iranian world, its powerfully innovative compositions, often poignant explorations of personality, and unprecedented documentation of contemporary life influenced the entire spectrum of later painting. At artistic centers from Istanbul, to Qazvin, Mashhad, and Agra, to India's Deccani plateau and, eventually, far into Rajasthan, motifs, compositions, and aesthetic concepts envisioned by Shah Tahmasb and his artists illuminated and changed the courses of entire schools of painting. Had not Aqa Mirak portrayed Shah Tahmasb so revealingly, and had not Mirza-'Ali and Mir Sayyed-'Ali so meticulously studied and rendered all of the trinkets, dry goods, and impedimenta of the Safavid court, later painting throughout the Muslim world would have been different, and probably be less compelling. Above all, however, this *Shahnameh*, a work of literature and art, stands as a monumental achievement over many centuries, the quintessence of an entire culture.

STUART CARY WELCH[6]
PARIS, 1997

1. For a monumental study of this great manuscript and of the Safavid style, see Martin Bernard Dickson and Stuart Cary Welch, *The Houghton Shahnameh,* 2 vols. (Cambridge: Harvard University Press, 1981). Note that we now consider Shah Isma`il's and Shah Tahmasb's manuscripts of the *Shahnameh* to represent two stages of a single project. It was initiated between 1515 and 1520 by Shah Isma`il.

2. See Dickson and Welch,*The Houghton Shahnameh,* 1: 15–16, figs. 4–5.

3. For the more elaborate of these, a miniature painting, see Dickson and Welch, *The Houghton Shahnameh,* 1: fig. 43. This and an equally compelling drawing of a single figure are contained in Album H.2154, assembled for Shah Tahmasb's brother, Bahram Mirza, in 1544.

4. See Dickson and Welch, *The Houghton Shahnameh,* 1: 30, 32, figs. 28–32; and Stuart Cary Welch, *Wonders of the Age* (London: T. Agnew, 1979) 19–20, fig. 5.

5. See Welch, *Wonders of the Age,* 36–37. Other rejected miniatures for this project can be found in Leipzig and in Istanbul.

6. I am deeply indebted to my late friend Martin Bernard Dickson, coauthor of *The Houghton Shahnameh,* for his invaluable readings and interpretations of contemporary documents and other historical information. Without his brilliant collaborative work, my discoveries based upon pictorial evidence would have been difficult to argue. Were he alive today, I sense that he would be pleased to know that a considerable section of this *Shahnameh,* which was presented in 1567 by Shah Tahmasb himself to Sultan Selim II of Turkey, has been returned to Iran, in exchange for a painting by William de Kooning of a seemingly distraught woman.

CREDITS AND ACKNOWLEDGMENTS

The appendix, "A Summary of the Complete *Shahnameh*," was adapted by Dick Davis from pages xxiv–xxxii of his book *Epic and Sedition: The Case of Ferdowsi's Shahnameh* (University of Arkansas Press, 1992).

The Publishers would like to thank Abolala Soudavar for generously allowing the use of miniatures from his private collection and for sharing his knowledge of other images available in collections around the world. We are also much indebted to Stuart Cary Welch for ensuring our access to four of the most magnificent of the Shah Tahmasb *Shahnameh* miniatures. Special thanks are also due to Prince Sadruddin Aga Khan for generously allowing us to use images from his collection. In addition we wish to express our gratitude for the advice and aid of Maire Swietochowski and Deana Cross at the Metropolitan Museum, Mohammad Isa Waley at the British Library, Graeme Gardiner at the Royal Asiatic Society, Elizabeth Gombasi and Liz Hansen at the Harvard Universities Art Museums, and Felicia Hecker at the University of Washington.

Many other people helped bring this book into existence. We would particularly like to thank Robin Bray of Redruth for helping with the design of the book and Rostam Batmanglij for silhouetting the flowers for the chapter headings, George Constable for his astute editorial suggestions, Ann Rollins who copyedited the book, Harry Endrulat who proofed it, and last but not least, Tony Ross who typeset the book and saw to its every detail, calmly putting on whichever hat was necessary at Mage Publishers.

GUIDE TO THE ILLUSTRATIONS

The following twelve pages catalog the *Shahnameh* illustrations used in the book and provide sources and credits. The list is organized in order of the painting's first appearance in the text and by manuscript and collection, beginning with those images that come from the Shah Tahmasb *Shahnameh* manuscript and then going on to images from other collections and manuscripts. Where details have been used to illustrate the text, the appropriate page numbers have been provided. Information such as the name of the painter and the date of the painting have been given wherever available. In some cases, painters are identified simply by a letter (e.g., "Painter A"). These designations refer to specific painters whose works have been identified, but whose names remain unknown. The references to "r" and "v" indicate whether the original paintings were on the right (recto) or left (verso) side of the manuscript.

Ferdowsi and the Three Poets of Ghazna
Painted by Aqa Mirak c. 1520-30 / folio 7r
Courtesy of Collection Prince Sadruddin Aqa Khan
Details on pages: 244, 251

The Court of Kayumars
Painted by Soltan Mohammad c. 1520-30 / folio 20v
Courtesy of Collection Prince Sadruddin Aqa Khan
Detail on page: XII, 258, 272

Hushang Slays the Black Div
Painted by Soltan Mohammad c. 1520-30 / folio 21v
Private collection
Details on jacket and pages:II, 14, 15, 17, 55, 62, 94, 95

The Feast of Sadeh
Painted by Soltan Mohammad c. 1520-30 / folio 22v
Courtesy of The Metropolitan Museum of Art, gift of Arthur A.
Houghton, Jr., (1970.301.2). Details on pages: V, VI, VII, 16, 18, 19, 36
162, 239

Tahmures Defeats the Divs
Painted by Soltan Mohammad c. 1520-30 / folio 23v
Courtesy of The Metropolitan Museum of Art, gift of Arthur A.
Houghton, Jr., (1970.301.3). Details on pages: 20, 21, 22, 52, 204

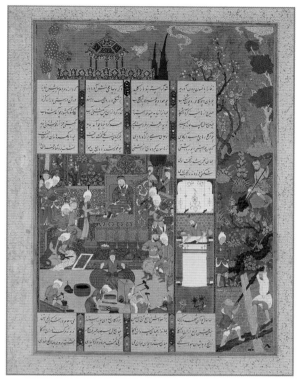

The Court of Jamshid
Painted by Soltan Mohammad c. 1520-30 / folio 24v
Private Collection
Details on pages: 27, 163, 207

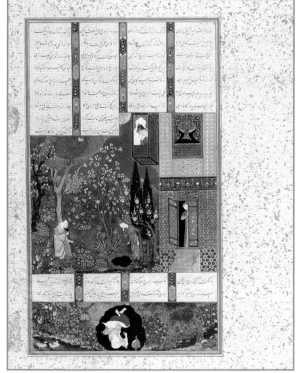

Death of Merdas
Painted by Soltan Mohammad c. 1520-30 / folio 25v
Private Collection
Details on pages: 28, 29

The Nightmare of Zahhak
Painted by Mir Mosavvar c. 1520-30 / folio 28v
Private collection
Details on pages: 30, 32, 34

Zahhak Hears his Fate and Faints
Painted by Soltan Mohammad c. 1520-30 / folio 29v
Courtesy of The Metropolitan Museum of Art, gift of Arthur A.
Houghton, Jr., (1970.301.4). Details on pages: 25, 35, 38

Zahhak Slays the Ox Barmayeh
Painted by Soltan Mohammad c. 1520-30 / folio 30v
Private Collection
Detail on page: 37

Feraydun Crosses the River Arvand
Painted by Soltan Mohammad c. 1520-30 / folio 33v
Private collection
Details on pages: 41, 42, 48

The Death of Zahhak
Painted by Soltan Mohammad c. 1520-30 / folio 37v
Courtesy of Collection Prince Sadruddin Aqa Khan
Details on pages: 13, 49, 51, 165

Feraydun, in the Guise of a Dragon, Tests his Sons
Painted by Aqa Mirak c. 1520-30 / folio 42v
Private collection
Details on pages: 56, 59

Feraydun Embraces Manuchehr
Painted by painter A c. 1520-30 / folio 59v
Courtesy of The Metropolitan Museum of Art, gift of Arthur A.
Houghton, Jr., (1970.301.5). Details on pages: 60, 79, 80, 83

Zal is Sighted by a Caravan
Painted by painter D c. 1520-30 / folio 62v
Art and History Trust courtesy of the Arthur M. Sackler Museum,
Smithsonian Institution, Washington, D.C.
Details on pages: 50, 86-87, 89

Mehrab Pays Homage to Zal
Painted by Mir Mosavvar c. 1520-30 / folio 67v
Private Collection
Details on pages: 90, 104

Zal Consults the Magi
Painted by Soltan Mohammad c. 1520-30 / folio 73v
Courtesy of The Metropolitan Museum of Art, gift of Arthur A.
Houghton, Jr., (1970.301.8). Details on pages: 98, 99

The Wise Men Approve of Zal
Painted by painter D c. 1520-30 / folio 86v
Courtesy of The Metropolitan Museum of Art, gift of Arthur A.
Houghton, Jr., (1970.301.13). Details on pages: 106, 107, 110

Qaren Slays Barman
Painted by Soltan Mohammad c. 1520-30 / folio 102v
Private Collection
Details on pages: 71, 126, 132-33

Zal Slays Khazarvan
Painted by painter C c. 1520-30 / folio 104r
Courtesy of The Metropolitan Museum of Art, gift of Arthur A.
Houghton, Jr., (1970.301.15). Details on pages: 130, 135, 137, 138-39

Afrasyab on the Iranian Throne
Painted by painter E c. 1520-30 / folio 105r
Courtesy of The Metropolitan Museum of Art, gift of Arthur A.
Houghton, Jr., (1970.301.16). Details on pages: 136, 141, 142, 145

Rostam Lassoes Rakhsh
Painted by Mir Mosavvar c. 1520-30 / folio 109r
Art and History Trust courtesy of the Arthur M. Sackler Museum,
Smithsonian Institution, Washington, D.C.
Details on pages: 146, 150-51

Rostam's First Trial
Painted by painter A c. 1520-30 / folio 118r
Art and History Trust courtesy of the Arthur M. Sackler Museum,
Smithsonian Institution, Washington, D.C.
Details on pages: 171 (lower), 172-73

Rostam's Fourth Trial
Painted by painter A c. 1520-30 / folio 120r
Courtesy of The Metropolitan Museum of Art, gift of Arthur A.
Houghton, Jr., (1970.301.17). Detail on page: 177

Kay Kavus and Rostam Embrace
Painted by painter A c. 1520-30 / folio 123r
Courtesy of The Metropolitan Museum of Art, gift of Arthur A.
Houghton, Jr., (1970.301.18). Detail on page: 183

Rostam Brings the Div King to Kay Kavus for Execution
Painted by Mir Mosavvar c. 1520-30 / folio 127v
Courtesy of The Metropolitan Museum of Art, gift of Arthur A.
Houghton, Jr., (1970.301.19). Details on pages: 187, 191, 193

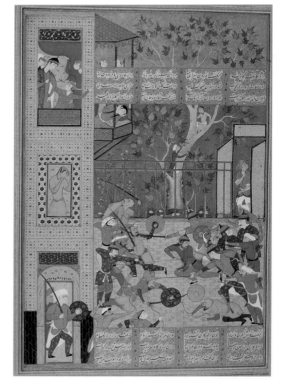

Sohrab Gains the Upper Hand
Painted by painter A c. 1520-30 / folio 153v
Private Collection
Details on pages: 219, 225, 229

Feraydun Strikes Down Zahhak
Painted by unknown artist in the Shiraz style, c. 1576
By Permission of the British Library (MSS. 3540 / folio 25r)
Details on pages: 44, 45

The Taking of Zahhak's Palace
Painted by unknown artist in the Shiraz style c. 1590
By permission of the British Library (MSS. 741 / folio 40r)
Detail on page: 47

Defeat of Tur
Painted by unknown artist in the Isfahan style c. 1604
By permission of the British Library (MSS. 966 / folio 26r)
Detail on page: 76

Rudabeh Lets Down Her Hair for Zal
Painted by unknown artist in the Qazvin style c. 1590
By permission of the British Library (Add. 27257)
Detail on page: 96

Zal Embracing Rudabeh
Painted by unknown artist in the Shiraz style c. 1576
By permission of the British Library (MSS. 3540 / folio 44r)
Details on pages: 114, 116

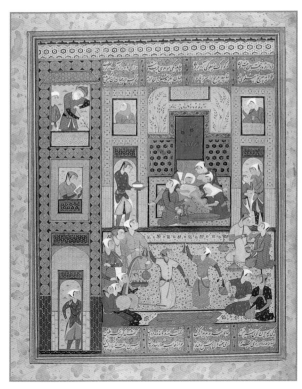

Birth of Rostam
Painted by unknown artist in the Shiraz style c. 1576
By permission of the British Library (MSS. 3540 / folio 54r)
Details on pages: 118, 119

A Warrior on Mount Damavand
Painted by unknown artist in the Shiraz style c. 1398
By permission of the British Library (OR 2780 / folio 213v)
Detail on page: 152

Rostam Lifts Qalun
Painted by unknown artist in the Isfahan style c. 1604
By permission of the British Library (MSS. 966 / folio 56r)
Detail on page: 156

Rostam Lifts Afrasyab
Painted by unknown artist in the Isfahan style c. 1604
By permission of the British Library (MSS. 966 / folio 57r)
Detail on page: 159

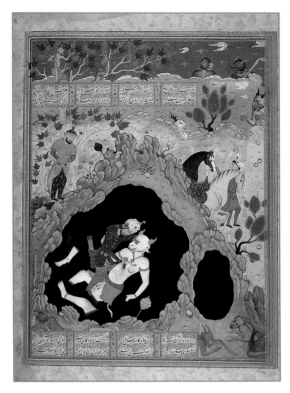

Rostam Kills the White Div
Painted by unknown artist in the Shiraz style c. 1576
By permission of the British Library (MSS. 3540 / folio 71v)
Detail on page: 185

Sudabeh Escorted to Hamaveran
Painted by unknown artist in the Isfahan style c. 1604
By permission of the British Library (MSS. 966 / folio 71r)
Detail on page: 199

Battle Between Iranians and Turanians
Painted by unknown artist in the Isfahan style c. 1604
By permission of the British Library (MSS. 966 / folio 74r)
Detail on page: 201

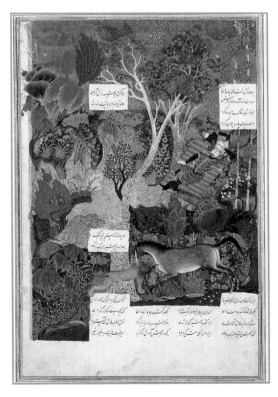

Sleeping Rostam
Painted by Soltan Mohammad c. 1520-30
Courtesy of the British Museum (1948-12-11-023)
Details on pages: 175, 258

Assault on a Castle
Attributed to Behzad c. 1475-1500
Courtesy of the Arthur M. Sackler Museum, Harvard University
Art Museums. Bequest of Abby Aldrich Rockefeller. (1960.199)
Details on pages: 214, 216, 217

Tahmineh Comes to Rostam's Chamber
Painted by unknown artist in the Herat style c. 1410
Courtesy of the Arthur M. Sackler Museum, Harvard University Art
Museums. Gift of Mrs. Elise Cabot Forbes, Mrs. Eric Schroeder, and
the Annie S. Coburn Fund. (1939.225) Details on pages: 208, 210

Battle Scene
Painted by Mahmud Mosavvar c. 1530
Courtesy of the Freer Gallery of Art, Smithsonian Institution,
Washington, D.C. (54.4) Detail on page: 74

The Child Rostam Kills the Mad Elephant
Painted by unknown artist c. 1444
Courtesy of the Collections of the Royal Asiatic Society, London
Detail on page: 121

Sohrab Slain by Rostam
Painted by unknown artist c. 1444
Courtesy of the Collections of the Royal Asiatic Society, London
Details on pages: 233

Rostam Kills the White Div
Attributed to Soltan Mohammad c. 1525
Art and History Trust courtesy of the Arthur M. Sackler Museum,
Smithsonian Institution, Washington, D.C.
Detail on Page: 179

Murder of Iraj by His Brothers
Painted by painter A c. 1560
Art and History Trust courtesy of the Arthur M. Sackler Museum,
Smithsonian Institution, Washington, D.C.
Details on pages: 65, 67

King Jamshid Carried by the Divs
Painted by unknown artist c. 1441
Art and History Trust courtesy of the Arthur M. Sackler Museum,
Smithsonian Institution, Washington, D.C.
Detail on page: 24